Star Tangled Murder

Nancy J. Cohen

ORANGE
GROVE
PRESS

Chapter One

"I can't imagine why anyone would want to dress up in a hot costume, ride through the woods on horseback, and shoot at moving targets between the trees," Marla told her husband while on their way to a battle reenactment. She supposed as a history lesson, it would bring home the point that war wasn't a game.

Dalton focused on driving as they sped along the western fringes of Broward County in Southeast Florida. Shady oaks, melaleuca trees, and palms dotted a landscape consisting mostly of agricultural fields. Their destination was Pioneer Village, a recreation of early Florida life.

"It's the U.S. Army versus the Seminoles," Dalton said, casting an aggravated glance her way. He took his history seriously. "This skirmish actually took place north of here in 1836."

"Then why hold it at Pioneer Village? I thought their focus was early twentieth century life in Florida."

"It's part of their mission as a living history museum to keep our past alive. They only do the reenactment once a year over July Fourth weekend. It's their biggest fundraiser."

"How sad that we have to remember a massacre this way. I guess we were lucky to get tickets," Marla said to mollify him.

She'd been attempting to understand his interests better, especially when he was slated to retire from his job as a homicide detective in a couple of months. She'd even taken today off from work to attend this event despite Saturdays being her busiest day at the salon.

"It was kind of Becky to tell you about it, but she did have

1

an ulterior motive in mind," Dalton said, raking his fingers through his silver-streaked black hair. "Will she be there today?"

Becky Forest was the curator of the local history museum and a friend of Marla's. She had scheduled a book signing for her new cookbook at Pioneer Village. Her studies involved early Florida food practices, but she modified her recipes for modern kitchens.

"I'm not sure which day she'll be stopping by," Marla replied. "I'll get a copy anyway. What's the fairground like? I've never been there before." Pioneer Village was located on a segment of the county fairgrounds.

"Pam used to like their antique shows," Dalton said in an offhand manner.

Ugh. Marla recalled when she'd first met Dalton. His house had been filled with heavy furniture pieces and knickknacks that had belonged to his deceased first wife. She'd refused to advance their relationship until he'd agreed to make changes. It was hard to believe they'd been married three years now.

"Did you ever bring Brianna with you?" she asked. His teenage daughter had made plans for today, or she might have joined them.

Dalton shook his head. "Brie never cared about the shows at the annual fair, and Pioneer Village didn't exist back then. I didn't even know about it until you told me."

"Maybe we can find something fun for her in the gift shop. That's where we'll find Becky's book on display."

Dalton gave Marla a lopsided grin. "If I remember, I wasn't too fond of her dishes last time you made them."

His comment sparked an idea. "Hey, maybe we can take cooking classes together after you retire. Or it might be something we could do as a family when Ryder is older."

They'd left their thirteen-month-old son at home, figuring a battle reenactment wasn't the proper place to bring him. Dalton's parents had offered to babysit for the day.

"Are you kidding?" Dalton said. "Ryder will be into sports as soon as he can throw a ball. We can go to games together."

True, but in the meantime, I'm afraid you'll get bored after a few months at home. Dalton had put in for retirement after twenty years on the force. She had mixed feelings about this major change in their lives.

"When will you hear back on the instructor position at the academy?" she asked. "It'll be nice to know when you might be starting there. Otherwise, you could put out feelers for the consulting work you'd mentioned."

"I'll get to it."

His annoyed tone didn't stop her from saying what else was on her mind. "I hope you realize I have a salon and day spa to run. Between Ryder and work, I won't have much spare time to spend with you."

He gave her a surprised glance. "Is that what worries you? I'm hoping to have more time to help you out. That's a big reason why I'm stepping down now, in addition to the safety factor."

"I know." She couldn't wait until he was no longer at risk of being shot by murder suspects. Although his current duties were mostly administrative, he chose to be hands-on for select investigations. Having Ryder had muted his enthusiasm for being out in the field.

Then again, who was she to talk? She'd put herself at risk numerous times with her amateur sleuthing. They both needed to focus on the home front.

Dalton followed signs to the fairground. Once inside the hundred-acre property, they veered toward the village and drove under an arched overhead sign. The gravel parking lot was already crowded as they searched for a space.

Pebbles crunched underfoot as she and Dalton trudged toward the ticket booth. Today's event would bring thousands of visitors, according to the fairground's website. People streamed in a steady flow toward the gate, beyond which spread grounds graced by tall, shady trees.

The sleeveless top she'd worn with a pair of Capri pants stuck to her back in the hot and humid summer air. Dalton had on

3

a comfortable polo shirt with khakis. They'd been smart to wear sneakers, anticipating they would be walking over grass for the reenactment.

Marla showed the confirmation email for the tickets she'd bought online. The clerk handed her a map along with a sheet of paper listing the day's activities and a flyer asking for donations to help with renovations. A box on a pedestal with a slit for cash stood next to the booth for the same purpose. Marla wasn't surprised. Most museums asked for contributions these days.

After they passed the turnstile, she paused to survey the scene ahead. Pines and oaks shaded a maze of concrete walkways with a broad grassy square in the center. Numerous buildings dotted the site with signs labeling each structure.

"There's so much to see," she said with a swell of interest. "We'll never do everything in one day."

Dalton tapped his watch. "The battle reenactment isn't until two, and it's only ten o'clock. We have plenty of time to look around. Let me see the map."

She handed it over, more intrigued than she'd expected by the prospect of a living history museum with costumed actors. She couldn't imagine living in an earlier era without modern conveniences, but people had managed. They'd even considered themselves more fortunate than their predecessors.

"Awesome; there's an old jail. Let's go there first," Dalton suggested.

Naturally, where else?

"What about these buildings by the entrance? We'll be skipping by them."

"We can come back." He led the way along the path and approached a small building painted white with green trim and a slate gray roof.

The paint had peeled off along the edges and the roof lacked a few shingles. If they were going for the antiquated look, it worked. Otherwise, repairs were definitely needed.

A sign labeled "Jail House" hung above a large front window. Off to the side swung a noose on a post. Marla grimaced as she considered how many criminals had met their ends there if it was a true relic.

A rangy fellow wearing a shiny badge stepped out from the interior. He wore a tan cowboy hat that covered his dark hair except for a few stray tufts. His keen hazel eyes regarded them from a sun-speckled complexion as they climbed a set of rickety steps to the porch.

"Howdy, folks. Welcome to the historic jail. I'm Marshal Phileas Pufferfish, although everyone calls me Phil," he said with a drawl. "Is this your first time visiting our village?"

"Yes, it is," Marla replied. "Pardon me for asking, but how come you're a marshal and not a sheriff? What's the difference?"

"A sheriff is an elected official. I was appointed as town marshal—unrelated to the federal marshal system—by the town's aldermen. I also serve as tax collector, fire chief, and building inspector." He stuck his hands in his pants pockets, the motion giving sparkle to the fancy silver buckle on his belt that matched his badge. He wore black jeans with an embroidered steel-gray western shirt.

"That's a lot of duties," Dalton remarked with a rapt look on his face.

Phil chuckled. "We're cross-trained to do various jobs in case someone gets sick. In a real-life parallel, I'm also the administrator for the village."

"How does that work? We're not familiar with the organizational structure."

"I'm stepping out of character to tell you this, but we're owned by the fairground, which is a nonprofit corporation. It's run by a board of directors and a group of advisors. Each tract has its own administrator like me."

"What do you mean by tracts?" Marla asked.

"The fairground consists of four sectors. The village is one of them." Phil made a sweeping gesture. "The parking lots, amphitheater, and exhibit halls make up the rest. The latter includes a barn for animal shows and competitions. During the annual fair, the southern parking lot turns into a midway with games, rides, and concessions."

"And the nonprofit runs the whole shebang?" Dalton said.

"Yes, that's correct." His sardonic tone hinted at a sense of dissatisfaction.

Did he feel overburdened by his dual roles, or did he not care for the oversight by detached directors?

"Tell us about this building," Marla said to get them back on track with a historical perspective. Dalton was peering at a plaque detailing the jail's history.

Phil's face brightened. "As you can read on that sign, the jail house is a calaboose built in 1895. It's twenty feet in width and the same in length. The walls are made from pine and are twelve inches thick. See how the structure is built on runners with a slatted wood floor? That's so the entire building can be moved when the smell gets too bad, as happens with prisoners. Please, come inside for a short tour."

Wary about the stench, Marla stepped across the threshold and sniffed. An odor of dust and mildew met her nose but not much else. With a sigh of relief, she glanced around and focused on a mannequin staring straight at her.

Dressed in a striped prison uniform, the figure stood inside a single barred cell. A secured window faced the rear of the property and helped to brighten the interior, lit by a lone overhead bulb.

To her left stood a couple of roll-top desks. A colorful Mexican blanket hung on the wall along with a black cowboy hat, a horseshoe, and various "wanted" posters. A round wooden tabletop sat on a barrel with two chairs off to the side. The quarters were tight but serviceable.

"Take my picture," she said, shoving her smartphone at Dalton. "Brianna will get a kick out of it." She entered the open cell and posed with her hands on the bars, careful not to dislodge the mannequin.

Dalton complied, then went over to one of the desks. He ran his fingers lovingly over the surface. "I've always admired these pieces of furniture," he told the marshal, who then launched into a detailed description of the desk.

Marla's ears closed. It was too hot inside this small space for her to concentrate. Without waiting for Dalton, who listened intently to the marshal's spiel, she descended the steps outside to wait for him in the fresh air. The two-story Edwardian mansion across the village square drew her attention. It was painted yellow with white and cocoa trim and served as a bright beacon among the other ramshackle structures. She'd like to see how the rooms were decorated.

"I want to tour Baffle House before the battle," she told Dalton when he finally emerged. "And then we have to stop by the general store so I can buy Becky's book."

"Let's do that at lunchtime. They sell snacks and we'll be hungry by then. We have to backtrack first if you want to see the buildings we missed by the entrance."

They took a quick peek at exhibits showcasing an antique printing press, fire engines, a telephone switchboard, and a railroad depot with a switching station and caboose. Marla admired the model trains, especially the motorized one running around an overhead track.

"Ryder would love this when he's older," she told Dalton.

He nodded. "It would be a great place to bring him. It's sad how many of these crafts are lost arts." His gesture encompassed the adjacent shoe repair place redolent with the smells of leather and polish.

"These artisan shops remind me of Scott Miller's clock repair place," she said. She'd met a horologist during a previous investigation after a murder at her friend's wedding. Horology involved the study of timekeeping, and graduates were able to design or fix clocks and watches. The memory of all those timepieces ticking and chiming in Scott's shop still rang in her ears.

Dalton took her elbow and steered her along the outdoor path. "Butter house, blacksmith shop, or smokehouse? Or should we check out the fishing hut next?"

"Let's go to Baffle House before it gets too crowded."

They had to pass by the jail again. The marshal stood in the doorframe talking to a wiry fellow in a denim overall.

Dalton's cell phone buzzed. He'd put it on silent at the jail house. "I have to answer this text. It's from Captain Williams. Wait here a minute," he told her before walking away.

Marla's steps lagged as raised voices reached her ears.

"You won't get away with it, Phil," the man in overalls said in a gruff tone. "Don't try to cut in on my operation."

"It isn't yours, Simon. You may have some fancy title, but you're not in charge." The marshal adjusted his cowboy hat while glowering at the other man.

Marla froze in place, hoping they wouldn't notice her. Just in case, she made a pretense of looking at the site map.

Simon jabbed a finger in the air. "They couldn't have gotten far without me. So don't imply that my contributions aren't important."

"I'm just saying they're using you. You're too blind to see it."

"Oh, and you're perfect? You think you're so high and mighty bossing it over on us. But let me tell you something, I can bring you down like an avalanche if you don't leave this alone."

Marla's bones chilled at the hostility in the man's tone. Was he another cast member?

Phil gave a nasty chuckle. "You wouldn't dare, because then you'd bring attention to yourself. That's the last thing you want, isn't it?"

"There are other ways of blocking you. Be warned," Simon said before scurrying off.

A tap on her arm startled her. Dalton had returned. He gestured that they should move on. Keeping pace beside him, she dared a glance over her shoulder. The men were nowhere in sight. Phil must have disappeared back inside the jail house.

"Did you hear any of that argument?" she asked Dalton. "And what did the police chief want? I hope it wasn't a new homicide case."

"Nah, he had a question about some paperwork I'd turned in. What argument?"

Marla repeated what she'd overheard. "Maybe this Simon fellow wants to be marshal. I wonder if the staff are required to audition for their roles. It can't be easy to learn the history and stay in character all day."

Dalton pointed to an older woman wearing a long skirt and a high-buttoned blouse along with an apron. She stood a couple of buildings over. "You could ask her about the requirements."

Most of the early visitors had already made it past this section, leaving it rather empty. The woman hummed a tune while stoking a campfire in front of a derelict shack. Her eyes sparked at their approach.

"Hello. I'm Millie Bleecher. If you have a few minutes, I'll teach you how to make homemade biscuits in an outdoor oven."

Marla hesitated. She wanted to tour the large residence, but the mention of cooking tempted her. The aroma of freshly baked bread convinced her to stay.

"Something smells divine," she said with a friendly smile. "I'd like to see your demo."

"If you don't mind, I'll head over to the blacksmith shop," Dalton told her. "Let's meet at the church when we're done and then we can go to Baffle House."

"Okay. I won't be too long."

He gave a two-finger salute and headed off. Marla turned back to Millie. "What ingredients do you use for the biscuits?" she asked to get the conversation flowing.

Freckles spattered the woman's face, while wisps of ash blond hair escaped a bonnet that tied under her chin. Millie looked to be in her forties and had the sturdy form of a Swedish masseuse. Maybe she got her strength from kneading dough or from lifting those heavy cast iron pots. Either way, she looked capable of managing a campsite on her own.

"All you need is flour, baking powder, salt, butter and milk. I use milk left over from our buttermilk project."

9

"What about equipment?" Marla's glance roved to a wooden plank that sat atop a series of buckets. Various items lay strewn across the makeshift worktable.

Millie regarded her with a kindly expression in her deep-set blue eyes. "You don't need much. A cardboard box with a lid, aluminum foil, wire coat hangers, aluminum pie pans and a baking tray will suffice. If you have food in the freezer that needs baking and the power goes out, you'll be able to prepare it with this handy pioneer method."

Marla moved closer to observe Millie's movements. Birds twittered among the trees as she stood in the dappled sunlight.

"First, we'll cover this carton and the lid on both sides with foil. Be sure to double layer the bottom. We'll double the pie pans as well. Then place them on the bottom of the box to hold your charcoal. Each briquette changes the temperature of the oven by eleven degrees. This means that for three hundred and fifty degrees, you'll need thirty-two briquettes."

Marla's brows raised at this tidbit of info. Dalton liked to barbecue. She'd have to pass on this tip to him, not that he'd be baking bread outside. Still, it might be useful when he grilled foods with the lid on.

She leaned over to peer inside the box. "What do you do with the coat hangers?"

Millie lifted one to show her. "We take each wire and stretch it out lengthwise. Use a screwdriver to poke three holes horizontally about one-third down the box on each side. Then fit the wires into the holes like this and twist them on the ends with a pair of pliers. I like to snip the extra lengths with these cutters."

"How clever. It looks just like a grill with those racks," Marla said, impressed by the simplicity of the design.

"Once the charcoal is ready, we put our baking pan on top of the rack and seal the lid. The bottom of the box will get very hot, so be careful where you place your oven."

Marla doubted it was something she'd want to try in her backyard. She'd probably set fire to the entire neighborhood.

Millie picked up a basket. "Here, you can taste one of these freshly baked biscuits. I'll slather on some of our homemade butter for you. They're also good with honey or molasses."

Marla bit into the baked good, bending over so as not to get any crumbs on herself. The butter helped to moisten the biscuit, otherwise it was too dry by her standards.

"Have you been working at the village for long?" Marla asked after swallowing the last morsel. She could use a drink of water to chase it down.

Millie chuckled. "I've been here for a couple of years, but you won't always find me baking biscuits. I'm also in charge of the sewing circle. Our meeting room is over yonder," she said with a wave. "You should stop by there for a tour."

"I will, thanks. I suppose you've met most of the other villagers who act as guides."

"Sure, we're all passionate about explaining our way of life to visitors. See this fire pit, for example?" Millie walked a few feet away to where a campfire burned. "Historically, flint was used to start fires. When struck with steel, it can produce enough sparks to ignite a fire with the proper tinder, such as hay or dried leaves. Today, you can buy fire starter kits online."

"Is that so?" Marla wrinkled her nose. She'd never been good at outdoor-type skills.

"See these tools? This part is a ferro rod and this one is a steel striker. The rod contains ferrocerium, an alloy composed of iron and cerium, a rare-earth element. You scrape the metal blade along the rod to get a spark." Millie showed Marla how to do it.

"That's a lot easier than using two rocks to start a fire," Marla said, visions of cavemen coming to mind. However, she was more interested in getting the woman to talk about her colleagues. "I didn't realize you had to be so skilled to work here. Would you know a man named Simon? I saw the marshal talking to him at the jail. He looked like a cast member."

Millie nodded, the skin crinkling beside her eyes. "Simon

Weedcutter is the town's farmer. You'll want to stop by his place to view his crops."

"What does he grow?"

"An assortment of vegetables. If we had an on-site restaurant, we could use them to prepare fresh food for guests. You haven't tasted anything until you've had my black-eyed peas over rice with cornbread and dandelion greens."

"Have you met Becky Forest?" Marla asked out of curiosity. "You two would have a lot in common. She's the curator of our local history museum. Becky recreates old Florida recipes for modern kitchens. She's doing a signing at the store this weekend for her latest cookbook."

"I know Becky. We've shared recipes for hominy grits among other southern specialties."

"I like the idea of a café on site," Marla said, realizing the only snacks available now were prepackaged items at the gift shop. "A restaurant would bring in more revenue. From what I've seen, this place could use it. Many of the buildings need repairs. Isn't the fairground responsible for the upkeep?"

Millie's shoulders slumped. "They provide our funding, but the last budget cuts are killing us. Phil has a plan that would give us more control."

"I noticed a donation box by the entrance. My husband and I might contribute if it's for a worthy cause. Is that what you mean?"

Millie lowered her voice. "Phil has proposed that we should buy the village from the fairground. He's looking for investors as well as donors if you're interested."

Marla gave her an astonished stare. "That would be a major change."

"True, and not everyone is pleased by the prospect. But I'm losing sight of my role."

"I understand." No, she didn't. Did the staff really want to be responsible for this burden? Sometimes being a tenant was less worrisome than being a landlord. And what did Phil personally hope to gain from his proposal?

Maybe he truly was dedicated to the village and feeling stumped by the directors. If the village fell into further disrepair, it might end up having to shut its doors permanently.

A glance at her watch told her she'd better move on. Dalton had said to meet up at the church and yet he wasn't in sight. However, a minister exited the sanctuary as she glanced that way. He headed in their direction.

Millie quickly grabbed a wooden spoon. "As you can see, it's easy to bake biscuits using this simple pioneer method. I hope you've learned a thing or two from my demonstration."

"Oh yes," Marla replied, wondering if the woman was afraid she'd said too much. "I might use a regular oven, but I like your recipe for homemade biscuits. Thanks so much for your time."

The minister sped past without lifting a hand in greeting. Clearly, he was in a hurry to get somewhere else.

Millie cleared her throat. "If you don't mind, I have work to do before the battle begins."

But instead of moving off, Millie watched the minister disappear behind the bait and tackle shed. Her mouth curved down and her eyes slitted, making Marla wonder what she had against the man.

Let it go, Marla. This tranquil setting might not be all it appears from what you've observed, but you're here for enjoyment and not to stir up trouble.

With those thoughts, Marla ignored her prickle of unease and left to find her husband.

Chapter Two

"I'm hungry," Dalton said when they finally met up again. He glanced at the site where she'd had her baking lesson and lifted his brows. "Did you eat a biscuit? Maybe I should have asked for one."

Marla grimaced. "It was too dry, although the homemade butter helped. The villagers need an air-conditioned restaurant that serves moist scones instead of Millie's pastries. They were too doughy as well. Nor was being near an outdoor oven fun in this heat."

He must have noticed her flushed skin. "You need to get cooled off. We'll still have time to eat lunch by noon if we stop at Baffle House first. It's probably air-conditioned."

They headed in that direction. "How was the blacksmith's shop?" Marla asked.

He gave her a quick grin. "It's hard work hammering molten metal, not something I'd ever want to do. Angus said he learned the trade from his father. He volunteers here full-time and makes products useful to the village, such as horseshoes, nails and farm tools."

Marla glanced at him. "What about swords and bayonets?"

"He serves the community, not the military. Did you know that around 1860, blacksmithing was the fourth most popular trade in the U.S. after lumber, flour milling and shoemaking?"

"No, I didn't." She could see the appeal of a simpler time with artisan shops, but she'd miss her modern conveniences.

They climbed the front steps of the house where a group was gathering. Green plants in ceramic pots sat on the porch along with two rocking chairs and a small wicker table. The single wood front door held an autumn-themed wreath.

While they waited, Marla told Dalton about Phil's plan to buy the village. "I don't understand why the fairground would consider the offer unless the village wasn't profitable. Maybe revenues are down, and Phil feels this is a good time to make an offer."

Dalton's brow creased. "He has a good position here as administrator. Why rock the boat?"

"The man I saw at the jail arguing with him was Simon Weedcutter, the town's farmer. Maybe he was blaming Phil for the state of disrepair. As liaison to the fairground, it would be Phil's job to request more funding for improvements."

"Seems like the army soldiers versus the Seminoles aren't the only conflicts around here. We can visit the farm later. I'd like to see their tomato plants."

Dalton took pride in his home garden. Maybe she could encourage him to expand his efforts in that regard once he retired. She'd love to have a source of fresh herbs for her kitchen. She'd had little time to cook since Ryder was born, relying on quick prep meals and take-out, but it would be nice to use her cooking skills again.

A middle-aged woman dressed in an old-fashioned rose blouse with a cameo brooch and a long skirt appeared in the historic home's doorway. She smiled at the crowd, making lines crinkle beside her warm maple-colored eyes.

"Welcome to Baffle House, folks. I'm Miss Lizzy. Please step into the parlor." She spoke in the refined voice of an upper-crust aristocrat. Marla liked the way she'd secured her champagne blond hair into a twist with a jeweled comb.

They entered a cozy sitting room with white lace curtains adorning the windows. Marla didn't know what to look at first—the ornate fireplace mantel, the oil paintings on the walls, the fringed lampshades, or the porcelain doll with large eyes sitting on a couch.

Lizzy began her lecture, while the guests held back at a polite distance.

"I'm a descendant of Adam Canfield, who bought this property in 1859. It had been a thriving sugar plantation until the price of sugar declined. Then Adam switched to citrus groves. He built this house for his wife, Elizabeth, in 1860. All went well until the Civil War came along, and our luck plunged downhill after that."

"How so?" a woman in the back called out.

"Adam was sympathetic to the Confederate cause, and he paid the price with his life. Later, the Great Depression forced his grandson, Zachery Winthrop, to sell most of the land. The house remained in the family along with the last hundred acres."

"How did the fairground come to own it?" Marla asked.

Lizzy's gaze turned thoughtful. "In 1956, the county donated land to establish a fairground. Our property was adjacent. Zachery's son, Ian, owed debts due to a gambling addiction. He sold our remaining acreage, including this house, to the fairground. Rumor says he was tricked into selling. But that's another story, and we need to move on."

"Why is this place called Baffle House?" Dalton queried as Lizzy led them toward a spinet piano in one corner.

"The house has a secret I'll tell you about later. It's baffled people for generations." She proceeded to describe the furnishings and pieces of art before they entered a hallway with a staircase to the second level.

In the hall, Marla paused to admire a fancy framed mirror. Beneath it was an accent table with a vase of fresh wildflowers. The leaves fluttered in a draft from an air-conditioning vent. Marla went to stand under it, removing her hat to let the breeze cool her scalp. The chilled blast felt so good that she wished she could linger.

Afraid to be left behind, she hurried after the group where they gathered in the dining room. A rectangular table set for six stood in the center. Ivory lace curtains, a crystal chandelier and

16

floral-patterned wallpaper decorated the room. Lizzy pointed out a walnut sideboard.

"My father crafted this piece. He was a carpenter and did beautiful work. Dad could have sold his furniture, but he never had the ambition."

Dalton ran a hand over the surface. "He was a highly skilled craftsman. It's too bad he didn't take his artistry more seriously."

"I know, right? I'll show you his other pieces as we move through the house."

Dalton's remark sparked an idea in Marla's mind. "Hon, maybe you should take up woodworking in your spare time. We could use extra shelving in the laundry room and a couple of chairs for the front porch."

His brows arched. "That's not a bad idea. I'll think about it."

"I can look into online classes if you like."

"No, thanks. If I'm interested, I'll do it myself."

Marla realized he must be getting tired of her constant suggestions of things to do in his retirement, but she didn't want him to get bored. He'd be home alone when Ryder was in day care and she went to work.

They entered the kitchen and her attention diverted to their surroundings. Appliances from the 1930s ringed the room while a big square table took up the middle space. An old-fashioned electric refrigerator and range drew her interest before she noted a carved wooden ship on the windowsill.

"Dalton, look over there. You could make toys for Ryder if you got into wood crafts. It's not only about furniture and shelving."

"True. I did like the set of model trains we saw at the depot. Railroad barons played a large part in Florida history. If anything, I'd like to learn more about that subject."

Bingo! He could follow the history trail for Florida's railroad industry. He might even become busier than before retirement, especially if any of his part-time jobs panned out. That would ease her concerns that he might regret his decision.

She and Dalton trudged upstairs after the group and strolled through a series of bedrooms, including a nursery with a handmade crib and shelves holding antique cast-iron toys. A dollhouse occupied one corner, while a child-sized table and chairs took up another.

Marla gravitated toward a tall hat rack. A fireman's helmet, cowboy hat and boat captain's cap would be fun for boys to try on, while girls would like the frilly hats bedecked with ribbons.

She gave a quick glance at a trio of porcelain dolls sitting on a crimson settee. Their placid faces and staring eyes reminded her of horror movies, same as the doll downstairs.

I'd rather have my Barbies. They might be skinny, but they're not creepy like these dolls.

"You said you'd explain why this residence is called Baffle House," Dalton reminded their hostess before the tour concluded.

Lizzy eyes twinkled. "It's an interesting story. Folks, if you have to leave, don't be shy about it. I know you want to get over to the bleachers before the battle."

Most of the crowd dispersed at her words, leaving only a few people lingering along with Marla and Dalton.

"As I said earlier, my ancestor, Adam Canfield, sided with the Confederates during the Civil War. He housed Captain Matt Lowry and his men who were marching north to deliver a Confederate payroll. When they heard a troop of Union soldiers was headed this way, they hid the gold and escaped to the Everglades."

She paused for dramatic effect before continuing the story. "Adam and his wife, Elizabeth, stood on the front porch and faced the Union troops. When Adam wouldn't tell them where Captain Lowry had gone, they shot him."

Marla clapped a hand to her cheek. "That's horrible."

"What happened to the gold?" Dalton asked, while Marla was still absorbing the scene in her mind. Imagine Adam's wife seeing him killed before her eyes.

"Captain Lowry's men failed to return, so the coins were never recovered. Nobody knew what happened to them. People have tried to find the lost payroll, but the ghost of the White Lady chases them away."

"Who's the White Lady?" Marla liked this legend. After her encounter with a playful spirit at Sugar Crest Plantation Resort, she believed in otherworldly phenomenon.

"Elizabeth is still here, searching for the gold so she can stave off the Union soldiers and save her husband. She's wearing the same dress she had on the day he died. Meanwhile, the secret of the missing treasure continues to baffle people."

"Do you believe this story is true?" Marla asked, remembering her own treasure hunt at the resort on Florida's west coast.

Lizzy winked at Marla. "Maybe. If you want to learn more, join our nightly ghost tour. Now, you'd better hustle along if you want to get a good seat for the battle. The bleachers get filled fast."

The other guests left, leaving Marla and Dalton dallying on the front porch. Marla still had some questions she wanted to ask.

"I gather you volunteer to act as tour guide?" she asked the other woman.

Lizzy gestured. "Who else could provide this much background information? As a descendant of the property's owner, I'm the best person for the job."

"It must be distressing to know Baffle House would have belonged to you if your ancestor hadn't gambled away his inheritance."

"This is true, although I'm hoping to make things right."

"How so?"

Lizzy leaned forward and lowered her voice. "I've offered to buy back the house along with the land it sits on, but the directors won't budge."

"Why would you want it?" Marla's curiosity spiked as they moved from past issues to present. Or was this part of the story?

"I know this place better than anyone, and I'd make sure it's properly maintained. That bunch of old fogies opposes anything to do with progress."

"I've heard about Phil's proposal. Do you think it will be accepted?"

Lizzy expression soured. "I doubt it. Besides, his plan wouldn't give me any advantage since I still wouldn't own this property. However, we are united in trying to get the directors to make changes."

Why would Lizzy go to such an expense when she couldn't live there? The house was a museum, not living history in the literal sense. Taking control of the house's maintenance didn't seem like a good enough reason to want to own the place. There had to be something Lizzy wasn't telling them, if this wasn't another fabrication meant to entertain.

Marla and Dalton departed after promising to consider the ghost tour.

"This village keeps getting more intriguing," she said once they were out of earshot. "What did you think about Lizzy's tale?"

"Which one? She told us a lot of stories. I'm not sure how much was truth and how much was fiction." He poked her arm. "I thought you were more interested in the décor than the history lesson."

Marla shrugged. "I got caught up in her spiel. Lizzy is a good storyteller either way. She seems devoted to keeping her part of the legacy alive. Do you believe she really is a descendant of Adam Canfield?"

"You can look it up when we get home. Meanwhile, let's grab lunch." He set a pace toward the general store. "We need to eat fast and head over to the battle site."

Marla squealed with delight as they entered the gift shop. Its old-time atmosphere drew her in along with a dazzling array of goods for sale. The air smelled like orange blossoms.

"Look at these," Dalton said, pointing to a selection of metal dinner bells and souvenir horseshoes. "I'll bet the village blacksmith made them."

"A lot of these things appear handmade." Marla wandered off to browse the shelves while Dalton headed across the wood-planked floor toward the refrigerated section. He'd pick out their lunch choices.

Marla fingered some aprons and bonnets that must have been crafted by the sewing ladies. Further over was a collection of handmade soaps and candles. Her nose filled with a bouquet of scents as she skirted a stash of logo mugs, baseball caps, tee shirts, and shot glasses. She paused to eye a colorful set of ceramic canisters then shook her head. They were pretty, but she didn't need any more tchotchkes to clutter her kitchen.

She glanced at a display of jams, jellies, tea, and honey on her way to the kids' section. Buckets and barrels spilled over with toys. Ryder was too young for most of them, but she could buy a book to read to him at bedtime.

After she found a couple of stories she liked, she grabbed a copy of Becky's new cookbook from a display stand. Dalton stood perusing a section on local history. He handed her their packaged sandwiches and sodas.

"I'm sorry to miss the book signing," she told the store-keeper as she paid for their purchases. "Becky is a friend of ours. She's the one who told us about the battle reenactment."

"Is that right? I expect her books will sell well after today's event." The manager, whose name tag read Uriah, spoke in a gravelly voice. He wore a button-down dress shirt and a vest along with charcoal pants. His receding dark brown hair needed a trim over his ears.

She took the shopping bags from his outstretched hand. "We've only been to see the jail, the blacksmith shop, and Baffle House so far. What else do you recommend?"

He pushed his wire-rimmed spectacles to the top of his nose. "You don't want to miss the schoolroom. Miss Violet is great with children. Do you have kids?"

"We have a son. Ryder is thirteen months old."

"When your boy is older, Miss Violet holds workshops for children on weekends. We have field trip programs for local schools, too. You can view the full list on our website."

21

"Thanks, I'll do that. What's this remedy for arthritis?" she asked, picking up a labeled bottle on the counter. "My mother could use it."

"That's one of my formulations. When my mom got sick, the docs said she wouldn't have long to live. It was holistic medicine that saved her. I'm a licensed pharmacist and would offer tonics and elixirs in the store if we had an apothecary. Phil said I could add one once his proposal gets approved."

"I've been informed about his plan. Do you support him, then?"

"As long as he keeps his promises. I like his idea of opening a café where guests could get freshly prepared foods instead of these packaged items. I'd convert our refrigerated section into my chemist's corner."

Marla pictured the village map in her mind. "There doesn't appear to be any available space for new buildings. Would one of the existing structures have to be modified?"

Uriah's expression soured. "Yes, it would, and not everyone is happy about that idea." A chime tinkled as other guests entered the shop. "Now if you would excuse me, I need to help these customers."

"One more minute. Do you have any portable fans? It's hot as an oven outside."

He retrieved several items from a drawer. "We have these paper ones. They're handmade by our sewing circle ladies and cost five dollars each."

Marla made her final purchase and then left with Dalton. In a hurry to head over to the reenactment site, they gobbled down their turkey and cheese sandwiches at a picnic table. While they ate, she told him about her conversation with Uriah.

"It sounds as though he's in favor of the marshal's proposal," Dalton said. He finished off his cola and stood to gather their trash.

Marla swiped a dribble of perspiration from her face. "Maybe they have a petition we can sign, although nobody has mentioned one. Or we can give a donation online if you want to support the village."

Dalton lifted an eyebrow. "We could also become members and visit when it's less crowded. Anyway, let's get going. We need to find seats."

Marla grabbed her shopping bags and stood, ready to see what the fuss was all about with the battle. Hordes of people milled about the exhibits along the way. Demonstrations were offered for barricade building, musket loading, tomahawk throwing, and basket weaving. Animal skins flapped in the breeze at one tent where a costumed fellow described the tannery process.

Marla glanced at a table holding a wooden apple press. An apple cider demo would be fun to watch, but they didn't have time to linger. Too bad these exhibits were only here during the reenactment.

They found seats a few levels up on a hot bench. Thank goodness she'd worn a wide-brimmed hat and sunglasses. She'd also had the foresight to apply sunscreen.

Soldiers wearing blue uniforms with high collars, shiny brass buttons, and tall hats marched past to take their places on the field. They carried muskets and had canteens strapped to their chests along with other equipment.

A man's voice on a loudspeaker rang out, welcoming the guests. She recognized the marshal's southern drawl.

"Today we are commemorating a massacre that occurred on July 3, 1836. That was one year after the Dade Battle in Bushnell that started the Second Seminole War. One hundred and ten U.S. Army troops were on a mission to deliver a cannon to Fort King in Ocala. Along the way, they were attacked by one hundred and eighty Seminole warriors. Only two soldiers survived."

"They must have been terrified," Marla said to Dalton. "It's so sad."

"Hungry and wounded, the two men made it to the fort," the marshal continued. "They explained what happened and a contingent returned to bury the dead."

The blue-coated soldiers moved forward in a column. They followed a narrow dirt trail among the pines and scrub brush but still in view from the bleachers. A small group wheeled the cannon, the only artillery in sight. Three officers rode on horseback behind the troop's drummer. The soldiers looked weary, as though they'd been on the road for days.

The narration resumed. "The troops weren't ready for action. Their muskets were not loaded, and their ammunition was stuffed under their jackets. They'd grown tired and didn't notice the tribesmen following them."

Suddenly, shots rang out.

"The captain is hit!" the marshal exclaimed as the other officers shouted orders. The soldiers scrambled for defensive positions. Then the lieutenant toppled from his horse.

"Another officer down! The Seminole chief is a wily fellow. He knows which men are commanding the force, and he's taking out the leaders one-by-one. Oh, no! There goes the sergeant. Now the rest of the troops will be mowed down like blades of grass."

Did the army troops even stand a chance? Marla watched with dismay as they seemed to realize they were surrounded and outnumbered.

From beyond the trees, Seminoles carrying weapons closed in on them. Riders on horseback set covering fire with the crack of rifles. Meanwhile, the troops fired the cannon with an explosive blast. Smoke filled the air.

Marla could barely hear what the marshal was saying over the constant pop of gunshots and the screams of the troops. The scene became a haze of moving figures.

Dramatic music swelled as the scene progressed.

"See how the poor chaps are attempting to build a barrier with those logs," the marshal's voice boomed. "Unfortunately, their efforts will be in vain. The Seminoles are encircling them. You can feel their desperation."

Dalton nudged Marla. "The army soldiers had muskets that were smooth-bore and more suitable for short-range firing. The

Native Americans used Deringer percussion rifles given to them in the Treaty of Paynes Landing. These had greater accuracy from a distance but took longer to load."

"Why was that?" Marla asked, following his cue.

"Both were muzzle-loaders, at least until 1850 or so. This means a powder charge and ball had to be inserted into the end of the barrel and pushed down to the firing mechanism. It was easier to do this for a smooth-bore musket with a larger barrel. Pushing the same ball down a tighter-fitting rifle took longer. However, the spiral grooves, termed rifling, inside this barrel meant greater accuracy. For tribesmen shooting at a distance on horseback, it gave them the advantage."

Soon most of the soldiers lay motionless on the ground. The Seminoles prowled among them, checking for survivors. Their colorful costumes made them stand out amid the greenery. Then they scuttled off into the woods leaving a dead silence behind.

"This concludes our show," said an unfamiliar voice on the speakers. "Let's give a big round of applause for our reenactors, many of whom have come from across the state to join us."

The cast of characters lined up and bowed to the audience, who cheered and clapped. Then pandemonium ensued while everyone descended from the bleachers. Several actors remained for guests who wanted to speak to them. These included a Native American with a ring through his nose and war paint on his face, an infantry sergeant in a blue uniform and tall hat who introduced himself as a Second Seminole War reenactor, and a historical educator dressed as a hunter.

Dalton paused to engage the latter. "Why was this battle so important?" he asked. "It didn't even take place here."

The man shrugged, rattling the necklace of pointy teeth around his neck. "This massacre was one of the key incidents in the Second Seminole War. We do our best to portray it as closely as possible to actual events. Andrew Jackson was President then, and he wasn't fond of the indigenous population. His policy was to remove them so settlers could come in."

"Yes, I read that Florida had recently become a territory of the United States," Dalton said. "The government wanted to move the tribes to Oklahoma, but the Seminoles refused. It was a sad and shameful part of our history."

"No matter how painful, we don't want the past to be forgotten." The man clapped a hand to his chest. "I'm a fourth-generation reenactor, and I believe in living history. You can see it, smell it and taste it through our recreations."

"What about those guns?" Marla asked. "Couldn't someone get hurt for real?"

"Nah. There's a lot of inspectors who make sure the weapons are safe and that everyone knows what they're doing."

"That's good to know. Thanks so much for your time," Dalton told him before steering Marla away and back toward the village.

"I'm surprised the marshal didn't conclude the festivities," she said. "You'd think it would be the perfect opportunity to ask for donations."

Dalton shrugged. "Maybe he got called off site for some reason."

They strolled along until a high-pitched scream tore through the air and shattered the peace.

Oh, no. Marla had heard similar cries before, and it hadn't ended well. She hoped history wasn't about to repeat itself.

Chapter Three

A horde of guests swarmed toward the noise while others scurried in the opposite direction to escape the scene. Marla and Dalton, already on the edge of the woods, rushed toward the bait and tackle shed from where the screams seemed to originate. She hoped someone had merely spotted an alligator on the grounds.

They approached the derelict wooden shack with its tilted sign and barged inside. Through a rear window, Marla spotted a deck that extended over a pond to a covered landing. A woman stood frozen on the planks, her horrified gaze fixed on a man lying face-up at her feet.

Dalton headed that way. As Marla followed him outdoors and got a closer look, she swallowed a surge of bile in her throat. The man down had an axe planted in his forehead. Blood pooled behind his head and seeped through cracks in the boardwalk.

Her heart jolted. The dead guy was the missing marshal. *Oh. My. God. We just met him. This can't be happening.*

As she grappled with reality, bystanders crowded onto the deck to gawk at the scene.

"Folks, stand back," Dalton said, taking command. "I'm with the Palm Haven Police Department. We need to secure this area. Please wait over by the shed." He yanked out his phone, presumably to call for backup, while Marla wondered if this fell under his jurisdiction.

A couple of guests led the witness to a bench, while Marla gave one more glance at the body. She knew she'd wrack her brain later for clues, especially if Dalton took over the case. Her gaze zeroed in on the swirls of paint and colorful feathers decorating the weapon's handle.

Wait, was that an axe or a tomahawk? It did share certain similarities to the ones in the battle scene, although those had to be fakes. The Seminoles had brandished tomahawks along with rifles, clubs, and spears.

A brackish scent from the pond invaded her nose and made her stomach churn. Good thing Phil hadn't ended up in there, or he'd be alligator meat.

They'd only spoken to him a short while ago, and he'd sounded strong during his narration. How could this have happened to him?

She swung around to regard the woman who'd sounded the alert. Her period dress indicated her role as a villager. What had she been doing back here? Did she run this shop?

Realizing their trip home would be delayed, she fumbled for her phone and texted Dalton's mom who was babysitting their son. Ryder was doing fine, Kate replied. He was down for his nap. She and her husband, John, could stay through dinner if necessary.

Relieved on that score, Marla stashed her phone. She forced her gaze to the woods bordering the pond. The tranquil scene belied what was happening on the boardwalk. Dalton was keeping onlookers at bay while urging anyone late to the scene to leave.

Her heart sank. She'd been praying that his last few months at work would be easy ones. Now he might have another case to solve.

Perhaps she should make herself useful and see what she could do to help him. They'd worked as a team before.

She approached the woman on the bench. With her sickly pallor, the lady looked as though she might pass out. Tendrils of honey blond hair escaped her bonnet.

"Let's give her some breathing space, okay fellas?" Marla told the crowd.

Her words galvanized them into action. The throng dissipated, while the woman gave Marla a grateful glance.

"Thank you," she said in a quiet voice. "Can I go inside the shed to wait? I don't want to stay out here where I can see poor Phil. This is unbelievable. Who would do that to him?" She rubbed a hand over her face.

"You tell me, ma'am. I'm Marla Vail, by the way. My husband is a homicide detective with the local police force." She gestured over to where he was speaking into his phone.

"Yes, I heard him say he was a cop. It's a good thing he's here. My name is Violet."

"I'm sorry for your loss, Violet. Phil must have been one of your colleagues."

"He played the village marshal. He was also our administrator. Now someone else will have to be appointed in his place." Violet didn't sound too distressed by this prospect.

"Do you have any idea who might be next in line?"

"Who knows?" Violet fanned herself. "I'm not feeling very well. It's too hot out here."

"I agree." Anxious to get out of the heat and feeling somewhat shaky, Marla signaled to Dalton where they were going. She led Violet inside the air-conditioned shack and seated her on an empty chair behind the cash register. It took a few moments of leaning against a counter before Marla's racing pulse slowed to a normal rate.

Glancing around, she noticed small details she'd missed during their initial rush through the place. Stuffed fish along with framed photos of prize catches decorated the walls. Various items related to fishing were for sale, including a selection of boat motors.

The rustic decor reminded Marla of seafood restaurants where she'd rather eat the fish than catch them. She wondered if the ramshackle exterior was intentional. A real old-time fishing shed would have open windows to let in the fresh breeze.

"May I ask what role you play?" Marla asked, turning her attention to the lady in the chair.

"I'm the schoolteacher." Violet removed a tissue from her purse and dabbed at eyes that were the same color as her name.

29

"Oh, really? I've heard good things about your classes from the gift shop manager."

Violet gave a shy smile. "Uriah is such a sweet man."

"I would have liked more time to browse in his shop, but we had to move on," Marla explained, hoping to cajole her into revealing more.

"Uriah really enjoys managing the store. He'll be disappointed that Phil's proposal will be dust now that he's gone. Phil had such great plans for our village."

"Such as?"

"He was trying to save our jobs, or at least, most of them," Violet said in a soft tone. "Thanks to budget cuts from the fairground, I won't be able to renew my classes for next season. You should see how the kids' faces light up when history is presented to them in an entertaining manner."

"Uriah said not everyone would be pleased by Phil's plan. What did he mean?"

Violet cast an anxious glance toward the boardwalk. "I shouldn't talk ill of the dead, but his proposed café would have displaced one of our more popular features."

"Which one would that be, if you don't mind my asking?"

Again, Violet's gaze flickered toward the rear exit. Was she nervous about someone she knew showing up there?

"I think I've said enough." The schoolteacher fluffed her skirts, her fingers plucking at the fabric.

Marla gritted her teeth. Getting information from this woman was as difficult as curling a stubborn strand of hair. "Are you a real teacher?" she asked to refresh their conversation.

Violet nodded, her eyes cast downward. "I used to teach full-time until... well, I'm happy to use my skills here. And I love keeping history alive the way we do at the park. Have you visited the schoolroom?"

"We didn't have time today. I'll come back when it's quieter." Marla was aware Violet had changed the subject away from herself. Was she hiding something?

"You might want to visit during the week. It's less crowded then."

"I work during the week, although I am off on Mondays." Marla handed Violet a business card.

Violet scanned the info then stuck it in her bag. "Thank you for looking after me. I feel better now, as long as I don't have to see Phil again. Can I go?"

Marla caught Dalton's eye outside and gestured to him. He said a few words to an onlooker and then stepped indoors.

"Violet, this is Detective Dalton Vail. Hon, the lady would like to leave the premises. Could you ask her your preliminary questions and get her contact info for later?"

"Sure, I can do that. May I suggest you take the car and go home to Ryder? I'll catch a lift from one of my team members."

"All right." Her heart sank. This case fell under his territory after all. While wishing she could stay and listen to their conversation, she realized her presence might prove distracting. She said her farewells and left.

Once back at the village square, she glanced at her watch. It was only three-thirty. She could spare another half hour if she wanted to depart at four as per their original plan. While anxious to get home to Ryder, she also wanted to learn more to help Dalton solve the case fast.

As she stood on the green, the heat and humidity hit her like a briquette of charcoal in Millie's makeshift oven. She got out the paper fan from her purse and waved it to cool her face. A rumble in the distance drew her gaze to the sky, where cumulus clouds gathered into towering columns. Likely, a storm was on its way, and she should be well inside her car by then. Where could she go right now that would be quick?

She should check out the Seminole camp. Not only might the murder weapon have come from there, but if the warriors had taken part in the reenactment, maybe one of them had slipped out during the battle scene. She could launch a few probes and then leave the park.

31

Her steps in that direction faltered when she came face-to-face with her cousin, Corbin Weinstock, rushing the opposite way. He halted upon their encounter.

"Corbin, is it really you?" she asked, after closing her gaping jaw.

"Marla, I can't believe it. What are you doing here?" He scratched at the plaid shirt he wore tucked into a pair of pants held up by suspenders.

"I can ask the same. Do you work at the village?" She waved at his outfit. "You're dressed for the part."

His blue eyes narrowed. "So what if I do?"

"It would be nice to let the family know that you're okay. I haven't seen you at any recent holidays when we've gathered together. Is your sister aware you work here?"

"Cynthia knows I'm all right. Otherwise, I keep a low profile."

Marla hadn't seen him since their extended family reunion four years ago at Sugar Crest Plantation Resort, when Aunt Polly had died. Corbin didn't look much different today for a man in his mid-forties except for a slight paunch. His hair had receded more, but he had the same sullen expression on his face.

She was one of the few family members who knew Corbin's history. Cousin Cynthia had hired an attorney to defend her younger brother when he was accused of a felony offense, but the man had screwed up and Corbin got convicted. Later, when the attorney turned up dead, Marla had briefly considered Cynthia as a potential suspect.

And here you are, Marla, at the site of another murder.

"Your cousins would like to see you," she told Corbin. "You should come to Rosh Hashanah dinner. Julia is hosting this year."

"Family get-togethers aren't my thing. And don't go telling people where to find me, either."

"I'm here with Dalton. He's a big fan of history but this was our first reenactment," she said in a friendly manner to put him at ease. "What role do you play?"

She didn't want to probe too deeply, but she did care about his welfare. And he was missing out by not joining family functions. If he realized not everyone would be judgmental, he might return to the nest, so to speak.

He hooked his thumbs into his waistband and squinted in the sunlight. "I work with Simon Weedcutter, the farmer, as his apprentice. We tend the crops and care for the livestock."

"I'll bet the children like the animals."

"They do. We have a petting zoo that your son might enjoy. Congrats on having a baby, by the way. My sister told me."

"Thanks. I'm glad you two keep in touch. Ryder is so cute." Marla showed him a photo on her cell phone. "Dalton is retiring in September so he can spend more time at home."

"Good for him. How is Brianna doing? She's a smart kid and must be all grown up by now."

Marla warmed at his interest. "She got accepted into college at Boston. She's leaving next month. It'll be exciting for her, but we'll miss her terribly."

"I'm sure the baby will keep you busy. Come by the farm next time you visit, and I'll give you a tour."

"You sound happy, Corbin. I'm thrilled you've found something you enjoy." She adjusted her sunglasses. "Where were you off to just now?"

His face reddened. "I have an errand to do for Simon."

"Oh? Is he at the farm, then?"

"No, he ran off earlier... I mean, he's busy elsewhere."

Marla gave him a startled glance. Simon had run off? Was that before or after the victim was murdered?

"That's too bad. I was hoping to meet him. Tell me, is yours a paid position, or do you volunteer your time? The staff I've met are all passionate about the living history experience. It's a great way to keep the past alive."

He shrugged. "I get paid. It's not much, but the salary pays my rent, and the fairground provides benefits."

"Do you live nearby? It's expensive to rent a place in town.

Rates must be more reasonable this far west. We're almost at the Everglades."

"I have a place over by the nature preserve. It's a ten-minute drive."

"That's easy. Maybe Dalton would be interested in volunteering when he retires. How did you learn about the opening here?"

Corbin kicked at a pebble in the dirt. "A friend told me about the position. It was a guy I'd met… earlier, who had been released before me."

"I didn't realize you liked farming."

"I take care of the animals. I'd go back to school to become a veterinary technician if I had the money. It's hard getting funding with my history."

She felt bad for him. It couldn't be easy for ex-convicts who wanted to be gainfully employed. "Will your sister help? She'd be thrilled for you to do something you loved."

"Cynthia offered, but I'd never accept her money."

"How do you feel about the marshal's proposal to go independent?" She noted his wary glance. "Oh yes, I've heard about it."

His mouth curved down. "I'm against the move. Better not to upset the apple cart, yes?"

"I understand his plan included an on-site restaurant. Your farm could have supplied the fresh vegetables. It's a shame that won't happen now."

"What do you mean?" Corbin glanced toward the fishing shack, where a hubbub of activity continued. "Hey, what's going on over there?"

Her gut clenched at the news she was about to impart. "I regret to inform you that the town marshal has passed away."

The blood drained from Corbin's face. "What? Phil is dead? How did that happen?"

"He was found on the boardwalk behind the bait and tackle shed. That's all I know for now." Dalton wouldn't want her giving out any further information.

"No way. I don't believe it." With those words, Corbin turned on his heel and dashed off in the general direction of the farm.

Or was he headed to the Seminole camp over that same way?

She envisioned the tomahawk imbedded in Phil's forehead. Dalton needed to visit the Native American site to see if one of the tribesmen could identify the weapon's owner.

Chapter Four

"Thank you for watching Ryder," Marla told her in-laws once she was home. Kate held the toddler in her arms, content to nuzzle her grandson in the family room. Marla's pleased glance took in her soft waves of auburn hair. Kate had been to her salon just last week for a touch-up.

"Where's Dalton?" John asked, glancing toward the kitchen where she'd entered via the inner garage door. His gray hair stuck out on one side as though the child had grabbed a tuft. It didn't subtract from his dignity. The former attorney stood tall and had sharp eyes behind his wire-rimmed glasses.

"Oh, um, he had something to do and will be along later. He's catching a ride home with friends." Marla didn't want to worry them about their son taking on another homicide case so close to his retirement. Besides, the events from the day had tired her out, and she didn't feel like talking about it. Taking care of Ryder was her priority now.

She sidestepped around the dogs who'd bounded forward at her arrival. Spooks, their cream-colored poodle, sniffed her ankles while Lucky, their golden retriever, pushed one of Ryder's balls across the tile with her nose.

"Remind my son about the art festival next weekend, will you?" John said, wagging a finger. "He promised to stop by."

John entered his stained-glass pieces into shows, a venture he'd pursued only after his own retirement. Marla hoped Dalton would be free to go next Saturday.

"I'll tell him. I wish I could come, but I'll be working."

"Here, your son wants you." Kate handed over Ryder, who was whimpering and reaching for Marla. "He's an active little boy. It won't be long before you'll be chasing him around the house."

"I know." Marla cuddled Ryder, who laid his head on her shoulder. "Thanks for coming today. Pioneer Village was fun. You should visit there sometime."

"It does sound intriguing. We're glad you could go. Call us anytime you need someone to watch Ryder."

"We'll see you at my brother Michael's birthday next Sunday, yes?" Marla asked. "It should be a nice party." Michael's wife, Charlene, had planned a celebration for him and had kindly invited Dalton's parents to join them.

"Sure, we'll be there. Get some rest, dear. You look tired." Kate's hazel eyes gazed at Marla with fond affection.

"Thanks again for watching Ryder. It was good to get away for a few hours."

Marla let them out, then shut and locked the front door. "Listen, sweetie, I have to get your dinner ready," she told her son. "You'll have to play with your toys on your own for a few minutes, okay?"

She sniffed his diaper to make sure he was clean and then snuggled his warm, soft body. Her lips brushed his cheek as she carried him into the family room adjacent to the kitchen. His skin tasted like nectar from heaven. She put him down, watching him scuttle away on all fours.

Before long, he wouldn't let her hold him at all. The years would go by too fast. He already pulled himself upright on the furniture, learning how to stand. She'd really have her hands full when he could dash around.

In the kitchen, she refilled the dogs' dishes and water bowls before cutting up food for Ryder. She'd prepare a plate for Dalton so he could reheat his meal when he got home. She sighed, wishing he was retired already. A fresh murder case would keep him busy for hours.

The front door slammed and the dogs raced toward the noise. Brianna's voice greeted the pets before she breezed into the kitchen.

"Hey Marla. How did you like the history park?" The teen tossed her keys and purse on the counter. She had on a halter top and shorts and sported a mild sunburn on her face.

Marla's heart lightened. "It was more exciting than I'd expected. How was the beach?"

Brianna's dark eyes danced. "We had lunch at the shrimp place across the street. I'm going to miss the ocean and palm trees when I live in Boston. That's the biggest downside to moving up north."

Marla glanced at her hair tied in a ponytail. "I hope you wore the hat with sunscreen that I bought for you."

Brianna waved a hand. "No worries. I only took it off when I was in the water."

While the teen went to shower, Marla put a portion of baked salmon on a plate for Ryder along with mac and cheese and diced cucumber. Then she retrieved her son and strapped him into the seat attached to the kitchen table. She helped him eat until Brianna rejoined them, wearing a pair of jeans and a tank top. She'd washed her long hair that had frizzed in the humidity.

"I like how I can air-dry my hair here. I'll need to use a blow-dryer in Boston when it gets cold outside," Brianna said, taking a seat at the table.

"You'll adore the city," Marla told her, rising to put their meals together. "My dad used to follow the Freedom Trail when we lived in New York State. Our family would spend weekends in Boston and the surrounding areas. In those days, I could have cared less about history."

"I've read about the places to visit. There are sites that date back to the American Revolution. Dad will love it when he can come and see them in person. Where is he, by the way?" Brianna glanced toward the bedroom wing.

Marla grimaced. "He's still at Pioneer Village. We saw

some of the buildings, got through the battle scene, and then there was, um, an unfortunate incident."

Brianna's expression turned shrewd. "Uh-oh. You look as though you've swallowed a lemon pit. Don't tell me—"

"Yes, you're correct, but I really don't want to talk about it now. I'd rather enjoy your company and have a peaceful dinner."

"Okay, but I'll expect to hear all the details tomorrow."

Brianna liked a mystery same as her dad, although she'd rather investigate diseases like the one that killed her mother rather than solve murders. However, she did come up with useful suggestions whenever they discussed a case and didn't shy away from the sordid details.

Dalton surprised Marla by coming home at eight, earlier than other cases that kept him up late. Brianna had gone into her room by then while Marla had bathed Ryder and put him in his crib. The dogs had settled into their doggie beds for the night.

After her husband disappeared inside the bathroom, she poured them both glasses of chardonnay to go with his reheated meal. Despite her fatigue, she wanted to hear what he had to say about today's events.

He waved her off when she broached the subject. "Let's exchange news in the morning. It's been a long day, and I'm tired."

She swallowed her disappointment and sat across from him at the table. The encounter with Corbin hovered on her tongue, but she postponed the tale. Instead, she described Ryder's antics and summarized Brianna's day at the beach. "Tomorrow is July Fourth. You're going to miss the fun at the park."

"Brianna is still going, yes? She'll help you with Ryder."

"I didn't tell your parents what happened at the village, although Brianna guessed from my expression. I promised to fill her in on events in the morning."

"That girl is too astute." He beamed with pride as he said it.

"Your father wanted me to remind you about his art show next weekend."

"It's on my calendar. I'll make it a point to stop by."

"And don't forget it's Michael's birthday on Sunday. I hope you can make it."

He gave an exasperated sigh. "I promised to be there, and I'll keep my word. I can always let Langley do the legwork that day."

Once he'd finished eating, Marla got up to do the dishes. He followed suit, picking up a dishtowel, but not before he kissed the back of her neck.

"I can't wait until I'm home with you full-time," he said in a gentle tone while she absorbed the faint scent of his spice after-shave.

"Then you need to wrap this case fast. Let me help by gathering information. Half the town will be at tomorrow's holiday event. I can sound people out about the fairground."

"That's not a bad idea. It is peculiar how we never heard of the village until recently."

"Tell me about it. I'll see what I can learn. It's the least I can do."

But not all, she thought as they completed their tasks and got ready for bed. She could think of many more avenues to explore, but they'd discuss it in the morning. That is, if Ryder let them have a few minutes of conversation over breakfast.

****

"You'll never believe who I ran into after I left you yesterday," Marla said the next day to introduce the topic. She'd fed Ryder and changed him into a tee shirt and khaki shorts. He was playing with a set of toy cars in the family room while she cleaned the kitchen.

Dalton had dressed for work in a button-down shirt and navy trousers. He looked handsome with his peppery hair slicked back and his features more relaxed.

"Who was it?" He picked up his keys from the rack of hooks on the wall by the garage entrance.

"Cousin Corbin. He works at the village farm as Simon Weedcutter's apprentice."

"No way! We haven't seen him in a while. How long has he been working there?"

"I didn't ask." She related the highlights of their discussion. "I never knew he liked working with animals. I'll bet Cynthia was surprised when he told her. She's been close-mouthed about it to me and never said a word."

"Corbin may have warned her off about revealing his whereabouts. The village would be a good place to lay low if he wanted to stay under the radar."

"He didn't seem elusive that way. I gathered he was more protective of Simon. Do you plan to talk to him?"

Dalton's shoulders hunched and a crease lined his brow. "I will now, since you've mentioned Simon left the farm around the time of the murder."

Marla pounced on his words. "Do you have a definitive time of death?"

"I didn't say that. Corbin told you the farmer ran off. You encountered your cousin shortly after you'd left the fishing shed. We know Phil Pufferfish died sometime between his last announcement at the reenactment and when the schoolteacher found him."

Marla put down the sponge she'd used to clean the kitchen table. "Did Violet tell you why she'd been there in the first place?"

"She claimed she liked to walk out on the boardwalk and sit on a bench to enjoy the view. The pond brought her a sense of peace. Her eye twitched when she told me this, though."

"Meaning she was lying? Why? To cover for herself or for someone else?"

"It's too early to tell." He let the dogs in from the backyard and then changed the trash bag while Marla pondered his remarks.

What was Violet's real reason for being at the scene of the

crime? Her excuse seemed lame. But she'd have to think about it later.

Needing to pay attention to her tasks, she packed her supplies for the day. Going anywhere with a child was a production. She marveled at how this had become her routine and couldn't imagine an earlier life without her son.

A memory flashed in her mind as she diced some strawberries. "You know who else entered the bait and tackle shed earlier in the day? The minister from the church. He hurried past Millie and me when I was watching her baking demo. Millie didn't appear happy to see him."

"Interesting. What else did you notice?"

"Haven't you wondered how the killer sneaked the tomahawk past everyone? Maybe the preacher hid it there to use later. He could have hidden it under his robe."

"That's rather far-fetched, but I'll add him to my list of people to interview. Anyone could have carried it that day as part of a costume."

"True. Did you identify the owner of the weapon?" Marla asked. "If it was authentic, it might have come from the Seminole camp."

"The tribesmen denied any knowledge of it. They're only hired for the reenactment. Their shaman works at the village and gives the tours."

Marla could understand their silence. "They'd want to protect their own. Have you considered a motive on the healer's part?"

"Whoa, let me do my job, okay? Is Brianna awake yet?"

Marla cast a glance at Ryder to make sure he wasn't getting into any mischief. "Brie is sleeping in. There's no rush in us getting to the park. The activities don't begin until ten o'clock. We'll take Ryder to the playground if we get there earlier."

"You know I'll miss being with you today, but duty calls." He gave her a quick kiss and then left.

The door sprang closed in his wake, and Marla stared after him, missing him already.

Brianna woke in plenty of time to get dressed and gobble down a breakfast bar. The teen was adept at getting ready in record time, especially when she'd often woken up almost late for school. Marla looked forward to spending girl time with her.

The town had gone all out for the Fourth of July. They'd missed the main street parade, which Marla figured would be too intense for Ryder.

Over by the bandstand, a couple of young men were setting up equipment and connecting wires for a series of concerts. Later the grassy field facing the stage would get crowded with spectators sitting in folding chairs and on blankets for headliner music and fireworks. This early, the shady concrete paths among the trees and around the lake were filled with families.

"Let's go to the playground," she suggested to Brianna. They'd head to the kiddy section later with its bounce house, petting zoo and face painting. She'd like to check out the vendors, too. Merchants were setting up their wares alongside nonprofit groups and civic organizations.

She pointed to the area reserved for the day's competitions. "I'll bet your dad would be good at the watermelon carving contest. He's missing out on the prize. He'd love a gift card to the local plant nursery."

Brianna snorted. "He'd be more interested in the biggest homegrown tomato award."

"You're right. I hope he expands his garden after he retires." A fragrant aroma from the food tents drifted her way, making her crave a chocolate croissant from a bakery cart.

She pushed the stroller, comfortable in a pair of shorts with a sleeveless top, a wide-brimmed hat and sunglasses. Brianna, keeping pace beside her, looked tall and slim in a short, flirty dress with strappy sandals. Her dark brown hair flowed loose down her back.

"I'm glad we have this time together," Marla told her. "You'll be gone before we know it. Your absence will leave an empty place in our house. I just want you to know how proud your father and I are of the young woman you've become."

Brianna rolled her eyes. "You sound like Dad. I wish he could have been with us today. I hate that he has another case so close to his retirement."

"I know." She'd told Brianna about yesterday's events during the drive there. "I promised him I'd sound out people today about Pioneer Village, but I don't know where to start."

"Don't worry about it. Just relax and enjoy the day for a change."

"You know that's hard for me to do. Will Jason be here today?" Brianna's boyfriend hadn't been able to sway her from her goals. Their parting would be bittersweet as he'd be heading to school in Manhattan.

"He has a family event. We might get together later."

"I hope you'll meet new people at college. Long distance relationships are hard to maintain." *Don't make the same mistake I did in choosing too soon and ending up divorced.*

"Marla, I'm not giving up on Jason, but we've both agreed to keep our options open." They reached the playground. "Can I push Ryder on the swing?"

"Sure, go ahead." She relented on offering advice and tried to ease her mind as Brianna had suggested.

Ryder squealed with delight with each higher push into the air. When he tired of that activity, Marla helped him climb onto the smaller slide while Brianna stood down below to catch him. They stayed there until it was time for his snack. Marla put him back in the stroller, inserted the tray, and offered the container with his mid-morning crackers and fruit.

She and Brianna resumed their stroll. Marla's stomach rumbled and she aimed toward the food section. "I could use a croissant," she said. "What about you?"

"I'd love a soft pretzel. It's too early for an empanada or an arepa. I'll miss our Cuban food in Boston."

"No, you won't. Not when you taste their seafood and New England clam chowder."

They meandered toward the food lane where Marla spied

friends among the throng. "Arnie! Jill! Hey, I'm over here." She waved at the couple who stood with their kids in line for a bag of popcorn. The aroma of cinnamon-coated pecans came from a nearby stand.

Arnie signaled for them to approach. Marla almost hadn't recognized the owner of Bagel Busters without his customary apron. His moustache and hair looked distinctly darker than the last time she'd seen him. He'd be forty-five in December, nearly five years older than Marla, but his energy kept him in youthful form. She greeted him with a hug and grinned when he praised Ryder and Brianna.

She regarded his children with affection. "Lisa and Josh, you've grown so much! I can't believe how tall each of you has gotten." Arnie's daughter was one year away from becoming a teenager. And Josh would be able to get his driver's license in the fall. Marla shook her head, unable to believe how quickly the years had passed.

Jill, a buxom blonde who wore a tight pencil skirt with a frilly blouse and heels on her feet despite the grassy turf, regarded Marla with a broad smile. As the widower's second wife, she'd inherited his brood and seemed disinclined to have children of her own. Marla figured she didn't want to ruin the figure she'd paid so much money to enhance.

"So tell me," Arnie said to Brianna in his New York accent. "Are you ready for college? I'll bet your dad is having a conniption about you going away." He winked at her, no doubt aware she was more ready than Marla and Dalton.

"I can't wait," Brianna said, exchanging high fives with the other kids. She and Lisa could pass for sisters with their dark hair and eye color, although the latter had a rounder face.

Jill leaned over, revealing her cleavage as she tickled Ryder on the chin. "Hello, little man. You are so cute with those big eyes. I can see your teeth are coming in."

Arnie peered around. "Where's Dalton?"

"He's on another murder case," Brianna stated in a nonchalant tone.

Arnie glanced at Marla for confirmation. "Oy vey. I hope *you* didn't discover the body this time."

"No, but we were close by." Marla summarized the incident.

"Leave it to you to find trouble," Arnie said, the affection in his tone softening his words. His turn in line came next. He paid for the popcorn then handed it to his kids.

"Have you guys ever been to Pioneer Village?" Marla asked.

Jill shook her head. "We've never gone, unless Arnie visited there before I swept him off his feet."

Marla laughed, remembering how her friends had met. Jillian Barlow had pretended to be an ugly former classmate who'd had a crush on him. Arnie had devised quite a ruse to avoid her and was blown away when he encountered her at Marla's salon. The astounded expression on his face when he got a look at the blonde bombshell would forever be imprinted on Marla's mind.

"Can't say that I've heard of the place," Arnie said, spreading his hands. "It sounds like a fun site to bring the kids, once Dalton solves the case."

Jill tapped Marla's arm. "Are you planning a retirement party? If so, I'd like to help."

Marla stared at her. "I haven't given it a thought. I mean, I figured his colleagues would be giving him a proper send-off."

"Are you sure? September seventeenth is only two months from now. They should be letting you know if they're planning a party, unless it's a surprise."

"Maybe it's a work-only event." Marla turned to Brianna. "What do you think? Should I throw a shindig for your dad?"

Brianna waved a hand. "His friends are bound to do something. Give them more time to contact you."

"I could ask Sergeant Langley if I see him around. Meanwhile, I know the restaurants that have private rooms for rent. I'd scouted them out for Ma and Reed's wedding, remember? I could always reserve a place just in case." A weight settled in her stomach. "Omigosh. Ma's first anniversary with Reed is less than a week later. Maybe I should consider a joint celebration, although that wouldn't be fair to Dalton."

"Calm down, Marla. You don't need to rush into anything," Brianna said.

Jill gave Marla a smile. "Whatever you decide to do, you can call on me. I know you have your hands full between Ryder and the salon."

Marla's heart filled with warmth. "Thanks, I appreciate it."

Ryder chose that moment to emit a series of cries. His face turned red, and he threw the rest of his crackers on the ground.

"He's pooping," Brianna declared in her no-nonsense voice. Once he'd stopped making his characteristic expressions, she unstrapped him and scooped him up along with his diaper bag. "I'll change Ryder. We just passed a family bathroom back by the bandstand. You stay here and chat with your friends." Brianna took in the bored look on Lisa's face and hooked a forefinger in her direction. "Wanna come and help?"

"Sure. I don't have a younger brother." Lisa set off with her at a brisk pace.

"Brianna has a big heart. She'll have a bevy of boys after her in college," Jill said, her southern accent becoming more evident.

"I agree, but don't tell Dalton. He worries incessantly about her as it is." It was bad enough getting her husband to acknowledge his daughter's independence. Things would become more difficult once she was away from home, more so for them than for the teen. Brianna would probably be happy to have a sense of freedom.

Marla's temples throbbed, too many thoughts hammering inside her skull.

"The party planning can wait," Arnie told her. "Dalton needs to solve this case before any celebrations are in order." He cast his son a reprimanding glance. Oblivious to his surroundings, the boy was texting on his cell phone.

Jill poked a finger at her husband. "We should visit Pioneer Village. It's odd that I've never seen any ads for the place."

"I thought the same thing," Marla said. "Surely Dalton would have gone before this. He loves history, and the village is right up his alley."

"The fairground has a huge local media blast for their annual fair. Maybe they advertise in out-of-state publications for year-round tourists."

"I suppose that's possible." Marla tilted her head. "Hey, you're in public relations. Why don't you ask around about their advertising?"

"Sure, I can do that." Jill grinned, clearly glad to be useful.

Pioneer Village must be allotted certain funding from which they had to pay all their expenses, Marla thought. Wasn't it the administrator's duty to disperse those funds? If so, who would take over for Phil now that he was gone?

This applied to repairs at the village as well as promotional campaigns. Were budget cuts really at fault for the lack of financial support, or was someone dipping their fingers into the history park's piggy bank? And if so, did that occur at the fairground's end or at the village?

Dalton should talk to someone from the fairground to ask these questions. Was it possible for him to examine their accounting records?

Brianna returned with Lisa and Ryder. Marla took charge of the stroller and parted ways with Arnie's family. She paused while Brianna bought a pretzel and then stopped by the French bakery stand for a chocolate croissant. They ate standing until Ryder banged his legs against the stroller, indicating they should move ahead.

"I know what you can do to help Dad," Brianna said after they'd discarded their trash and walked on. "You've met Millie, Lizzy and Violet at the village. Maybe you can find some other women there to approach."

"That's a great idea. They'd be more willing to talk to me than your dad." Intrigued by this notion, Marla wondered which cast members she might have missed during her initial visit.

Brianna's brows lifted. "You're off work tomorrow, and Ryder will be in day care. You could scoot over there for a couple of hours. I'd offer to go with you, but I have plans. Maybe ask our neighbor, Robyn. She's always eager for an adventure."

"This is true." Robyn Piper, in her thirties and still single, had given up her corporate job and worked as receptionist at Marla's salon. She also lived in the same development. Like Marla's friend, Tally, Robyn got a kick out of accompanying Marla on her escapades.

Sadly, Tally was tied up with her dress shop and her son Luke these days. Marla had hoped to meet them at the playground, but Luke had the sniffles and Tally was keeping him home.

Amazed at how their lives had changed since the birth of their sons, she licked a smidgen of chocolate off her mouth. Hopefully, her next visit to Pioneer Village would be as sweet.

Chapter Five

"Hey, Marla, how's it going?" called a familiar voice from behind. Marla whirled around to face Susan Feinberg, another neighbor. Susan was the same age as Marla, although she'd started her family a lot younger.

"Hi, it's good to see you here." Marla smiled at Susan's children. "Jess, I like your sundress. It's so cute," she told her friend's eight-year-old daughter. Donny, her older brother by four years, wore shorts with a preppy shirt. Marla gave him a high-five in greeting.

"I just dropped off my brownies at the charity bake sale," Susan reported. "We were headed over to sign up for the watermelon competition, but Donny said he was hungry. That kid eats constantly. You wait until Ryder is older. It's a challenge to keep the pantry stocked."

Marla chuckled. "I don't want my son to grow up too fast. Try the pastry tent. I just got a chocolate croissant there. Where is David?" she asked, inquiring about Susan's husband.

Susan's pert nose wrinkled. "He had a board meeting at the temple."

"On July Fourth? That's too bad."

"He'll meet us here later. They have another candidate to interview for cantor."

"I suppose that's a good thing." Marla, being a more secular type, celebrated the holidays but skipped out on religious services. "Dalton isn't here, either. He has another homicide case."

Susan's brown eyes rolled skyward. "Heaven help us. So close to his retirement? That's a *shandeh*."

"It is a shame. I just hope he solves it fast." She peered at Susan over her sunglasses. "Hey, have you ever been to Pioneer Village?"

"Can't say that I've heard of the place. What is it?"

"It's a living history experience with costumed guides and historic buildings. We visited there yesterday. They had a battle reenactment for a massacre that occurred in the Seminole Wars. Dalton enjoyed it, at least until the murder."

Susan gaped at her. "No way. That's where he picked up the case?"

"Yep. It's a fun place otherwise, although you really need more than one day to see everything." She glanced at Brianna. The teen was keeping Susan's kids occupied in conversation while rocking Ryder's stroller.

"Would there be anything I could use there for my magazine?" Susan asked. As consulting editor for *Ladies Town Post*, she worked at home for the publication that reported on tri-county social events. She also did a blog focusing on household tips with daily inspirational quotes.

"You know, you could do a feature article on women's roles at the village. I met a lady who's a descendant of a former plantation owner. She gives tours of their family residence, now owned by the fairground. There's a ghost story attached to the place."

"Awesome, I love it! What a great idea. Who else might be a good candidate for an interview?"

"I've met the schoolteacher and a lady who does cooking demos. I imagine all the village women can offer unique perspectives on the historical angle. Or you could ask them what got them interested in working at the park in the first place. I'm going again tomorrow," Marla said, ditching her plan to ask Robyn to accompany her. "Would you like to join me?"

"Really? That would be great. I'll be free at twelve-thirty if that works for you."

"Fantastic; I'll pick you up then. Better pack a snack if you don't eat lunch first. They don't have a café, and the picnic tables are outside in the heat. At least they're under cover so there's some shade."

Susan's brow creased. "Wait, why are you going back when you were just there?"

"I want to help Dalton, and your excuse of a feature article is the perfect reason for us to chat with people. The women might be more willing to gossip than the men." She swiped the sweat off her forehead. "That reminds me. I promised Dalton I'd ask around today about the village. You're not the only one who hasn't heard about the place."

Susan shrugged. "I don't pay much attention to notices about the fairground. Those big fairs have never interested me unless there's a person-of-interest story attached. I suppose it's a spot I've overlooked."

"I'll bet you will find lots to interest you tomorrow." Her attention diverted as Ryder chose that moment to cry out in his stroller.

Marla said a quick farewell and took over pushing her son's vehicle.

"If you see friends and want to run off, don't feel as though you have to stick around," she told Brianna. "I thought I'd take Ryder to the petting zoo to see the animals."

"No, I'm fine. I'm meeting friends later. I want to spend time with my baby brother."

"That's so sweet. What will we do without you when you go to college? Our house will seem so empty." Brianna's presence had become a comfort to Marla, and their home would seem strange without her there. But that was the way of life. Your kids grew up and left to forge their own paths.

"Are you kidding?" Brianna said. "Ryder takes up all of your time when you're home. You'll barely miss me. Besides, I'll be back for school breaks, and we can always video chat. I don't want to miss Ryder's milestones. I'm sure you'll send lots of photos."

At the mention, Marla snapped one of Brianna and Ryder to add to her collection. "What do you think about Susan accompanying me tomorrow? It'll give us the perfect excuse to ask questions."

"It's a good ploy. Just be careful you don't stir a snake sleeping under a rock."

They resumed their pace along the concrete path. The petting zoo was located inside the kiddie zone. Marla didn't spot anyone she knew in the throng of parents.

As Ryder patted a goat inside a portable fence, she addressed the owner of the kid-friendly site. His truck stood beyond with a large sign that read, "Mobile Petting Zoo. We Come to You."

"What a great idea for a birthday party," she said, handing Ryder over to Brianna. "Do you have a card?"

"Sure thing." The lean young man with a scruffy beard passed one over to her. It gave his name as Ross Madison. "We can bring goats and chickens or whatever you like. I can even borrow a cow if you want a milking demonstration."

"Do you do sheep shearing, too?" Marla asked in jest.

"Not me, but you can catch a demo in season over at Pioneer Village. They have a much larger area with all sorts of farm animals."

Marla cast a glance at Brianna who'd moved closer by a few steps. "Oh, do you know Simon, the village farmer? My husband and I just visited there, but we ran out of time before we reached the farm. I'm planning to go back tomorrow to see what I'd missed."

Ross shaded his face with a hand. "Simon has covered for me a few times when I've been overbooked. He's great with kids but is shy about leaving his little enclave."

"Why is that?"

Ross spread his hands. "I dunno. He's more comfortable tending his crops, I guess. His apprentice mostly takes care of the animals, although technically Simon owns them."

"The animals don't belong to the fairground?"

"Nah, they're part of his personal menagerie. He couldn't keep them in town with the zoning laws, so this gig works out well for him. I've always wondered why he doesn't get his own tract of land for a real farm, but I suppose he doesn't have the funds. Or maybe he likes the benefits the fairground provides. You should talk to Fern Hatfield. She sells her hats down one of the vendor aisles. She knows people from the village, too."

"Thanks for the tip. I'll check her out."

When his attention got drawn away by other guests, Marla put her son back in the stroller. He'd been squirming in Brianna's arms, restless to move on. She gave him a drink of water to keep him hydrated and pulled the vehicle's hood over to shade his face.

"That was an interesting conversation," Brianna said as they aimed toward the food lane. They'd check out the merchants after lunch. Marla didn't want Ryder to get off his daily schedule.

"Yes, it was. I need to learn more about Simon. His role as a farmer would have been critically important in pioneer days. You'd think he would want more visitors to come his way."

"Was he in favor of Phil's proposal? It might have provided him with more opportunities."

"Possibly. My cousin said he would rather keep things as they are. It's likely Simon felt the same way. I won't really know his opinion until I talk to him."

They passed a hospital display offering free Band-Aid dispensers and a realty firm that gave out key rings. The Boy Scouts had a table as did a local veterans' troop. Brianna plucked a chocolate kiss from a table sponsored by a solar energy company, while Marla halted by a dog bakery offering sample biscuits. She took a couple for her pets along with one of their cards.

After she and Brianna bought sandwiches for lunch, they found seats at a picnic table. Marla fed Ryder, while music blared from the stage where a band played top hits from the sixties. Ryder would never be able to take his nap with all this background noise. She'd have to take him home.

Once they'd finished, Brianna ran off to meet friends and watch the hot dog eating contest. Marla pushed the stroller among the vendors. No thanks, she thought to the plants spilling out from one tent onto the pavement. She had a black thumb and killed any potted greenery that came into her possession. Ditto for the ceramic painted pots. No use for those at her house.

She stopped in her tracks when she spied a booth selling handmade hats. A closer view showed a dazzling array of headgear decorated with ribbons, feathers, and faux flowers.

"These are amazing," she said, hoping flattery might loosen the proprietor's tongue. "I love this one." She pointed to a crimson brim hat with fabric roses but was also attracted to a teal fascinator with lace and a cute orange felt hat that would be great for the fall. "How did you learn to make these things?"

The woman grinned. She had a tanned complexion, curly blond hair, and proud blue eyes. "I've always loved millinery. It might be an old-fashioned art form, but I miss the days when people wore hats. Would you believe I attended a hat academy?"

"Really? I'd no idea such a thing existed. I'm Marla Vail, by the way. I own a salon and day spa." She handed over a business card.

"Fern Hatfield." The millinery lady pointed to Marla's sun hat. "I see you're sensible in protecting your skin from the sun."

"Always. This one has sunscreen protection."

Fern peeked into the stroller as Ryder whimpered. "Aw, your baby is so cute."

"Thanks. I need to take him home soon for his nap." She glanced at Fern's ringless fingers. "Do you have any kids?"

"Not me, but I have five nieces and nephews. Tommy loves his fedora and Angie wears a bonnet we bought her at Pioneer Village."

Marla's ears perked up at this opening line. "We just visited on Saturday. I met Millie who runs the sewing circle. She sells their goods in the general store. Do you have a shop in town?"

"No, I only do the arts and crafts shows or local festivals like

55

this one. I've met Millie. She's very talented with a needle and thread. Sometimes she'll come to these events and sell her handmade items. On occasion, she'll bring her guy friend, too."

"Who do you mean?" Marla asked. She'd been unaware Millie had a romantic attachment.

Fern waved a hand. "I don't know if they're together or are just friends. The man works at the village in the role of minister, but he isn't in the least bit priestly."

Marla digested this information. Was that why Millie had glared at the guy as he'd hurried past them without any acknowledgement? They'd had a lovers' spat?

"Millie is multi-talented," Marla said, hoping to learn more about her. "In addition to sewing, she likes to cook. She told me how she'd offer her southern specialties if they had a café on site. I tasted her biscuits at an outdoor oven demo."

Fern leaned forward and lowered her voice. "Sewing bonnets and knitting scarves is a hobby for her. Having her own restaurant is her real dream. She's a much better chef than she is a baker."

I should hope so, Marla thought, remembering the dry consistency of the sample she'd tried. "How come Millie is working at a history park instead of a job in the culinary field, then?"

"She was let go from her previous position at a restaurant and hasn't been able to get another one since," Fern confided, her words coming faster together. Marla figured she got bored sitting there all day. Plus, being chatty kept potential customers at her booth.

"What happened to drive her away?" It must have been something serious for Millie to have been ousted in that manner.

Fern pressed her lips together. "She doesn't like to talk about it, and I don't pry."

Marla got the hint and changed the subject. "I adore this orange hat. It'll be perfect for October. How much do I owe you?"

She made her purchase and left, wondering what had

occurred to propel Millie out of the kitchen and into the history village. Had Phil promised her that she could have the position as chef in his proposed café? And what was going on between her and the so-called clergyman?

Marla shrugged off these thoughts for later. Brianna had texted that she wanted to stay and would catch a ride home with friends. Marla could leave without her.

Peering into the stroller, she noted Ryder's flushed skin. She needed to get him out of the heat and home for his nap. It would have been easier if Dalton had joined them.

Soon enough, she told herself as she headed for the exit. *It'll be quicker if you help him solve this case.*

In the meantime, she'd write a list of the key personnel at the village and do an Internet search on their names. Dalton would be doing his own background checks as he had better resources. However, she had observational skills that could prove useful from a different perspective.

Finally at home, she put Ryder down in his crib and read to him before leaving him with his pacifier and favorite stuffed animal. The baby monitor accompanied her into the kitchen where she washed his dishes and tended to the dogs. A load of laundry later, she sat down at the computer. Dalton must be immersed in his case as she hadn't heard from him.

Before she could tap the keyboard, Robyn sent a text message that made her pulse soar.

Marla dialed her back immediately. "What do you mean, they have to shut the water off at the salon on Tuesday morning?" she said as soon as her receptionist answered. She envisioned irate customers as well as lost revenue.

"Sorry to bother you on the holiday, but there's been a leak in the supply line," Robyn explained. "Some valve needs replacement. They'll have to turn off the water for the entire shopping strip starting at nine on Tuesday."

Marla winced inwardly at the disruption that would ensue. "How long will the repair take?"

"They said to reserve a two-hour window, but we should play it safe and reschedule our morning appointments. I'll notify everyone today."

Marla sighed. "Why don't you wait until tomorrow? The plumber might be available earlier and get started on our job on Monday."

"All right. I'll call everyone tomorrow afternoon. How was the battle reenactment?"

Marla had told Robyn about their plans for Saturday since she'd needed time off from work. As receptionist, Robyn was responsible for scheduling along with salon publicity and other functions.

"It was exciting." *Especially the dead body on the boardwalk.* She didn't elaborate, not caring to get into a lengthy discourse before Dalton's office released a public statement.

"How was your date Saturday night?" she asked instead. Robyn had been shy of commitment until recently, when she'd resorted to online dating.

"Bor-ing. Chad talked technology the entire night. When he saw I wasn't wearing a smartwatch, I think he crossed me off his list."

"That's his loss, not yours. Are you going to see the fireworks later?"

"When have you known me to stay home? Of course, I'm going. I'll let you know if anything changes regarding the plumber."

"Okay, thanks. Have fun." Marla rang off, staring at her computer screen. Recalling her purpose, she typed in Phil Pufferfish's name. Nothing relevant popped up.

Drat, it might be a pseudonym he used in his role as marshal. How many of the other players used stage names?

When she couldn't find listings for the rest of the crew on social media, she input Baffle House. Several sites popped up, which mostly repeated the history Lizzy had related.

How about the murder weapon? Marla knew little about

tomahawks and looked this subject up next. Huh. There was a difference between a throwing tomahawk and a tactical one. The latter was a lightweight weapon built for multiple uses.

Each owner decorated his tomahawk according to personal tastes. Items used might include rawhide tassels, paint, feathers, beadwork, or even clips of hair from a favorite horse. Marla scrunched her eyes while trying to remember details of the murder weapon. The handle didn't seem to be too long, and it was decorated with feathers and paint. She couldn't recall an exact pattern but visualized red, yellow and black colors.

She couldn't wait to ask Dalton about it but delayed her questions when he finally got home. Instead, she followed her mother's advice and fed him dinner first before broaching the subject. Men mellowed after a meal, Ma had always said. He'd made turkey burgers the day before and had planned to grill them. Due to their change in plans, Marla had stuck them in the oven to cook.

He took a turn getting Ryder ready for bed while she did the dishes. Hopefully, the neighbors' firecrackers wouldn't bother their son. Marla hated the things. They kept her awake and scared the dogs. Why would anyone risk blowing off their fingers to light explosives at home? She'd never understood the fascination.

"How is the investigation going? Can you share anything?" she asked Dalton after their chores were finished. They sat in the family room watching the news on TV. Brianna still wasn't home, although she'd texted Marla her plans for the evening. The dogs had settled onto their cushions. All was quiet, at least for the moment.

Dalton ran his fingers through his hair. His face drooped like it did when he was tired. "I'm still establishing alibis. Nobody is giving me a straight answer."

"They're actors hired to play a role. Did you get their real names? I looked up the people we'd met and couldn't find them on social media, or at least, no one who lived in Florida."

He gave her a curt nod. "I have a list of the regular staff

members and volunteers. Then there's the exhibitors and reenactors who took part in the battle."

"That's a lot of people to cover. Do you have help with the interviews?"

"I've assigned a couple of other guys to do the minor players. Did you learn anything new today?"

"Yes, I did." She straightened her spine. "Arnie and Jill were at the park with their kids. So was Susan Feinberg from down the street. I dropped a hint that she might do a feature article on the women of the village, and she loved the idea. We're going there together on Monday."

"Good thinking. That's a great excuse to talk to people. What else?"

Now she had his full attention. "I met Fern, a lady selling hats at a crafts booth. She knew Millie from other events. Millie did the baking demo at the village, remember? And she runs the sewing circle. Fern mentioned that Millie's real dream is be a chef in her own restaurant. Do you think Phil promised she could be in charge of the kitchen when they opened a café?"

Dalton lifted an eyebrow. "If so, she must have supported his plans."

"Fern also said Millie is often accompanied at the craft fairs by the minister from the village. It made me wonder if the two of them have a thing."

"We'll see. Just be careful when you talk to these people. One of them might be guilty of murdering the marshal."

She bristled at his warning. "I'm always careful. What about the murder weapon? Has anyone admitted ownership?"

His eyes glinted. "The shaman claims it was his and that it had been stolen from their camp."

"Do you believe him?"

"It's an awfully convenient excuse if he's the killer."

"I read online that the markings on a tomahawk are distinctive to each owner," Marla said. "Depending on the handle length, they could be used as a throwing weapon or for short-range combat. They also had a ceremonial purpose. During important council meetings, a tomahawk would be placed on the ground. If the chief picked it up, this meant he approved going to war. If he buried it, the war plans were over. That's where the phrase *bury the hatchet* originated."

Dalton gave her an approving grin. "You have done your homework. Since you'll be talking to the villagers tomorrow, I'll let you in on a secret. We found a pearl button at the scene of the crime."

Chapter Six

Marla gaped at her husband. "What kind of pearl button? Where was it found?" She was surprised he'd share this information with her.

"Under the body. Ever see one like this?" He showed her a picture on his cell phone. The size of a pearl button earring, this one was lustrous and round with a gold shank.

She shook her head. "It looks like a genuine cultured pearl rather than a plastic one. If it were fake, the color would be whiter and the roundness more even. Is that real gold?"

"It's a metal shank on the underside." He showed her a second picture.

"Could the button belong to one of the uniforms from the battle?"

"I think the army soldiers wore brass ones, but I'll double-check."

"Is anyone's costume missing a button? That would be a telltale clue."

His mouth compressed. "We'll have to examine everyone's outfits to see, although there weren't any traces of fabric attached. If this button had been ripped off a player's outfit, you'd think part of the cloth would have come with it."

"Not if the thread got loose and it dropped off on its own." She felt her eyes blaze with excitement. "I could ask the sewing ladies about it when I'm there tomorrow. Maybe they offer sewing lessons."

He grinned and poked a finger at her. "I knew you'd come

up with a clever idea. It'll be more natural coming from you to talk about fabrics and such. Here, I'll send a copy of these photos to your cell phone." That done, he stretched and yawned. "Let's go to bed. I'm tired."

She followed him inside the master suite and took off her jewelry in front of the dresser. He got out a clean pair of boxers and removed his shirt.

"I'll put a bee in Susan's bonnet to ask the women about their costumes tomorrow," Marla said. "I'm sure they'll be happy to talk about what they wear for their roles."

"Where will you start the tour?" Dalton glanced at himself in the dresser mirror, wincing at his haggard face. Stubble shadowed his jaw and his hair hung limp.

"We'll begin at Baffle House," Marla replied. She wanted him to get his rest but wasn't ready yet to let him disappear into the shower. "Lizzy has the most interesting tale with ghosts and lost treasure. Then we can visit the schoolroom since Violet, the teacher, is the person who found the body. Susan's article will give us the perfect excuse to question everyone." She couldn't wait to go back with this cover story to see what they could learn.

Dalton gave her a sideways glance. "How about Millie? You could ask her what business the minister had at the bait and tackle shop that day."

"I'll see if I can find her since she seems to move around. Then we'll check out the Seminole camp and the farm. Is the encampment real, by the way?"

"It's not official Seminole land, if that's what you're asking. The shaman has Native American blood and may have recruited other members of his tribe to act as warriors in the battle, but the site isn't part of any reservation."

"Are there women among them?"

"Yes. They conduct the basket weaving classes. They might offer cooking demos, too."

"What are your plans for tomorrow? We can meet for lunch if you'll be there."

"I've assigned Sergeant Langley to chase down Simon and the preacher, whose name is Henry Godwin. I'm going to visit Phil's sister."

Marla pressed a hand to her cheek. "Oh, no. I'd totally forgotten about his next of kin. Poor woman. Did Phil have any other relatives? Was he married?"

Dalton removed his socks and pants and tossed them on his side of the bed. "He was divorced with no children. His parents are deceased. The sister is married, though. She'll be making funeral arrangements once we release the body."

An ugly image surfaced of a gaping wound in Phil's forehead. Marla hoped the mortician did a good job of patching him up.

As it grew darker, firecrackers shot off in the neighborhood, accompanied by whistling noises and loud booms. The dogs roused in their beds, and Lucky whined. Marla soothed the pets while Dalton hustled into the bathroom to take a shower. She checked the video monitor. Ryder stayed asleep, thank goodness. She'd better get ready for bed, too. Tomorrow would come soon enough, and she needed her wits about her.

Nonetheless, the incessant noise outside reminded her of the battle scene. She tossed restlessly in bed, unable to lessen her anxiety. Too many things were happening beyond her control.

She must have fallen asleep during a lag in the concussions outside because she awoke after dawn and Ryder was crying in his crib. Dalton lay beside her as still as an alligator waiting for prey. His light snores indicted he slept peacefully.

She stumbled out of bed and into the nursery, blinking in the dim light from a nightlight. As she changed Ryder's diaper and fed him, she thought about how her morning routine relaxed her mind. Caring for her son took priority over everything else.

Once Dalton woke up, he watched the toddler so Marla could get dressed. Then it was his turn. He rejoined her in the kitchen as she completed her chores. Looking handsome in a navy sport coat, he grabbed a breakfast bar before heading out.

"I'll check in with you later," he told Marla. "Be careful with your inquiries, you hear?"

She gave him a kiss. "Good luck with your interview. Love you." They spoke in soft voices as Brianna was still asleep.

Marla left shortly thereafter. She dropped Ryder off at day care and then checked for any updates from Robyn regarding the plumbing issue. Nothing. The work must still be scheduled for tomorrow morning.

Since it was too early to get Susan, Marla ran errands. Should she buy sandwiches to bring along on their excursion? Nah, it would be another thing to carry. Once again, she regretted that the park didn't have a café. She would have supported Phil's plan.

Except the village lacked any spare room for expansion from what Marla had seen. How had Phil meant to accomplish this goal? Raze one of the sites and rebuild? Or convert a building that was already there? Either way, it might have impacted someone's job at the park.

She picked up Susan and filled her in on their way to the living history experience. They both wore shorts, comfortable tops and sun hats. Marla had advised Susan to wear sneakers.

"I don't imagine there will be a lot of visitors there on a Monday morning," she said, focusing on the road heading west. "People came in droves for the battle reenactment, but I'll bet today will be a lot less crowded. The tour guides should be happy to see us."

Susan swiped a strand of brown hair behind her ear. "Tell me more about how the marshal died. I can't believe the schoolteacher found him. That must have been horrible."

"I agree. Poor Phil. No one deserves an axe in the head."

Susan grimaced. "Maybe somebody had it in for him. How did he happen to be on the boardwalk, anyway?"

"That's a good question. He'd been narrating the battle scene. Maybe he got a call that lured him away. If he'd cut through the trees, it would have taken him less than ten minutes to get there. I'll have to ask Dalton about his cell phone records."

Marla glanced in the rearview mirror and changed lanes to pass a slow driver. "The minister went there earlier that day. We should talk to him if we won't interfere with Sergeant Langley's investigation. Dalton assigned him to do interviews today."

If she could catch the sergeant, she'd ask him if anyone from work was planning a retirement party for Dalton. That would be another item to check off her list.

"Millie is the lady who gave the baking demonstration. She might be willing to talk if she's around," Marla told Susan.

"Does Millie work there every day or only on weekends?"

"I hadn't thought to ask. It's true that not everyone might show up on a daily basis if they aren't getting paid. However, Fern the hat lady said Millie couldn't get another job in town, at least not as a chef. That doesn't discount her from working in some other capacity, though."

"So what's our plan? You said the hostess at Baffle House has a cool ghost story, although a murder would be much more of a headliner." Susan's nose wrinkled. "Normally, our readers prefer lighter fare. The editor-in-chief is more likely to approve a women's interest story."

"Your focus *is* on the village women, although ghosts are always popular," Marla said. "And now another spirit occupies the grounds along with the White Lady. You can slip in a mention of Phil's death that way."

At the village, they headed toward the historic mansion. Hardly anyone else strolled the shady paths. With such a meager crowd, would all the actors be present today? Hopefully she and Susan would find several of the women to interview. They needn't worry about interruptions with fewer people present.

Susan oohed and aahed at the numerous labeled buildings and spreading oak trees, while Marla pointed out the jail as they passed by. The place seemed oddly empty without the marshal's presence. Would someone else be assigned the role? How about his position as tract administrator? Could he have had a competitor who wanted him out of the way?

Dalton or his associate should ask those questions. She'd suggest them later if she remembered. Meanwhile, they halted by the bait and tackle shed where yellow crime scene tape marked the entrance.

Susan's mouth gaped. "Is this where it happened?"

"Yes, out back on the boardwalk. There's a path off to the side that goes around to the pond. Let's see if we can gain access by that route. Maybe we'll see something that Dalton missed."

Unfortunately, that path was blocked by tape strung between a couple of trees.

Her neighbor looked relieved. "It's just as well. I can live without seeing the scene of a murder. Was there a lot of blood?"

The image of Phil's body surfaced in her mind. "Blood had pooled behind his head. But he'd have died instantly. I'm wondering how someone could approach him from the front with an axe. It would put him on guard unless it was someone he knew and trusted."

"Maybe it was part of the killer's costume. Wouldn't it have to be one of the Indians, then?"

"Native Americans, Susan. But you're correct. The weapon had to have either been planted on the boardwalk ahead of time or carried by one of the costumed actors."

"How about an Army soldier? A tomahawk could be considered a spoil of war."

Marla lifted an eyebrow. "With all the commotion during the battle, I suppose one of the soldiers might have slipped out to meet Phil. As for spoils of war, most of the Army soldiers were massacred. There were only two survivors."

"Was everyone among the troop a professional reenactor from out of town?"

"Dalton has a list of the participants. He can probably eliminate the actors who aren't part of the regular staff. I doubt the killer would wait a year to knock off Phil."

Marla moved along the concrete path, leafy branches providing shade from the scorching sun. Birds twittered overhead, lending a sense of tranquility that she knew to be false. They passed the fire pit on the way to the church. Millie wasn't there setting up for a baking demo. Hopefully, they could catch her later.

"There's the church," Marla said. "Let's go inside as long as we're here."

The double doors of the whitewashed building opened easily. Marla paused inside the vestibule to study the pristine interior. She liked the simplicity of the white walls and the polished wood pews that faced a raised dais with a pulpit. Tall windows let in sunlight on both sides. Dust motes floated in the air that had a faint lemony scent. In one corner stood an American flag. She didn't count the stars but wondered if it was era appropriate.

A gray-haired lady emerged from a hidden alcove in the back. She wore an ivory blouse tucked into a long cocoa and rose skirt with a colorful scarf around her neck. A floral scent accompanied her, reminding Marla of the lilac festival in upstate New York near where she'd grown up. It was the only part of the place she missed, along with the cooler summers.

"Hi, I'm Gilda Macintosh. Welcome to our church," the lady said with a faint western twang. "I'll be happy to tell you about this building if you're here for a tour."

"The minister isn't in? We were hoping to meet him," Marla said. Her glance swept Gilda's attire. No pearl buttons in sight.

"I'm sorry. He's been called out to attend a parishioner." Gilda held her gaze with eyes the color of golden rum set against a tanned complexion. Sunspots dotted her face.

"Oh, I see." Marla assumed the woman was playing a role. What about the clergyman? Was he for real or merely an actor like the rest of them? "How old is this building?" she asked in a friendly manner. Maybe she could get the lady to gossip about the preacher in his absence.

Gilda made a broad gesture encompassing the interior. "This church was constructed in 1894 in the Crystal River area. It's one of the few buildings in the village that was brought here from out of town. It looks grand, wouldn't you say?"

Susan pointed to an organ in one corner. "Do you hold services in the church?"

"Of course, miss. Church service goes on for two to three hours, so you'll want to wear comfortable clothes. That's not the original pulpit in case you're wondering. People used to be a lot shorter. We have better nutrition now, so we live longer and grow taller. This higher pulpit originated on the west coast in 1912 and was sent over from there."

"I see those chandeliers have candles." Marla indicated the overhead lighting.

Gilda gave her an indulgent smile. "We don't have electricity in the church. The windows are original, and they let in the light. For that reason, most of our functions are held during the daytime. As for air-conditioning, it consists of raising the windows and letting in the breeze."

"What else happens here besides religious services?" Susan asked with a curious glance.

"Our town meetings take place in the church. When we have an event, we ring the bell and call everyone to attend. We say the Pledge of Allegiance and offer a prayer before we start the business portion."

"Who runs those meetings?" Marla said. She had a notion but kept it to herself.

Gilda bent her head and clasped her hands together. "Phil Pufferfish, may he rest in peace. Phil was our late town marshal. He's just recently passed away. His absence will leave a deep void in our community."

"I heard the news. My husband and I met him when we toured the jail the other day. He was passionate about his history." She watched the woman for a reaction. Gilda appeared suitably sad, but it could be an act.

"Phil was our best advocate. He did a great job playing marshal and worked hard as our administrator."

"I understand the fairground oversees village operations. How soon do you think they'll appoint a replacement?"

"I have no idea." Gilda's eyes glittered. "Let's hope they don't hire an outsider. Phil understood our needs better than anyone."

"In what way?" Susan asked, running her hand idly across a polished pew.

Gilda's gaze swung her way. "Have you seen the other buildings? They're in a severe state of disrepair. Phil had a plan that would have fixed everything. Then we wouldn't be so dependent on the fairground for funding. We're lucky the church has held up so well."

Yes, and why is that? How come this structure looks so much better than the others? Marla wondered. "Who do you think will take up the pulpit next, so to speak?" she said aloud, meaning the job as administrator.

"I doubt it will be Henry, who plays the preacher. He would have lost his role if Phil's proposal succeeded."

"Is he a real ordained minister?" Susan asked with a wide-eyed glance.

Marla suppressed a grin. They worked well together. Susan acted sweet and clueless while Marla asked the more targeted questions.

Gilda fluttered her hand in the air. "Henry isn't a real chaplain. It's only a role he plays. Phil meant to bring in a real minister if his offer got accepted. He suggested we offer package deals for special events. Guests would have to use our chaplain's services and our catering menus, assuming Phil's on-site restaurant got established."

Marla's mind blossomed with possibilities. "That's a great idea. Here's another one. You could build a gazebo in the village square. Then you could do outdoor weddings with chairs set up on the grass. And on other weekends, you could use the gazebo as a stage for musicians. Attendance would increase with more fun things to do."

"Perhaps, as long as these activities didn't distract from the historical setting. Anyway, it's a moot point now with Phil gone. The fairground's directors will determine what happens next."

Marla wasn't sure which angle to pursue first, the mention of the fairground's authority or Henry's role. She decided to focus on the latter.

"How did Henry get this position? Are you able to choose where you're placed?"

"We can apply for specific posts. He's always been a devout sort, so it suited him."

"If he loves this role so much, how far would he go to keep the status quo?"

Gilda's eyes darkened. "I'm not sure I care for what you're implying. Besides, Henry also runs the bait and tackle shed. He wouldn't be out of a job altogether."

This was news, and it might explain why he was rushing there the day of the reenactment if he had some business to conduct at the place.

Uncertain what to ask next, Marla turned a frantic gaze on Susan. *Now what?* she signaled with her eyebrows.

Susan retrieved her sunglasses from her purse. "We need to be going, but I must tell you that I adore your scarf. Did Millie or one of the other sewing ladies make it? I'd love to buy one if they're sold in the general store."

Gilda fingered the item. "It's lovely, isn't it? Millie is very talented that way." Then her gaze shuttered, and her smile vanished. "Too bad she can't sew up her mouth as well," she murmured.

Whoa, I heard that. "Do you two ever cross paths in your roles?" Marla asked, pretending she hadn't caught Gilda's last remark.

"No, we don't," Gilda said in a curt tone, but then her voice softened. "I also give tours at the telephone exchange and the post office. You should stop by when I'm there sometime."

"Thanks, we'll do that. Speaking of Millie, I sampled her

biscuits during one of her outdoor baking demos," Marla said to swing their conversation back to the woman. "She expressed an interest in the café Phil proposed."

"Millie had sweet-talked him into hiring her as chef once his proposal went through. That's not an option anymore."

Stepping closer, Marla laid a hand on the older woman's sleeve. "I'm sorry, but I have to ask. Would you know anyone who might have wanted to harm Phil?"

Gilda shook her off. "What business is it of yours? And why are you asking all these questions, anyway? You're awfully nosy for tourists."

Susan stepped forward. "I'm a journalist, and I plan to do an article on the women of the village, if you'd like to be included. It would help bring publicity to the place and perhaps more donations. I noticed a box at the entrance for contributions."

"You should talk to Angus, but don't tell him I sent you. He's the blacksmith."

"Oh? How does he fit into things?" Susan switched her bag to her other shoulder.

"You'd best let him fill you in. Don't let his appearance intimate you. He's a big guy but he has a soft heart. Well, except for his skirmishes with Phil. Those riled him up plenty."

"What skirmishes?" Marla queried. She didn't want to press their luck and would move on if Gilda shut down. The tour guide must have been grateful for an audience, though, because she answered the question.

"At town meetings, he and Phil often clashed about their ways of doing things. More than once, Angus told the marshal he'd better keep his nose clean, or things would some crashing down around him. I got the impression they weren't discussing village rules and regulations."

Chapter Seven

"Thanks for talking to us," Marla said. "We appreciate the tour of the church."

"My pleasure. Enjoy the rest of your day, ladies."

Outside the building, Marla turned to Susan to offer her impression. "That was interesting. Gilda appeared to support Phil's plan, but I couldn't get a good reading on her. Every now and then, she'd give me a look I couldn't interpret."

"I know what you mean. At least she gave you a good tip to see the blacksmith."

"Or she said those things about Angus to purposefully misdirect us. Regarding the minister, I was surprised to hear Henry ran the bait and tackle shop. I suppose he could hide his costume for that role beneath his clerical robes." *Along with a tomahawk*, she added to herself.

"If so, Phil wouldn't have suspected a thing if Henry asked to meet him at the fishing shack," Susan proposed. "It must have been something urgent to draw Phil away from his narration of the battle. But what would be Henry's motive?"

"To keep his position as fake minister?" Marla replied. "Maybe he needs the extra money from both jobs, assuming he gets paid."

"Who doles out the paychecks?"

"I presume that would have been Phil's responsibility, unless the payments came directly from the fairground." Had Dalton asked the fairground people about this aspect? Marla would give him the idea later if he hadn't pursued it yet.

Susan shrugged. "Let's see what we can learn from Lizzy at the mansion." They started walking in that direction. "Did her ancestors really own this land?"

"So she said. You should ask the questions. Mention how she'll be the focus of an article in your women's magazine. In fact, it might be best for me to stay away. She's seen me with Dalton, and if she knows he's the detective on Phil's case, she might clam up."

"You're right. We could meet back up at the schoolroom to interview the teacher."

"Okay. I'm hoping to run into Sergeant Langley, so let me know if you see him. I noticed his car in the parking lot. Dalton will be retiring in two months, and I want to ask if his friends at work are planning anything. If not, I'll organize a party. It's the same month as my mother's first year anniversary with my stepdad."

"Wow, you have a lot on your plate," Susan said, detouring past a fallen branch in their path. "Too bad Brianna will have left for college, or she could have helped."

"Tell me about it." Marla glanced up as they approached Baffle House and heard loud voices coming from somewhere off to the side.

"I'll find someone to cover for you, but you shouldn't have come here," a woman said, her voice recognizable as Lizzy's by her refined enunciation. "Now go away before anyone sees us together."

"Be sure to ask Simon about it when his assistant isn't around," a man replied. His tone held a note of menace. "We don't want him involved."

Marla's heart thudded in her chest. Did he mean Corbin, her cousin? And what were Lizzy, this fellow, and Simon the farmer engaged in that they needed to keep under wraps?

Before she could speculate further, the man darted from the shadows and vanished behind the trees. Lizzy made her way back inside the house.

Marla stared after the guy, wondering if she should attempt to follow him.

Probably not, since their time was limited, and she had other people to visit. Still, that conversation left her curious.

She nudged Susan. "See if you can find out anything about that man. It's clear Lizzy is involved with him in some manner. I'm heading over to the sewing circle."

Susan nodded and aimed toward the mansion's front porch.

Marla set off down the path. She found the building labeled Sewing Room from a plaque outside and read the brief history inscribed on the wood.

The small white building had originally belonged to a historic home in the city. It had served as a detached kitchen. Doing the cooking away from the main residence had been a common practice in case of fire so it wouldn't destroy the house.

Marla knocked on the single door. After getting no response, she stepped inside the unlocked structure and faced a large space filled with crafting supplies. Cubby holes against the wall held skeins of colorful yarns, spools of thread, and rolls of fabric. An ancient sewing machine with a foot pedal took up one corner while a hat rack holding a collection of bonnets stood opposite. Countertops held scattered sewing supplies. A colorful quilt hung on a ceiling rod at the far end.

Anxious to see if they had any pearl buttons among the goods, Marla stepped past a circle of folding chairs and dodged a mannequin in period dress. She stopped at a series of drawers built into the shelving and opened them one-by-one. They held an abundance of ribbons, feathers, faux flowers, and other adornments.

Her eyes widened as she opened one of the final drawers. Here were buttons fixed to cards like the ones you bought in stores, but she didn't see any pearl varieties. A sigh of disappointment escaped her lips.

Now what? Her gaze flitted to a series of lidded ceramic canisters on the countertop and vintage glass jars. Loose buttons in all shapes and sizes nestled inside.

Memories of her visits to Aunt Polly came to mind. Her mother's sister had allowed her to play with a box full of the things when she'd been a child. She liked to pretend they were jewels. Ma kept a container of loose buttons at home, too, although she'd never taught Marla how to sew. Or maybe Marla had been more interested in styling her dolls' hair than learning crafts.

She was just reaching a hand inside one jar when a shrill female voice stopped her.

"Don't touch those."

She withdrew her hand and whirled around. A girl in braids and dressed in a pinafore regarded her with a stern expression.

"Sorry," the child said, "but Millie would get angry if we messed with her stuff. Are you here for a tour?" She looked like a younger version of Brianna with her dark hair and eyes.

"Yes, I am. No one answered when I knocked on the door, so I've been looking around by myself. Is that not allowed?"

"We encourage self-guided tours throughout the park," the girl said as though from rote. "However, I'm happy to help. Did you read the sign outside?"

"Yes. I understand this building had been a detached kitchen for a house in town and was moved here to be part of the museum. Your sewing circle looks to be quite industrious. I've seen their products in the general store. But how is it that you're here and not in the schoolroom?"

The girl gave a silly grin. "It's July, so we're on summer break. Besides, I get credit for volunteering. If you're interested, I can describe what we do here."

"Sure, go ahead." In her innocence, perhaps the girl would reveal something important. "By the way, what's your name? I'm Marla Vail."

"Daisy Partridge. We girls are taught from an early age how to sew clothes. The men of the village wear shirts, pants with suspenders, and leather boots. The women wear skirts and blouses or dresses with long sleeves and high necklines."

Daisy was good at memorization, Marla thought. Maybe she

liked acting in her school drama club. "What materials do you use?" she asked, staying in character. She needed to keep the girl engaged until she could ask more targeted questions.

"We work with wool, cotton, and muslin. Sometimes, we'll dye the material. Most of the village women have only two or three outfits plus a good one for church days."

"I like their bonnets, and a guide we met at the church had on a lovely scarf," Marla remarked.

"You can buy those things in the store along with shawls and aprons." Daisy glanced at her wristwatch. "Would you be interested in a butter-making demonstration? I'm giving one in fifteen minutes on the side porch."

"I'm afraid I won't have time," Marla said with a hint of regret. "I have to meet a friend. She's touring Baffle House, but I've been there before. Does the sewing group hold lessons? I might want to sign up."

"The village has various workshops. You can pick up a schedule at the ticket booth." Daisy pointed to the containers on the shelves. "I saw you looking at the button jars. We all contribute."

"Have you come across any like this one?" Marla showed the girl her photos of the pearl button.

"Not that I remember. You might ask the store manager or the minister."

"Why them?"

Daisy fingered a piece of felt on the center table. "The store sells buttons along with other sewing supplies, but Minister Godwin is our expert on fashion."

"Oh? How so?" A man posing as a preacher was an odd person to be interested in style.

Daisy's glance darted to the doorway. "He's the one who orders our costumes, but don't tell anyone I said so. We're not supposed to talk out of character."

Marla hadn't considered where their clothing came from. But how did Henry get involved?

"Anyway, come by sometime when Millie is here. Did you

see the quilt our group just finished?" Daisy pointed to the bed cover hanging on a rod.

"I did. I like the green and coral colors." Marla moved closer for a better look at the stitching. She'd never had the patience for handicrafts but admired others who were talented that way. "Hey, is this a door behind the quilt?" She had almost overlooked it.

"That's a storeroom, but it's off-limits to the public. Now, you'll have to excuse me. I need to prep for my butter demo and was told to lock the door when I leave."

"Good luck. I hope you get a crowd." Marla made her departure, glad she'd at least learned something new from Daisy.

It appeared Henry Godwin was in charge of ordering costumes for the staff. That was a far cry from fishing and preaching. It also meant he was someone Phil couldn't have readily dismissed even if he'd replaced him as minister. This diminished Henry's motive as a potential murderer unless Phil had something else on him.

She glanced at her watch, realizing Susan might not be finished touring the great house. They'd do the Seminole camp and the farm after the schoolroom. Maybe she could slip into the blacksmith shop before heading over to the school.

She found the artisan craftsman outside his shed. Leafy oak branches provided shade as he sorted through a collection of scrap metal parts. He glanced up at her approach.

"Welcome to the Blacksmith Shop. My name is Angus," he said with a slight brogue.

"Hi, I'm Marla." She gave him an assessing glance. He was a brawny fellow, with unruly reddish hair and a beard to match. Sweat beaded his forehead and glistened on his hairy chest that she glimpsed beneath his shirt, its top buttons undone. Not pearl ones, her keen eyes noticed, although she wouldn't have expected any on a smithy's outfit. He'd tied a leather apron around his waist. It hung down over his pants to below his knees.

He gestured to her with a work-gloved finger. "Come inside and I'll show you my tools."

Marla hadn't been looking for gloves as much as pearl buttons. His hands were covered, but then all the ladies would have worn gloves in that era, too. She'd seen pairs for sale in the general store. Had Phil's killer worn gloves to avoid getting fingerprints on the axe's handle? She should ask Dalton if any prints had been found.

After making sure the door was propped open in her wake, Marla stepped into the log shed. Sunlight streamed in through two open windows to provide light. Various pieces of equipment lay scattered about the floor or hung on the walls.

"Blacksmiths have to be both tradesmen and businessmen," Angus began with a broad sweep of his arm. "We provide a wide range of services to the town, and we negotiate our own prices. We'll keep meticulous records of these transactions. Mostly, you'll find us creating or repairing equipment such as hoes, plows and rakes along with wagon wheels, farm tools and horseshoes."

"I've seen some of your goods for sale in the general store," Marla said, wrinkling her nose at the smell of burnt metal. "How long has your shop been set up in the village?"

"This building started as a barn in 1930 then was moved over here and converted into the blacksmith shop. Much of this equipment predates 1940, but some of it is over a hundred years old, like this drill press and antique oiler." He held up those items as he spoke. "See this chisel? I use it to etch veins on the leaves of this metal rose."

"That's very intricate," Marla said, impressed by his skill. She hadn't realized blacksmiths might create works of art.

He gave her a modest grin. "More often, I make the tools I'd mentioned from steel or wrought iron, like these door handles and gate hinges. It's a tiresome and grueling trade. The forge over here is our key piece. That's where we heat the metal in a charcoal fire until it's soft enough to manipulate. These bellows help to concentrate air into the forge to make the fire hotter. You have to watch it carefully, because steel can burn if it's left in too long."

Marla resisted the urge to step back when he hefted a mighty hammer that would have rivaled Thor's mythical weapon.

"After I take the metal out with those tongs, I'll shape it on the anvil. This one originated in 1891. You wouldn't want it to fall on your foot." He banged the hammer down onto the anvil then placed it aside. "Listen to this noise all day, and your ears will keep ringing."

He would have gone on except Marla put up a hand to stop him. "You wouldn't supply the axes the Seminoles carry in battle, would you? I thought blacksmiths made swords and other weapons. I've seen that scene in about every fantasy movie I have ever watched."

He chuckled and folded his arms across his chest. "Those are fantasies, all right. Most of the weapons you see in our reenactment are props."

Oh, yeah? Then how come a real tomahawk ended up in Phil's head?

"Does Minister Godwin supply them? I've heard he's the source of your costumes."

"Henry was in the garment business, so he has connections in that industry. Phil's the one who obtained our props. He used to manage a troupe of actors before he came to work here. Most of the professional reenactors bring their own gear, though."

Marla moved to a clear area of the wood-planked floor that wasn't covered with dropped nails. "Was Phil also an actor?"

"Aye. It's what made him so good at hiring the right cast members. Did you know him?"

"We met the day he died. He'd given my husband and me a tour of the jail before the battle started. I couldn't believe it when we learned what happened to him."

Angus's mouth curved down. "He got the role of his life when he landed this gig. His story doesn't have a happy ending, though."

"Do you mean his role as town marshal, or as the tract's administrator?"

His dark brown eyes regarded her warily. "Both, I suppose you could say."

"Did you approve of how he ran the village?" she asked, following up on Gilda's comments.

"My opinion doesn't matter now that he's dead. If you're done here, I need to go back to work. I've repairs to make to one of our wagon wheels." He picked up a wrench and weighed it in his hand.

Marla felt a sudden need to vacate the premises. "Thanks for the tour. It's great that you're keeping these skills alive and sharing them with visitors."

She hustled outside, wondering at his reticence to discuss Phil Pufferfish. Had there been bad blood between the two for some reason that would give Angus a motive for murder? Or did Angus mean to take over Phil's position as town leader?

As she entered the general store, she formed some questions to ask Uriah to further her investigation.

She sauntered up to the counter after a couple of customers exited. "I've been to the blacksmith's shop," she told the shopkeeper in a casual tone. "Angus seems very skilled at his trade. I noticed his products for sale here last time I came by."

"Angus learned smithing from his daddy," Uriah explained, a hint of admiration in his tone. "He's very talented. Did he show you his metal sculptures? I've told him he should enter them in art contests, but he doesn't think they're good enough. He won't let me sell them, either."

"I saw the rose he'd made. The etchings on its leaves were remarkable. Was he into sculpting before he got this job?"

Uriah chuckled. "Heck, no. Would you believe Angus was an accountant in real life? He hated the work, claimed his neck always hurt from bending over his desk. Doing paperwork for a living wasn't in his nature. When he took up his father's hobby, he found his calling."

"He was fortunate." She paused a moment, wondering how to phrase her next question. "Was Angus involved in any of the bookkeeping for the village? You'd think he would be the perfect person with his former career."

Uriah shuffled a collection of health tinctures on the counter. "No, that's the administrator's job. Phil kept all the records."

"Maybe Angus should apply to take Phil's place. He has the financial skills."

"Angus wouldn't compete with Lizzy. She wants the position."

Marla's ears burned at this revelation. "Really? Why it that?"

"It would give her control over the town's funding. The admin receives our allotment from the fairground. He's responsible for our paychecks as well as doling out the money needed for maintenance."

This confirmed what Marla had heard so far. "Why couldn't Angus also apply?"

He glanced toward the door. "Angus is fond of Lizzy. She isn't aware of his feelings, but the last thing he wants to do is challenge her."

That's interesting. Marla made a mental note about their potential relationship.

"Speaking of Lizzy," she said, "I accidentally overheard her talking to a strange man who darted off into the woods. I got the impression he didn't belong in the village. Any idea who this guy might have been?"

"I dunno, miss." Uriah shoved his hands into his pants pockets.

"What's beyond the tree line?"

"It's private property. I understand they guard that place like a fortress."

"And the village tract sits right up against it," Marla mused, half to herself. "What's over there? A neighbor's house?"

"Don't ask me. And if you're smart, don't ask too many questions of anyone else, either. That could very well be why poor Phil ended up dead."

Chapter Eight

Was Uriah passing on a friendly warning, or did this threat come from him directly? She couldn't ascertain his purpose and tossed out another query to test him.

"I visited the sewing circle. They said you obtain supplies for them, including buttons. Would you have seen one like this?" She showed him the pearl button on her cell phone, watching for his reaction.

"Where did you get that?" He backed away, his face suddenly washed of color.

"Someone lost it during the reenactment," she said without revealing the location. "I'll bring it to Lost and Found unless you know who might wear this type of button. Or do you sell them in your store?" Judging from his response, he'd recognized the item. But from where?

"They don't make those kinds anymore. It's a vintage design."

"Is it worth anything? I don't know much about buttons since I don't sew."

"You'd have to ask Minister Godwin. Henry is our button expert. It's a passion of his to collect them and explain their use through history. He's even founded a society for collectors."

"I understand Henry supplies everyone's costumes. Could this be part of a uniform, or perhaps a lady's blouse? Or even a bridal gown for a mannequin?"

"As I said, consult Henry on the subject. He's our fashion expert."

"We've been to the church, but he wasn't there." Clearly, Uriah knew something about the button that he wasn't willing to share. How could she get him to open up?

"Where are you going next?" he asked, stacking some brochures on the counter as though disinterested in her response.

"I thought I'd visit the schoolroom," Marla replied.

Uriah wagged a finger at her. "Don't go bothering Violet. She's still recovering from her shock of the other day, and she has a delicate constitution."

Was that genuine concern in his eyes, or something more?

"I know. I was there. She invited me to visit the school."

An unexpected wistful smile curved his lips. "She loves working with kids. It's a shame… well, never mind. She's happy in her role, especially since Phil can't plague her anymore."

"Oh? How is that?" Was Violet glad to see the former administrator gone for some reason?

"It doesn't matter now. Can I help you find anything?"

Marla purchased a painted wood caboose for Ryder, hoping the toy would encourage Dalton to consider woodworking as a hobby. After stuffing the receipt in her purse, she passed on a business card to Uriah, identifying herself as a salon owner and stylist.

"You may notice my last name sounds familiar. I'm Detective Dalton Vail's wife. He's the lead investigator on Phil's case."

"No wonder you're so nosy," Uriah muttered.

"I'm only trying to help. I imagine you'd like business to get back to normal as soon as possible."

"That's true, although we'll be lucky if the fairground doesn't shut us down."

"Why would the directors want to do that?" she asked, not understanding the logic. "If anything, they should put more money into the place. Lots of these buildings need repairs. In addition, they could publicize the village better to draw more tourists here."

Uriah's face assumed a rueful expression. "Phil was our advocate in that regard, but I'm not sure he had our best interests at heart. He wanted us to secede from the fairground, which would have eliminated his cash cow. Or so Angus implied at our town meetings."

"Meaning what?" She surmised Phil had earned extra income as the tract's administrator in addition to his role as marshal. He would have lost that paycheck if his plan had succeeded. Maybe he figured the attraction would make more money on its own. Then the staff could all share in the profits.

Uriah glared at her. "Does it matter? It's a moot point now that Phil is gone."

Is it? The man was murdered. Any bit of information might be relevant.

Another set of customers entered the shop before Marla could pose her next question. She'd have to find out what Uriah knew some other time. She thanked him and left to go meet Susan.

Outside, she texted Dalton to ask if he'd talked to anyone from the board of directors.

Not yet. It's on my agenda for today. Busy now. Will catch up later, he wrote back.

Drat, she was hoping to discuss her findings with him. Uriah knew something about the button and seemed protective of Violet. He was afraid the fairground would shut the place down.

Angus, the blacksmith and a former accountant, hadn't been happy with Phil's leadership. Since Phil handled the village funds, did Angus suspect something shady going on in that regard? Could this be the cash cow Uriah had mentioned?

Uriah had revealed that Angus had a thing for Lizzy, who didn't necessarily reciprocate his feelings. For that reason, he wouldn't challenge her application to take Phil's place as administrator.

And what about Uriah's warning? Did he mean she shouldn't ask questions in general or inquire too closely into the village's affairs? In that event, what did he know that she didn't?

Frustrated that she couldn't share her discoveries with Dalton right away, she secured her phone, adjusted her bags, and headed for the schoolroom.

Susan was waiting out front and tapping her foot.

"Oh, there you are. I was about to call you." Her friend's face was either flushed from the heat or from impatience.

"I was in the store talking to the manager. How did your tour go?" Marla asked.

Susan's eyes gleamed. "I loved it, and like you said, Lizzy is an interesting lady. She doesn't live in the house. It only serves as a museum these days, but she feels she's the best person to represent the village because of her heritage. She's been lobbying the board of directors to appoint her the next administrator."

"Yes, so I've heard." Marla shared what she'd learned in a quick summary.

"You know this gives Lizzy a motive to get Phil out of the way," Susan said.

"Possibly, although there may be more to it than that issue alone. Is it true this entire acreage used to belong to Lizzy's family?"

Susan nodded. "It was a sugar plantation later converted to citrus. A series of economic downturns, hurricanes and bad luck caused her ancestor to sell most of it. I don't quite understand which part of the land belonged to them. Look at the map in the brochure. The village seems to jut out from the rest of the fairground. It seems odd to me that the boundary isn't even."

Marla pictured the property's shape in her mind. "We could drive around the fairground's perimeter when we're done. I get what you're saying. The edge isn't square. Maybe they just bought up whatever land they could get their hands on beyond the county's initial donation."

"We'll see. Anyway, I want to look up that story about the missing Confederate gold. Lizzy laughed when she told me about people's attempts to find the treasure. She's searched every inch of the place herself and came up empty."

"Did she mention the White Lady? Maybe she's rigged the place to show the ghost during their nightly tours. That would chase away any treasure seekers."

Marla remembered the hauntings at Sugar Crest Plantation Resort when she'd stayed there with Dalton to introduce him to her family. Some of the ghost stories were real and some had been the result of an elaborate ruse.

Susan tucked a loose strand of hair behind her ear. "I'll research the house's history to see if I can find out how Adam Canfield really died."

"Thanks, that would help. Lizzy told me and Dalton she'd made an offer to buy the village property from the fairground. Did she bring this up at all?"

"No, and neither did I. We focused on her role as tour guide and what had led her to volunteer for the position."

Marla moved under a tree where the shade dropped the temperature. "Did she mention that man we saw at the house? Maybe he's helping her win the post of administrator. He could be on the board of directors."

"If so, why did Lizzy mention Simon the farmer in their discussion?" Susan's upper lip beaded with perspiration. She took out a battery-run fan from her purse, turned it on, and aimed it at her flushed face.

"Maybe Simon supports Lizzy's bid. He might be hoping to expand the farm if she's in charge. I assume she would get paid extra for the admin position. Did she mention her home life when she spoke to you? Like, does she need the money?"

"Lizzy is widowed and seems to be well-off financially, so I doubt that's a motive. Her daughter is married and has two kids. They're in the Hammock Lakes subdivision. I couldn't get a straight answer from Lizzy about where she lives."

"What else did you learn from her?" Marla gestured that they should climb the steps to the schoolhouse. They went up and halted on the front porch. Marla tucked away her sunglasses and Susan stashed her fan.

"Would you believe Lizzy owns a doll shop at Papaya Corners?" Susan replied with a conspiratorial grin. Obviously, she liked her role as sleuth. "Her mother and aunt started a collection and then Lizzy got interested in the hobby. She went on to become a certified doll appraiser. She's the only one in our tri-county region."

"No way. I've been to that shopping center and never noticed a doll store there. She must make a good income to afford the rent. But how can she spend time there if she works here as a tour guide?"

Susan spread her hands. "Maybe she has a manager or else she has hours by appointment only. We should go visit."

A visual image surfaced in Marla's mind of the creepy doll with a shiny face in the living room at Baffle House. "Does she sell vintage or modern dolls?"

"I'm not sure. Does it matter?"

"Some of the older models can be scary, as in horror movies. I liked American Girl dolls and Barbies when I grew up, especially ones with long hair that I could style."

Susan chuckled. "Jess's favorite is a baby doll that came with a stroller. You could feed it and it would pee. She still has it in her closet." Susan's daughter was the spitting image of her mother with the same brown hair and eyes.

A sudden yearning gripped Marla with a surprising ferocity. Wouldn't it be amazing to have a daughter for whom she could buy kitchen sets and dolls and play makeup? She'd come into Brianna's life when her stepdaughter was a preteen and had missed those early years. Was it too late to think about giving Ryder another sibling? Would Dalton even consider the idea, or was he one and done where their children were concerned? Was it an idea she even dared to explore?

"What is it, Marla? You look kinda weird," Susan said, peering at her.

She sighed. "I'm wondering what it would be like to have a daughter of my own. Dalton probably doesn't want any more kids at this stage, and I'll be too old if we wait for Ryder to be potty trained. I never thought I'd have a family at all and should have started earlier."

Susan clucked her tongue. "You can't cry over spilt milk. If it's something you really want, talk it over with Dalton. He might be more receptive than you think."

"He's going to be forty-nine this year. The age difference hadn't bothered me before, but that's late to raise kids."

"It's never too late if this is something both of you really want. Anyway, we're just standing here and it's almost lunchtime. Let's go inside and meet the teacher."

Marla stepped across the threshold and surveyed the area. Electric lighting was noticeably absent. The doors had glass inserts to let in the sunlight along with several open windows. A wood-burning stove with fireplace implements took up one corner while an upright piano occupied another. Blackboards ranged across walls, vying for space with bookshelves in between the windows.

She eyed the student desks and chairs that sat in rows facing the teacher up front. It must have been uncomfortable to be seated on that hard wood all day. Maybe the kids left early to help with chores at home.

The place was warm but not unbearable with a cross-breeze. It smelled of old books, the scent reminiscent of the library where Marla had spent time as a kid. Her mother had taken her, hoping to inspire a passion for reading. Instead, Marla had paged through the pictures to admire people's hairstyles and clothes.

Violet stood behind a scarred wooden desk. She wore a muslin dress with a floral design and an ivory shawl. She'd knotted her hair into a bun.

"Marla, isn't it?" Violet said in her soft voice. "You've come for your tour! How lovely. And who is your friend?"

"This is Susan Feinberg. She's a journalist working on an article about the women of Pioneer Village."

Susan bobbed her head. "Marla and I are neighbors, and she

told me about her visit here. I'd never known this place existed and thought it would be interesting for my readers to learn more about it. Tell us about the schoolroom." She got out her notebook and pen.

"Each row represents a different grade. You come to school when you're six years old. The younger children learn how to read and write, while the older kids learn science, geography, and math. Students bring their own lunch or walk home to eat. The only supplies they need are pencils, paper, crayons and paste."

"Life was simpler in those days," Susan remarked, strolling around the room. She paused to examine a series of equations chalked on a blackboard. A poster of the alphabet hung across the top. The only chalk supplied was the white kind.

"As the village teacher, I have no one else to answer to except my class and the town aldermen who hired me. I live a quiet life and can manage quite well on my own."

"Isn't marriage encouraged?" Marla asked. "Or are teachers expected to be spinsters?"

Violet's face reddened. "Women without a husband are regarded as an anomaly. The role of females in this era is limited to certain roles."

Marla nodded. "In my mother's day, you could choose between being a nurse, a teacher, or a secretary. Thank goodness we're free to choose what we want to do these days."

Violet moved the inkwell back and forth on her desk. "Maybe so, but there will always be men who exploit women. Do you watch the news? Throughout the world, it's the men who suppress us and deny us true freedom."

Violet had gone completely out of character, Marla realized. Was this her true nature peeking out? Or merely her political viewpoint?

"We've seen progress, at least in our county," she said. "Here men are more careful about their behavior."

"No, they're not." Violet's eyes glittered. "Many of them still abuse women, and the laws support them. Famous people might be condemned by the media, but what about the rest of us? Not everyone can afford to fight for what's right. And even if they do, the odds are stacked against them."

Marla lowered her voice, aware Susan had halted and was listening in. "Is this what happened to you? You had a bad personal experience, and some guy was at fault?"

The schoolteacher sidestepped so abruptly that she nearly knocked her desk chair over. She straightened it then narrowed her eyes at Marla. "Did you stop by to question me?"

"Not at all. You'd offered to give me a tour, remember? I just came from the general store where I bought a toy for my son." She lifted her shopping bag as evidence. "Uriah spoke very highly of you and said you're wonderful with children."

"How many kids do you have?" Violet asked with a polite expression.

"I have a stepdaughter from Dalton's previous marriage. Brianna is eighteen. Our son Ryder is thirteen months old. How about you?"

"I've no little ones of my own, but I get pleasure from my pupils." Violet's brow smoothed. "Uriah is such a sweet man. He's a caterpillar among the snakes out there."

"He told me he's hoping to add an apothecary section to his store."

"That would make sense as he's a licensed pharmacist. He's really into the history of that profession. He could do so much more if we had the funding to expand."

Susan stepped forward. "Tell me more about your role. I imagine being the sole teacher for the village must be a challenge."

Marla cast her a grateful glance for bringing the subject back to Violet's position. She'd ask Dalton to check into the woman's employment record if he hadn't already done so. Perhaps she'd been sexually harassed in her previous job. Maybe that's how she'd ended up with this gig. She had quit or was let go from her previous position.

She wandered away while Susan asked questions and took notes but could hear everything they said in the single-room space.

"Where do you live when you're not working here?" Susan asked in an innocent tone.

Violet's lips curved upward. "I have a condo in Hollywood with an ocean view. It's a drive to get here to work, but I don't mind."

"Nice. What do you do on your time off? Our readers will want to know about your interests."

"I take long walks on the boardwalk and have joined a Tai Chi class on the beach."

Marla's ears perked up. Delicate Violet might be less helpless than she appeared.

"I've seen the yoga group there," Susan said. "We don't go east too often, but we'll take a walk with the kids and then do weekend brunch at a place by the Intracoastal."

"You have kids, too? If they're old enough, I do story hour at the Sunrise library branch."

"That's awesome. What else do you like to do?"

Violet gave a shy smile. "I love Latin music. It makes me want to dance, so I've started taking salsa classes." She shimmied her shoulders in a graceful movement that made Marla realize she must be agile between her dance lessons and Tai Chi.

"How about cooking?" Susan asked, smiling in return.

"Heck, no. I'm clumsy in the kitchen. I can't even boil an egg properly."

"Speaking of food," Marla said, "have you tasted anything Millie has made? I tried her biscuits and thought they were rather dry."

"You and me both." Violet made a face. "Her stew isn't any good, either. River is a way better cook over at the Seminole camp."

Marla filed that information for later. "I'd heard about Phil's proposal to gain control over the village. He planned to open a restaurant where visitors could get freshly prepared meals. Where did he mean to put it? It appears to me that every corner of the village is taken."

"He would have converted the Seminole camp. He spoke about it at a town meeting and said their settlement didn't belong as part of an early Florida village. The shaman was furious. He rang out a string of curses when Phil proposed the idea. The two of them nearly came to blows."

"Did you tell my husband about this?"

Violet clapped a hand to her cheek. "Oh, my. I'd forgotten all about it. I was too upset to think straight when he interviewed me."

"Don't worry. I'll pass it on to him," Marla said with a glance at Susan. Visiting the Native American site had just become a priority.

Chapter Nine

"Should we go see the Seminole camp before the farm?" Susan asked once they'd left the schoolhouse. She and Marla stood under the shade of a gumbo limbo tree.

"I don't know. Let's eat first. Then we can decide where to go next."

They purchased sandwiches and drinks at the general store and headed toward the picnic tables. Marla spied a familiar figure lumbering down the path from the opposite direction.

"Look, there's Sergeant Langley. You go and get seats. I'll be right back." Marla dashed off to meet him. "Joel, how are you? How are Elise and the kids?"

His somber face broke into a grin. He was a stocky fellow where Dalton was tall and lean. Together they reminded her of a classic comedy team, except for their roles in solving murders.

"They're great, thanks. What are you doing here? Wait, I should know. You're snooping around like you always do. Learn anything you want to tell me?"

"Actually, yes. Would you like to join us for lunch? I'm with my friend, Susan." Marla gestured toward the picnic tables. "I can share half of a turkey sandwich."

"No need. I ate a big breakfast, but I'll sit for a few minutes."

Marla made introductions to Susan, who'd claimed a shady spot under a leafy oak tree. She sat next to her friend, unwrapped her sandwich, and popped the lid on her soda can.

"So ladies, what have you got?" Langley said, folding his hands on the table. His florid face held a bemused expression.

Marla related the highlights of their conversations, while Susan filled in the details. "Is there anything you can share?" Marla asked at her conclusion.

Langley nodded and shifted his seat. "Billy Cypress is the shaman, and he's the genuine article. River Osceola is the woman who plays his wife. They're both present today at the camp if you go there next. During the reenactment, River was teaching basket weaving at an exhibit tent. Billy played the role of Indian chief at the battle. He claims someone stole his tomahawk the day before. He only realized it was missing that morning when he put on his costume."

"Do you believe him?"

Langley shrugged. "He said he'd armed himself instead with a rifle and spear. He'd taken shooting lessons so his actions would appear more authentic. He's freely admitted the murder weapon belonged to him."

Marla chewed and swallowed a bite of her sandwich. "Was he present at the battle scene the entire time or did he step out?"

"He didn't say. In the haze of smoke, nobody could tell who was where. We've spoken to the history advisors and reenactors. They say it gets confusing. There's a certain script to follow but actors improvise. One guy said he thought he'd seen the Indian chief whooping it up on his horse in the aftermath."

"Then if Billy had stepped out momentarily, it might have gone unnoticed. Is there a path from the woods to the fishing shack?"

Langley's face took on a morose expression. "There isn't a distinctive trail, if that's what you mean. But you could get from Point A to Point B by cutting through the trees."

Susan jabbed a finger in the air. "Did Billy mention anything about Phil's plan that would displace their site?"

"I hadn't heard about that aspect before you told me, but it would give him a possible motive. I was more concerned with his alibi. Maybe it's something you can bring up when you speak to him."

"How about Simon, the farmer?" Marla said. "My cousin, Corbin, is his assistant. He let slip that Simon had run out either during or after the battle."

"The farmer wasn't all that forthcoming. It was hard to get a reading on the man. He showed me his crops but not the herb garden."

"I wonder why. Billy and Uriah must use herbs in their health tonics. Those plants are important to the village."

"Maybe Simon doesn't want them contaminated by visitors tramping through the place," Susan suggested. "We'll see if we can get a peek when we're over there."

Langley stood to take his leave. Marla rose, one last question on her lips. "Joel, I've been meaning to ask you about this. Dalton's retirement is set for mid-September. Are the guys at work planning any sort of celebration?"

He lifted his brows. "I believe there's something in the works. Captain Williams has mentioned it, but nothing will happen until this case is solved."

"I'm thinking I should arrange a separate event for our extended family and friends, but I don't want to conflict with whatever date you guys are planning."

"It's two months off. Why don't you wait until things are more settled? Anyway, if you'll excuse me, I need to move on. Please don't do anything to jeopardize our investigation."

As if! Don't you know me by now?

"We'll be careful," she said aloud. After he left, Marla turned to Susan. "I'll plan something for Dalton. I could start by compiling a guest list. Hey, that will give me an excuse to see Corbin. I can tell my cousin to expect an invitation."

"There you go. Good thinking." Susan took Marla's trash and added it to her own before tossing the goods into a nearby trashcan. Other tables had filled with visitors, while an older couple stood by waiting for Susan and Marla's spot.

"We should head over to the Seminole camp," Susan said. "I'll interview the woman while you talk to Billy."

"Okay." As they plodded along the concrete path under the shady trees, Marla's eyes widened at the sight ahead.

"Look, Millie is there," she said, unable to stem the excitement from her tone. She pointed to the older woman standing behind a black-clothed table.

Millie grinned upon recognizing Marla. "Hi there, you've come back! Are you here for my apple cider demonstration?" She indicated the equipment covering the table.

Marla exulted in this opportunity. Now she could ask Millie more questions.

"Sure, I'd love to see what you're doing. This is my friend, Susan Feinberg. She's writing an article for her magazine about the women of the village."

Susan got out her notebook and pen. "I'd love to include you."

"Is that right?" Millie tugged on the apron that protected her high-necked blouse and long skirt. Wisps of ash blond hair escaped the edges of her blue bonnet and fluttered in a light breeze.

Marla glanced at the sky. The air had been still up until now. In the distance, she noted a line of storm clouds. Great. She'd like to be finished here before it rained.

"How come you're not over by the church like last time?" Marla asked, curious.

Millie's eyes twinkled. "I like to move around. It gives me a different vantage point to watch the goings-on."

She had a point. But who was Millie watching—the visitors or the staff?

Susan piped in. "I understand you're in charge of the sewing ladies. Do you actually make clothes and repair costumes? I mean, do you really sew or is it all for show?"

"We do minor repairs, but mostly we make things to sell in the general store. We're quite crafty." Millie laughed at her pun.

"We met Gilda earlier," Susan continued in her innocent tone. "She gave us a tour of the church. Gilda said she fills in where needed. Is your job like hers?"

Millie lifted her chin. "My duties are more specific, like the sewing circle and the cooking demos. Gilda gives a good spiel, but she doesn't always get her facts straight. Be sure to verify whatever she says."

Was this true, or was Millie resentful towards Gilda for cutting in on her territory?

Marla stayed Susan's arm when she was about to hand over a business card. She'd cautioned her friend earlier not to leave any contact information. It would be safer for her that way with a killer on the loose. Giving her own info was different since her husband was the detective on the case.

"Can you show us how the apple press works?" Susan asked with an avid expression on her face. Marla made a mental note to buy a copy of Becky's cookbook for Susan. She'd appreciate it after today.

Marla was impressed by Millie's knife skills as she cut up the apples. She tossed the pieces into a bucket and then mashed them with a wooden tool. That part required strength, she thought, noting how the woman's arm muscles bulged.

The mash went into a press lined with a muslin cloth. Millie folded the cloth to cover the fruit then secured this with two wooden half rounds to make a circle on top. She added two levels of rectangular blocks and finally attached a handle. As she turned the crank, juice poured from a spout into a pail. A funnel and sieve stood by for transferring the liquid to a jar.

"Want a taste?" Millie offered, pointing to a stack of paper cups.

"Sure," Marla said to be polite. She took a sip. The warm juice didn't have much taste.

Susan smacked her lips. "It's not as sweet as I'd expected."

"That's because the level of sugar depends on the type of apples and the ripeness. You're probably used to sweetened drinks. This is a natural product."

A large group of guests headed their way, about to infringe on their privacy. Drat! Marla had things to ask but would have to save it for another time. She nudged Susan to indicate they should move on.

"We have to go, but it was nice meeting you," Susan told Millie. "If I have more questions for my article, I'll catch you later."

Marla waved to Millie. "Thanks for the demo. It was fun."

Heading toward the Seminole camp, Marla and Susan passed an arched bridge that stretched across a canal. Apparently, it led to the rest of the fairground. A gate blocked access on the other side.

Marla supposed the gated entrance made sense. Pioneer Village was a paid attraction, while the fairground itself was not unless the annual fair was going on. The other buildings that housed exhibits or shows had their own requirements. Fairground officials probably had a code to get in through this rear entrance, but visitors would have to come by the ticket booth in front.

At the encampment, a series of chickee huts with palmetto thatched roofs stood in a circle amongst the trees. A round hut on stilts took up space in the center. That must be the meeting hall, Marla surmised. Colorful blankets strung on a rack flapped in the breeze.

Since the shaman wasn't in view, Marla approached a woman who was stirring something in an iron pot suspended over a campfire. She had thick wavy black hair that spilled down her back, long-lashed eyes, and high cheekbones enhanced by an expert application of makeup. Marla's admiring glance took in her patchwork dress with its red, yellow and black design, the set of beads around her neck, and the silver bracelets on her wrists.

The woman put down her spoon and rose to address them. "Hi, I'm River Osceola. Welcome to our site. Have you come for a tour?" she asked in a melodious voice.

"I'm Susan Feinberg, and this is my friend, Marla Vail," Susan said, taking the lead. "I'm writing an article for *Ladies Town Post* on the women of the village. Would you like to be included? If so, you could start by explaining your role in this exhibit."

"That's easy. I play the tribal shaman's wife. We're both

members of the Seminole Nation. Would you like me to share a bit of our history?"

"Please, go ahead," Susan said, retrieving her notebook and pen.

River gestured for them to follow her into a patch of shade. Marla noted the moccasins on her feet. They looked more comfortable but less sturdy than Marla's sneakers.

"In the 1700s, bands of Creek Indians migrated here from Georgia and Alabama. They were joined by other tribes and runaway slaves. These groups united to form the Seminole Nation. Despite attempts by the government to chase us away, hundreds of tribesmen fled into the Everglades to hide after a series of wars. Fast-forward to 1957, when tribal members voted in favor of a constitution. This established the official Seminole Tribe of Florida. We have several reservations throughout the state."

"You mentioned how the natives fled into the Everglades," Marla said. "If I had to rely on my survival skills in the woods, I wouldn't last long." She thought about Lizzy's tale and how the Confederate soldiers had fled into the wild, never to return.

River chuckled. "Our men did the hunting and fishing. They had plenty of game to snag, such as deer, rabbits, and gators. Women helped tan the alligator skins, took care of the children, and did most of the farming and cooking."

"What crops did you grow?" Susan asked. "I know corn must have been one of them."

"Corn, beans, and squash were staples of our diet." River pointed to the cookpot. A fragrant aroma emanated from its contents. "I'm making a stew with sweet potatoes, venison, onions and rice. You can have a taste when it's ready. In the meantime, try our sofkee drink made from corn. See this ladle? It's carved from guava wood. Each household has a spoon like this with a unique design."

River removed the lid on a covered pot that rested on a trestle. She ladled a sample into disposable paper cups and handed them over.

Marla took a tentative sip, rolling the warm substance on her tongue. It had a thick consistency closer to porridge than water.

"Interesting," Susan said. "It fills the stomach. I see how this can be satisfying."

River lifted a screen cover off a platter. "Have one of these coontie cakes and a sweet potato biscuit. They're my favorites."

Susan eagerly helped herself while Marla took a bite from each one. They tasted a lot better than Millie's efforts. She finished each moist sample and chased it down with the sofkee.

"What's coontie?" she asked, never having heard of it before.

"Coontie is a plant. We make flour from its roots, but you must be careful because certain parts can be poisonous. Back when our ancestors lived in the swamps, coontie plants helped them to survive."

Marla didn't hear much beyond the mention of poison. In one of Dalton's earlier cases, a suspect who did gardening as a hobby had tried to kill her using poison derived from a plant. Herbs could be dangerous, too, without the proper knowledge. River might be someone to watch, along with Billy and Uriah who used herbal remedies.

Then again, Phil had died from an axe in his forehead. That was a more blatant way of murdering someone.

"I think food is so representative of a culture, don't you?" she said aloud. "We've met Millie, who made apple juice from a press. Have you two ever exchanged recipes? I understand she fancies herself as a chef. I've tasted her biscuits, and yours are better." Marla waited to gauge the other woman's response.

River bristled. "Millie isn't on my favorite person list. She supported Phil's views. He was our town leader who recently passed away. Have you heard about his proposal?"

"Yes. I'd met Phil on an earlier visit, and he mentioned his plans," Marla replied.

"He wanted the village to buy our tract from the fairground. If his bid had succeeded, he meant to build an on-site restaurant. He would have kicked us out for the space. Millie talked about the menu for the café as if it were a done deal."

"I can understand how that would upset you. How did Billy react when he heard this plan?"

"How do you think? We're relegated to this corner as it is. It's just another attempt by white people to chase us off the land."

"I like the idea of a café," Marla admitted, "although I'd think it should be more centrally located, like near the picnic tables. Surely there's some other building that could be converted." Like the sewing room, she thought. That structure had been a detached kitchen back in the day. Why not restore the place to its original use?

"That'll be up to the next administrator. The fairground has yet to appoint someone."

"Who would you like to see take over the job?" Susan asked, while Marla cast her a grateful glance for posing that question.

River shrugged. "Somebody who cares about the village and who is willing to put money into repairs. How did you learn about this place, anyway?"

"My friend Becky Forest told me," Marla said. "She's the curator of our local history museum. Maybe you've run into her. She studies ancient Florida food practices and writes cookbooks."

River's face brightened. "I know Becky. She included some of our native dishes in her latest volume. I like how she offers related commentary on the meanings of each item."

"I bought a copy on Saturday at the general store but missed her signing."

"My name is in the acknowledgements," River said with a proud grin. "It was thoughtful of her to recognize me that way."

"How did you come to work at the village?" Susan asked, scribbling notes while they spoke. "Have you always been interested in educating people about your heritage?"

"Yes, although I worked as a model to earn money to go to college. I'd even won the title of Miss Florida Seminole. But I had enough of that life and wanted to go somewhere quiet. It's peaceful here. I can do my crafts and listen to the birds when I'm not giving tours."

Star Tangled Murder

River wasn't the only one who felt that way, Marla realized. Other cast members had also come there to find peace or to escape their pasts. Her cousin Corbin was one of them. Millie and Violet could be included. Who else had settled there to hide away from reality?

"Do you live on a reservation or do you have a place elsewhere?" Susan continued.

"I have a house in Davie with my boyfriend. It's close to NSU where I'm an adjunct professor of history." River noted their surprised expressions. "Hey, this isn't a full-time job. I might have wanted to leave modeling, but I have an education and put it to use."

"That's great." Susan gave her an admiring glance. "How does the scheduling work here? Do you each make your own hours? I imagine you'd need a flexible schedule with a day job outside the park."

"The paid staff have regular hours. It's up to the volunteers when they want to come. If I can't be here, Gilda fills in for me."

"We met her at the church," Marla said. "She seemed very knowledgeable about the building's history."

River's gaze narrowed. "Be careful what you say around her. Gilda has big ears and a loose mouth."

Marla would have liked to ask why River held that opinion but just then she spied a robed figure with light hair darting from one of the chickee huts. It couldn't be the shaman. This guy wore clerical garments. Was he the minister?

She excused herself and hurried over. Susan could continue the interview with River on her own. That had been their initial plan, anyway.

"Hi, are you Henry Godwin? I've been wanting to talk to you."

The man whipped around, his robe swirling at his booted feet. His footgear made her wonder what he wore beneath his ecclesiastical garments. His fishing outfit or regular clothes?

"And you are?" he asked with a squint of his blue eyes. He spoke in sonorous tones suitable to a preacher.

"Marla Vail. I met Gilda over at the church. She gave a wonderful tour and mentioned how much you enjoy your role there."

He patted down his robe. "Yes, I like to describe the church in detail to our guests. Sorry I missed your visit."

She gave a dismissive wave. "I heard about Phil's proposal. In truth, I don't understand why he meant to replace you with an ordained clergyman. Couldn't guests bring in their own officiant for special events?"

His gaze chilled. "Maybe so, but Phil wanted to offer a package deal. In addition to a rental fee, folks would have to use our clergy and our catering staff. Simon would supply the flowers. It would be mostly an in-house affair except for music."

"Seceding from the fairground seems a drastic move. What about the loss of benefits for the paid staff?"

"Phil said we should wait to address that subject until after the split happened and we'd formed our own corporation. Even if he'd succeeded, I would still work here. I'm in charge of the bait and tackle shed. Fishing is a true passion for me. But why are you asking these questions?"

"I'm Detective Dalton Vail's wife. He's investigating Phil's murder. The sooner he wraps this case, the sooner things will return to normal. Anything you can tell us will help."

He stiffened. "Well then, stop looking my way and set your sights on Angus Roundhouse. There's something about our blacksmith that you should know."

And you obviously can't wait to tell me. Is it to throw suspicion off yourself?

"What's that?" she asked as expected.

"Angus participates in axe-throwing competitions. It's his favorite sport."

Marla's mouth gaped, not only because of the blacksmith's alleged prowess with an axe but because the manner of Phil's death must have been leaked beyond the initial witnesses.

Chapter Ten

"Where does Angus do his axe-throwing?" Marla asked. "Is it a bar game, or is it part of the annual Highland Games held at the fairground?"

Henry ran a hand through his golden blond hair. "You'd have to ask him for more details."

She'd heard of hammer and log tosses at the traditional Scottish spectacle but not this type of competition. She recalled passing a booth for it at the battle reenactment. Was that Angus's exhibit, or had he stayed at the blacksmith shop during the event?

She glanced at Susan, who was still engaged in conversation with River. "I understand Angus and Phil had different views at town meetings," she said. "Did they ever get physical?"

Henry's eyes glittered. "No, they hashed it out verbally, but you could tell Angus was ready to punch Phil."

"What got him so riled?"

The brackets deepened on the sides of his mouth. "Angus wouldn't say, but I could guess. Phil received the funding for our parcel. You've seen the state of these buildings. Did the fairground really institute budget cuts like Phil claimed, or was he dipping his fingers into the pie?"

Marla stared at him. "Are you saying Phil lied about it, and Angus suspected this?"

"Angus has an accounting background. He would know more about these things. It may have only been conjecture on his part, but if he was right, then Phil got his just rewards."

Those were harsh words. Regardless of the reason, nobody

105

deserved to die that way. Plus, this death seemed more personal. Would somebody really plant an axe in the marshal's head if he was appropriating village funds? Or had he betrayed someone who cared about him?

"I understand you're a button collector," she said to appeal to his ego. "What's the fascination in a bunch of buttons?"

His boyish face brightened. "Buttons tell our history better than many other items. They've been around for five thousand years."

"That's a lot older than zippers. I imagine most of the costumes worn by the staff have buttons. I've heard that you do the ordering. How did that come about?"

"I used to manufacture fabrics. I get the material wholesale for the costumes and then contract with a company that makes period clothing."

"Do any of the outfits use pearl buttons like this one?" Marla showed him the photos.

His jaw clenched. "Where did you get that?"

"My husband found it on the village grounds," she said, unwilling to reveal the exact location. "I'm asking because it looks valuable."

"It belongs to me. I'd picked it up at a garage sale and gave it to Uriah to research. The vintage design would be a good match for our fabrics in the store, if he could find something similar. He must have dropped it."

"Then this button didn't come off anyone's costume or uniform?"

"Not to my knowledge."

If Henry is telling the truth, that means Uriah was the last person in possession of the item.

Henry checked his wristwatch. "If you'll excuse me, I need to go. I've an appointment for a fishing lesson in ten minutes."

Marla raised her hand. "Wait, I have one more question. The day of the reenactment, I was watching Millie's cooking demo at the fire pit near the church. We saw you hurrying out of that

106

building and heading toward the bait and tackle shed. What was your purpose in going there?"

A shadow flitted across his face. "I'd forgotten to put the lid on a container of live bait and didn't want it to dry out."

"Do you have much contact with Millie?" she asked to assess their relationship.

"She helps me out on occasion. Millie is a woman with many skills. Besides sewing and cooking, she's handy with a paintbrush. She helped me give the church exterior a fresh coat of paint."

"I did notice how that building looked better than most others. Millie said she'd like to see a café added to the site. She would have applied for the chef's position if it had materialized under Phil's plan. Rumor says she'd lost a previous job in the field, though. Do you know why?"

He nodded. "The restaurant where she'd worked went up in flames. Nobody was hurt, but there was substantial damage. The owners accused her of setting the fire because she was about to be dismissed. She denied it, saying they wanted to claim the insurance and used her as a scapegoat. Nothing was ever proven, but due to their allegations, the door was closed to her at any other kitchen."

Considering the woman's baking skills, perhaps her former employers were glad to be rid of her. Marla would have to ask Dalton to check into Millie's employment record and the fire inspection report. If she'd been wronged, the former chef wouldn't take lightly to being betrayed a second time.

"Millie is very talented at sewing," she said. "Maybe that's a better occupation for her to pursue." Certainly, her hand-sewn aprons had to be more appealing than her dry biscuits.

"True," Henry said, bobbing his head. "You can find her at craft shows. She'll often rent a table to sell her handicrafts. Sometimes, I'll join her to look for buttons. Anyway, I've said more than I should. Enjoy your tour." He gave her a priestly bow and turned away.

Marla had hoped to gauge Henry's personal feelings toward Millie, but he'd only spoken about her in a casual manner. If Millie had a special fondness for him, it might be a one-sided affair. Why else would she have glared at him as he strode past that day?

She'd mention this potential twist to Dalton along with the blacksmith's disagreement with Phil. Had Angus been correct in surmising the village records had financial discrepancies? If so, did he have any proof?

That scenario didn't seem likely, because then Angus might have been the one to end up dead if he'd confronted Phil about it. Or if Angus had evidence, he could have brought it to the attention of the fairground directors and avoided Phil altogether. Meanwhile, he voiced his opinions at the town meetings. Was this to alert his fellow villagers to Phil's misdeeds or to purposefully cause dissent among them?

Susan rejoined her and they headed inside the chickee hut to find the shaman. They agreed to exchange news later.

A man stood on a ladder repairing the thatched roof. He had stark black hair tied in a low ponytail and wore a long tunic in red, yellow and white over a pair of dark pants. A necklace of silver ornaments hung from his neck.

Upon spotting them, he descended to the planked floor. "Hi, are you ladies here for a tour?" he asked in a raspy tone. "I'm Billy Cypress, the village shaman."

Marla sniffed, detecting an odor of cigarette smoke that accompanied him. She introduced herself and Susan. "We were hoping to learn about your role," she explained. "We've already spoken to River outside."

He gave them a white-toothed grin. "People seek the help of a shaman for healing in the physical and spiritual sense. We work in conjunction with traditional medical practice."

"What's that?" Susan asked, pointing to part of a costume on the floor.

"Oh, I should put this on so you can get the whole effect.

Visitors like to see me in my native regalia." He picked up what turned out to be an elaborate headdress decorated with feathers and shells. It fastened on his head with a leather band.

"This is what's known as a roach headdress. It's made from animal hair dyed in bright colors and attached to a leather base. See how it stands straight up from the head like a crest?"

Marla nodded. "Is that what you wear when you play the Indian chief at the battle scene? I saw the reenactment with my husband. It was so smoky from the gunfire that all the figures were shadowy. Were you on horseback the entire time?"

"Naturally. My warriors check the soldiers on foot to make sure they are all dead. Looting is forbidden. We respect our enemy and leave them for burial by their own kind."

"Did you notice anyone among the company slipping out during the event?"

He shook his head. "Not really. I was paying attention to my own part in the drama."

"Were you there the entire time? Or did you leave for a brief interval?"

His mouth thinned and his eyes narrowed. "What is this? Why all the questions?"

Marla laid her cards on the table. "I'm married to the lead investigator on Phil's case. I've heard about your boss's plan of secession. He would have replaced your exhibit with a café."

Billy scowled at her. "Phil claimed our site wasn't authentic to a pioneer village, but he was wrong. We would have traded with the inhabitants and been essential to their survival. Besides, it's critical to educate people about our culture. Phil would have swept us aside as though we don't matter, and we've experienced enough of that throughout history."

"I can see how his plans would have made you angry."

He folded his arms across his chest. "Not so angry that I killed him, if that's what you're implying."

"What do you do when you're not working at the village?" Susan asked in her sweet tone.

"I own the gift shop at the casino, but my hours there vary. I spend most of my time here where it's more peaceful. My staff manages the store when I'm not available."

That meant finances wouldn't be a motive, Marla thought. He probably didn't even need this job for its meager salary. Like River, he did it to share his heritage with others.

"What's your relationship to River?" she said. "Do you always pair up together?"

His expression softened. "I like working with her. She's very talented. At least now she doesn't have to worry about..." He cut himself off and glanced away.

Had he been about to mention Phil? Marla bit her lower lip. Uriah had said almost the same thing about Violet. Had the late marshal gone around hitting on the female cast members?

She sought another line of questioning but came up empty. A glance at Susan indicated her friend had come to a dead end as well. Maybe they were both tired and needed to regroup.

Susan must have read her thoughts because she addressed Billy for both of them. "We appreciate your time in explaining things to us. Thanks for sharing."

Marla got out a business card and handed it over. "Here's my contact info if you think of anything that might be related to Phil's case. I'll pass along any news to my husband. I know it can be intimidating to talk to the police."

Billy accepted the card with a frown. She figured the tribe had their own authorities and he regarded Dalton as an outsider. Then again, this wasn't reservation property.

They left the chickee hut and went outdoors. The air was redolent with the aroma of cooking meat. River sat by the stew that simmered in the pot. She pecked at her cell phone, flushing when she noticed them.

Marla waved goodbye and aimed in the direction of the adjacent farm. They'd barely have time to meet Simon if he was there. The farmer was the only main player they hadn't met yet. She was hoping he'd shed light on the others.

No one was visible at the animal pens that stank of dung, so they headed for the fields of crops. These stretched into the distance, framed by a line of trees on one side and by the bridge to the rest of the fairground on the other. A canal wound around that side, providing a natural barrier. Was Susan right in that the village stuck out from the rest of the fairground? They should take a drive around as her friend had suggested.

The farmer stood in his denim overalls by a row of corn. He squinted at them with wary brown eyes beneath a straw hat. Stubble shadowed his weak chin. Lean as a scarecrow, he grinned at them. A front tooth was chipped and another one was missing, giving Marla the impression that he needed a good dentist.

"Howdy, folks. Can I help you?" he asked in a gruff voice.

"I'm Marla Vail and this is my friend, Susan Feinberg. We were hoping to learn more about the farm," Marla explained. She looked around but didn't see her cousin anywhere in sight. He must not be working there that afternoon.

"I'm kinda busy. I have to take care of the weeds."

Marla didn't see any tools in his hand. Was he trying to put them off?

"Are you the farmer? Can you at least tell us what you grow here?"

"Yes, ma'am," he said with obvious reluctance. "My name is Simon Weedcutter. We grow pumpkins, potatoes and corn. Are you aware Florida accounts for twenty percent of the nation's fresh market sweet corn? We plant the crop from August through April. You need at least four rows for pollination to take place."

"How do you know when an ear is ready to be picked?" Marla asked, wondering if Dalton would want to grow corn in his vegetable garden.

"The silks turn brown. After you buy corn at the marketplace, don't let it sit too long in your kitchen. You'll want to eat the ears as soon as possible, or the sugar will convert into carbs."

"Good to know," Marla said with a nod. "I cook it in the

husk in the microwave for four minutes then slice off the ends. The husk peels right off."

"Oh, cool," Susan said. "I'll have to try that method. We usually boil ours."

"Sweet corn has more sugar than field corn, which is grown for livestock consumption," Simon added, tucking his thumbs into his pockets.

"Speaking of livestock, we'd hoped to see the animals today," Marla said.

"My assistant, Corbin, manages that sector, but he's out getting supplies. You'll have to come by another time."

"Right." Too bad Marla had missed him on this trip. "We stopped by the Seminole camp earlier and tasted their corn drink."

Simon chuckled. "Did Billy tell you about their green corn dance? It's a Native American ceremony held in May before the harvest. He does a show here that's popular with the ladies."

"It's a seasonal celebration?"

"Billy can explain the meaning better. Spiritually, it's a time for reflection when your sins are forgiven, and you repent for anything you've done wrong in the past year."

Marla exchanged glances with Susan. That sounded like Rosh Hashanah, the Jewish New Year. "The native encampment would have been eliminated if Phil had his way. We heard about his proposal. How did you feel about it?"

Simon's brows drew together like the overhead clouds that had begun coalescing into thunderheads. "Phil was full of hogwash. Why rock the boat when things are good?"

Things don't look so well to me with most of these buildings in disrepair.

"I understand he wanted to establish a restaurant. You could have supplied fresh vegetables from your farm. A sit-down café would enhance the park and encourage visitors to stay longer."

"We don't need to expand. Then more people might come by to see the crops. Guests can stick to the petting zoo and not bother me about my plants."

"What about your herb garden? Does the shaman use herbs in his potions? Or Uriah for his holistic tonics? Aside from use in cooking, your plants could be valuable to them that way. Where is this patch of land, anyway? My husband is into gardening. Maybe I can get him interested in growing herbs for my kitchen."

A muscle twitched in Simon's jaw. "Our herb garden is private. Nobody goes there."

His tone had turned hostile, same as the gleam in his eyes. Why would he work at a living history museum as part of the attraction if he didn't want visitors?

"What's over that way?" she asked, gesturing toward the woods by the far border. She remembered Uriah mentioning private property. That's where the man had gone whom she'd seen talking to Lizzy.

"Belongs to a neighbor. Now if you'll run along, I have chores to do."

Marla glanced at Susan. Her friend's shoulders sagged, and she looked as tired and wilted as Marla felt. Since she'd packed away her notebook, Marla surmised Susan had no further questions. They thanked Simon for his time and hurried off.

"Did you get the feeling Simon was hiding something?" Marla asked as they headed toward the exit. "He wasn't happy about Phil's plan and clearly doesn't like people visiting his farm. Yet it's his job to explain the site to guests."

"I know. There are too many things to consider right now, and my brain is fried. It's too hot to think clearly."

Marla agreed. Watching her steps on a square of uneven pavement, she barely registered the whoosh of air rushing past her ear. She heard a twang and glanced up.

Susan pointed to a nearby tree where an arrow pierced the bark. "Look out! Someone is shooting at us."

"What?" Disbelief slowed Marla's steps. Her veins turned to ice as another arrow whizzed past and landed with a *thunk* on the ground.

"Let's move!" Her feet took flight, and she dashed toward the park exit with her heart thumping in her ears.

Chapter Eleven

Marla ran in a zigzag pattern, her pulse racing and her breaths shallow. *Twang.* Another one almost found its mark. Her feet hammered the pavement as she headed toward the front gate.

As they neared the exit, she realized the attack had abated. Silence met her ears as she paused to lean over and catch her breath.

She held her stomach with a trembling hand. "Are you okay?" she rasped to Susan, barely able to speak. Her breathing gradually slowed along with her heart rate.

"I think so." Susan's face had gone pale. "What was that?"

"We must have upset someone today. It could have been anybody. But was the intent to scare us or to cause real harm?"

Susan gave her a puzzled glance. "Lizzy seemed nice when I talked to her. And River was cooperative."

"My bet is more on the blacksmith. If he throws axes for a sport, maybe he does archery as well." She glanced over her shoulder. All seemed quiet. Even the ticket booth lady had vacated her stand.

They aimed for the parking lot at a hasty pace. Marla didn't feel safe until they were in the car with the doors locked. A rumble of thunder sounded overhead, increasing her tension.

"Are you going to tell Dalton someone shot arrows at us?" Susan asked.

Marla made sure no one followed them as she exited the lot and entered the main road. "Not yet. I don't want him ordering me off the case."

Susan pointed at the intersection ahead. "Wait, make a right turn there. I'd like to drive around the perimeter. I'm still thinking the fairground's shape is uneven."

Marla grew befuddled as the land they circled seemed to form a perfect rectangle. "This can't be right," she said, turning a corner to repeat the run.

Susan peered out the window. "Look at these woods. I don't see a mailbox, but this has to be where the neighboring property is located."

"We must have missed the driveway. I'll check it out another time." Marla glanced into the rearview mirror, still unnerved by their panicked flight. Nobody seemed to be tailing them. She changed directions to head for home. "I didn't mean to put you in danger today."

Susan gave her a weak grin. "Don't worry about it. I'm glad I came. I've gathered enough information for my article, and I loved Lizzy's tale of lost treasure."

"It is a great story. I wonder how much of it is true." Marla's shoulders tensed as her cell phone trilled. Now what? She answered on the car's speaker system.

"Hey, it's Robyn," said her salon receptionist. "I received a message confirming the plumber will be arriving for the valve repair tomorrow morning at nine. It's supposed to take two hours or so. I've rescheduled our morning clients and offered them a discount off their next service. Your first appointment starts at noon."

"Got it. Let's hope the plumber doesn't run into any unexpected issues. Give me a heads up if things change," Marla advised before ringing off.

Susan's face brightened. "Now you have the morning free. What will you do?"

Marla considered her options. "I'd like to talk to my cousin, Cynthia. She must know how I can get in touch with Corbin. Her brother can give me a rundown on the village staff if I can get him to talk."

"Maybe Dalton has made progress on the case and you won't have to waste your time."

"It's no bother. I haven't seen Cynthia in a while, and I can mention Dalton's retirement party to her. That will be my excuse when I talk to Corbin."

"Would you want to visit Lizzy's Doll Emporium on Thursday before you go into work? I know it's your late day. It would be a good chance to interview Lizzy away from the park, and I could buy my daughter a gift while we're there."

Marla heard the excitement in Susan's tone. "Okay. I'll set up an appointment to make sure Lizzy will be present. Maybe the store will have things for boys so I can buy Ryder something."

After she'd dropped Susan off and was on her way to pick up Ryder from day care, Marla fielded two more calls, one from her mother and one from her friend, Tally. She let them both go to voicemail. It had been a trying day, and she wanted to have some quality time with her son. She'd return their calls later.

At home, she watched Ryder tinker with his indoor play garden while her mind wandered. Too bad she hadn't had the smarts to take one of those arrows at the history park. Dalton might have been able to trace the source. For now, she wouldn't tell him about the incident.

Nonetheless, she wanted to share her discoveries and approached the topic after he'd arrived home and they had time alone. Dalton ate dinner while she put Ryder to sleep and finished her evening chores.

"How was your visit to Phil's sister?" Marla said once they'd prepared for bed.

Showered and dressed in his pajamas, Dalton lay next to her with a book in hand. It was the one he'd bought at the village store about the railroad era in Florida. He smelled of soap and his favorite shampoo.

With a resigned sigh, he inserted a bookmark and put down his book. "Her name is Kathy. She was broken up by her brother's death, especially because it was unexpected."

"I imagine so. Were they close?"

"He came over for holidays, otherwise they didn't communicate that often. She works as an office manager for a novelty company. They make fancy tools with decorated handles like the kind you buy for gifts. She said Phil lived in a townhouse. He'd paid off the mortgage, which set off an alarm in my mind. The guy was only making fifty grand from his job, so where did he get the money for the balance due?"

"If he was single, maybe he didn't have many expenses. Did you ask Kathy who might have wanted to harm her brother?"

"She pinned it on someone from work. Phil had been excited about his plans for the park, but not everyone was thrilled by the idea. He didn't see that they had a choice."

"You mean, because the alleged budget cuts were killing the attraction?"

Dalton drew the sheet over his legs. Marla, feeling hot despite the air-conditioning, lay on top of the covers.

"No, I mean the offer from a development company to buy the village tract."

"What? The fairground was considering a sale to someone else?"

"Yes. I'm wondering if this offer extends to the adjacent property as well. I haven't had time to trace things further."

"Lizzy had a visitor who disappeared in that direction. Maybe he was the elusive neighbor. If he'd opposed a sale, he might have been conferring with Lizzy on how to fight the deal. She wanted to buy the village tract herself, remember?"

"Then again," Dalton mused, "Phil had also put in a bid to the fairground on the village's behalf. Maybe someone wanted him out of the way to clear the path, so to speak."

"What does the developer mean to do with it? Is it a land sale only, in which case the fairground could rent the tract back and keep the village intact? Or would the property be razed and rezoned? I still don't understand why the fairground isn't more supportive of the history park. It could be made more profitable with an infusion of funds and better publicity."

"I don't know the answers, but I'll have my team investigate this offer. Meanwhile, what did you learn today?" Dalton tickled her arm. "Langley said he ran into you and Susan."

She flushed, remembering their discussion about a retirement party. "He'd just come from the Seminole camp. Susan and I went there after lunch. Billy, the shaman, is an authentic member of the tribe. He's passionate about sharing the history of his people. He wasn't pleased by Phil's proposal because it would have eliminated the camp's site."

"That's understandable. I doubt anyone else will pick up Phil's cause now that he's gone."

Marla tended to agree. "Billy played the Indian chief during the reenactment. He claimed he was on horseback the entire time, although in the smoke and haze, it would be hard to tell."

"None of the reenactors could pinpoint exactly who was where," Dalton admitted. "Billy did identify the murder weapon as belonging to him, but he's adamant that it had been stolen."

"Can River corroborate this?"

"She agreed with his statement. The other tomahawks used in the battle scene were props."

"Supposedly, Phil supplied these props through his former acting connections. Have you interviewed anyone from his troupe?" Marla reached for the water bottle she kept at her bedside and took a deep gulp.

"Not yet, but it's on my list. The village shaman is still a strong lead. He could have lied about the tomahawk being stolen. And it would have been easy for him to leave the battle scene amid the smoke and confusion. He had a motive since Phil intended to eradicate the Seminole camp."

"I'd look further into Simon," Marla suggested. "The farmer is secretive about his herb garden. It's possible Millie and River use herbs in their recipes. Uriah and Billy could also use them for their medicinal tonics. So why wouldn't Simon let anyone see what he grows there?"

"Where exactly is this plot of land located?"

"I'm thinking it's at the rear of the farm near the neighboring property. Corbin wasn't there when we visited, or I might have asked him. Can you tell me again why he'd been sent to prison? I don't remember the details, only that Cynthia believed him to be innocent."

"He worked at a financial firm that was engaged in investment fraud," Dalton explained. "When the executives went down, so did all their minions. Corbin served two years in prison for his part in the fiasco, even though he claimed to have been duped." Dalton's noncommittal tone didn't give away his thoughts on the subject.

"It's interesting how Corbin worked in the financial field," she said. "Angus, the village blacksmith, was an accountant before trading in his computer for a leather apron."

"Yes, I recall that came up in our initial background checks."

"It appears Angus suspected Phil of misappropriating money from the town's coffers. Phil was the one who received village funds from the fairground. I doubt Angus had any proof or he would have told someone in authority."

Dalton twisted on his side to regard her. "It would certainly account for Phil's ability to pay off his mortgage if he'd been embezzling money. But would somebody murder him because he was stiffing the village?"

"Possibly, if the killer is passionate about the place. However, I think Phil's death was more personal. Planting an axe in someone's head is almost like making a statement. As for the weapon, it had to have been hidden on site in advance or carried as part of someone's costume."

"If not Billy, how about River?" Dalton suggested. "She could easily have taken the tomahawk when he wasn't looking."

"I like River. I'd rather think Billy is the more likely suspect. He mentioned how with Phil gone, River won't have to worry anymore. Uriah said almost the same thing about Violet, the schoolteacher. It made me wonder if Phil hit on the women there."

"If so, River would have a double reason to get rid of Phil. She'd get her revenge and save the Seminole camp from displacement at the same time."

"What about Uriah? The shopkeeper is interested in Violet and may have acted protectively for her benefit."

Dalton snorted. "Uriah wanted Phil alive. If his plan had succeeded, Uriah would have been able to expand his shop and establish an apothecary."

Marla ran with this train of thought. "Millie would have had a café where she could be chef. Listen to this. According to Henry, she was let go from her previous job at a restaurant that subsequently had a fire. She'd been suspected of arson by her former employers. You should look up that fire report along with Millie's employment record."

"Good idea."

"That's not all," Marla added when he opened his mouth to say more. "Henry used to be in the garment business and collects buttons. I showed him your photos, and he admitted the pearl button was his. He said he'd given it to Uriah to research for his store."

Dalton sat up straight. "That's news to me. Did you follow up with Uriah to verify this statement?"

"We ran out of time. It was getting late, and I had to get Ryder from day care."

"What else did you learn?"

"We met Gilda, who gave us a tour of the church. I noticed how that building along with Baffle House are the only ones in the village that are well maintained. Henry told me later that Millie had helped him put on a fresh coat of paint. I think she has a thing for him, but it was hard to tell if he returns her regard or not."

"Interesting. Oh, I confirmed the story about Lizzy's ancestor, Adam Canfield, being shot to death by a Union soldier. It's mentioned in several different sources along with the missing Confederate payroll."

"Then what purpose does the legend of the White Lady

serve? Nobody stays overnight in the house. Is it purely for entertainment?"

Dalton shrugged. "You'd have to ask Lizzy."

"She told Susan how various treasure hunters have searched for the gold coins. Maybe her ancestors made up the ghost story to scare people away."

"That would be a reasonable explanation. But don't you believe in spirits since you encountered them at Sugar Crest Plantation Resort?" Dalton asked with a teasing grin.

Marla shuddered at the memory of being pinched in the rickety hotel elevator. "Don't forget your uncle's dude ranch in Arizona. That place rivaled the nearby ghost town with its own set of spooks. I guess I'd have to see this one for myself."

Dalton yawned and stretched. "On a more practical plane, I'll check out Phil's townhouse in the morning, and then I'll do more digging into the village finances. The administrator was bound to have left a paper trail if he'd been skimming funds. I've already requested his bank records."

Marla covered herself with the top sheet. "I'll have the morning free since the salon will be closed for plumbing repairs. I'd like to meet Cynthia for breakfast if she's available. She can tell me how to get in contact with her brother. Corbin might be more willing to talk to me away from the history park. Also, Susan suggested we visit Lizzy's doll shop on Thursday."

She still had to return her phone calls and set things in motion for Dalton's retirement party. Too much to do and never enough time.

Her gaze swept to the baby monitor. Ryder lay restfully in his crib, his sweet little face so precious in repose. For his sake, they needed to wrap this case fast. Then they'd all be safe and snug without worrying about killers on the loose.

She'd put their security alarm on but still worried that she and Susan might have painted targets on their backs after their visit today. Her last images as she drifted to sleep were deadly arrows zinging through the air.

Chapter Twelve

Tuesday morning, Marla rushed through her morning chores after Dalton left to drop Ryder off at day care. At nine, she figured her cousin must be awake. She sent Cynthia a text asking to meet for brunch.

Aren't you working today? Cynthia typed back.

Plumbing repairs. No water until noon, so the salon is closed. I need to talk to you about Corbin.

All right. The usual diner at ten-thirty? I can't get there any earlier.

Sure, that's fine. See you then. They met at their favorite breakfast place every few months. Cynthia liked to hear about Marla's crime-solving exploits while Marla listened to Cynthia's entertaining descriptions of high society events.

Marla had helped once with Taste of the World, an annual fundraiser held at Cynthia's seaside estate. She'd overseen the chefs who donated their time for the event. Marla hadn't counted on her efforts being sabotaged. When the chefs started dropping off the roster one-by-one, Marla had chased down the culprit. Cynthia had helped her solve the case and developed an adventurous streak in the process.

Marla ran some errands until the designated time to meet. She got to the diner first and claimed a booth. Her cousin breezed in looking as put-together as always with a printed Palazzo pants set, freshly styled golden blond hair, and mascaraed blue eyes. In her fifties, she could still pass for a woman in her late thirties.

Marla waited until the waitress served their order before she brought up the subject at hand. She didn't want to be interrupted during their conversation. After taking a bite from her sesame bagel with nova and cream cheese, she began. Always watching her figure, Cynthia had stuck with scrambled eggs, tomato slices, and whole wheat toast.

Marla cupped her coffee mug as she plunged into the topic. "Dalton and I visited Pioneer Village. Imagine my surprise when I ran into Corbin there. Did you know where he was working? He said the two of you kept in touch."

Cynthia snorted. "We chat on occasion but not as often as I'd like. I wanted him to live with us, at least temporarily, when he got out of prison, but he turned me down. Poor guy deserved a break."

"I know you believed he was innocent, and that Ben Kline failed his job as a criminal defense attorney. Was there any evidence that Corbin wasn't part of the investment fraud?"

"No; the executives made sure to cover their tracks. They didn't care who got hurt in the process." Cythnia took a noisy slurp of her coffee. Usually, she followed the polite niceties of society. Did talking about her brother upset her?

"How did Corbin get his job at the history village? He'd mentioned a tip from a friend who'd had an earlier release. I assumed he meant one of his prison buddies."

Cynthia scowled. "That would be Simon, the village farmer. Corbin must have mentioned how he liked working with animals. They wouldn't betray him like his former employers."

Wait, Simon has a prison record? Does Dalton know this?

He'd run background checks on the main cast members. This must have come up in his research. If so, why hadn't he told her?

Maybe he'd wanted to get her impression of the man before coloring her perception. She'd be sure to ask him about it later.

"Corbin told me he'd like to become a veterinarian assistant," she said, "but he lacks the funds to go back to school."

Cynthia studied the salt and pepper shakers on the table.

"It's veterinarian technician. There's a difference. An assistant can be trained on the job or take classes. No certification is required. Corbin works in this capacity now when he feeds and exercises the animals."

"Then what does a technician do that's a level up?"

"They need an Associate Degree from an accredited school, must pass a credentialing exam, and have to keep up with continuing education. I'd offered to subsidize Corbin's tuition, but he wouldn't accept my help."

"What other duties can a tech perform that an assistant can't do?" Marla drained her coffee cup and waved at the waitress who was circulating around with a filled carafe.

"They take patient histories, collect specimens, do lab procedures and X-rays, assist in surgery and clean teeth, among other things."

"Huh. I've never noticed when I take Lucky and Spooks to the vet. I'm surprised Corbin would switch from the financial sector to a hands-on career. He didn't make the change to avoid coming into contact with people. At the history park, he manages the petting zoo and meets guests on a daily basis."

"Simon helped him get the job. With his background, Corbin would have had trouble getting a post elsewhere."

"Is he barred from ever working in finance again?" Had Phil been aware of Corbin's background when he'd hired her cousin? He might have given him the role with the intent of using his skills to cook the books for him. She sincerely hoped that wasn't the case.

"Corbin's not interested in the financial field anymore," Cynthia replied, crunching down a piece of toast and chasing it with a gulp of water. "If he becomes a vet technician, he'd have different options. For example, he could get a position at a zoo. He wouldn't be limited to a private office or an obscure corner in a tourist attraction."

Marla tossed out another probe as she dug into the home fries that came with her bagel and nova sandwich. "Did Corbin mention why Simon had been in prison?" She didn't need to wait on Dalton's response if her cousin knew the reason.

Cynthia gave her a cynical glance. "Simon had studied horticulture in college. He was working at a plant nursery when he was accused of growing marijuana on a vacant portion of land. Simon claimed the guilty party must have framed him when they heard the authorities were moving in."

Interesting how the two former jailbirds had ended up at Pioneer Village, and both of them claimed to have been set up to take a fall.

Marla steepled her hands. "Did you hear about the man who played the town marshal at the village? Phil Pufferfish? He also served as administrator for the tract. He was killed during the annual battle reenactment."

Cynthia's jaw gaped. "No way. Did he get shot accidentally, or what?"

"He had an axe planted in his forehead. Dalton was on the scene. He's managing the case."

"Surely my brother isn't a suspect!" Cynthia gripped her coffee mug with tight fingers.

"Not really, but Simon is a person of interest. I'd like to ask Corbin about him. Has he mentioned anything about the other staff members at the village?"

"He did mention how the administrator had some wild plan to buy out the place from the fairground. Simon got into a snit at the town meeting when the idea was introduced."

"Simon impressed me as a man who wouldn't support any disruption to the status quo," Marla said. "He's supposed to describe the farm's operation to visitors, but he wasn't very friendly when I met him. He likes to keep to himself."

Cynthia arched a penciled eyebrow. "Maybe he disliked Phil's plan because it would bring more scrutiny to his patch of land. According to Corbin, Phil meant to keep better tabs on which sites guests visited. He might have had other cuts in mind besides the Seminole camp."

"I'm surprised your brother shared that much with you."

"I think I just caught him in a grumpy moment. I hope Corbin won't be blamed for anything that's not his fault." She regarded Marla with an anxious frown.

"Don't worry. We have plenty of other suspects." Marla gave Cynthia a quick description of the main characters. "I'm leaning toward Billy. The shaman would have had the most to lose if Phil's proposal had succeeded. He identified the tomahawk and admitted it belonged to him. Supposedly, it had been stolen the day before."

Cynthia patted her mouth with a napkin. "Sounds fishy to me. Then again, why would he admit to owning the thing if he's the killer?"

"To assert his honesty, perhaps. The other tribesmen in the battle scene carried tomahawks but they were props."

"Were they actors or real Native Americans?"

"I'm not sure. Billy may have called upon his friends to give an authentic performance. Not that it matters if their weapons were fakes."

"Let me see if I have this straight." Her cousin's eyes sparkled. "The chief suspects include the shopkeeper, the blacksmith, the farmer and the minister."

Marla ate her last bite of bagel. "Don't exclude the women. There's the schoolteacher, the shaman's wife, the tour guide at the grand house, plus Millie and Gilda who fill in for the rest."

"How heavy is a tomahawk? Could a woman use one to crack a man on the head?" Cynthia winced as though imagining the scene.

"If she were angry enough, I'd say yes. Phil didn't appear to put up a struggle, so he couldn't have guessed what was coming."

"How hard is it to hide the weapon in the folds of a woman's gown?"

"Perhaps as easy as under a clergyman's robe. But if it truly was stolen the day before, it could have been hidden on the boardwalk earlier. Henry said he'd rushed over there to seal a container of bait. What if he went to stash the axe inside a pail or a barrel, instead?"

"Then what? How did Phil end up on the boardwalk at the time of the murder?"

"Good question. The battle scene drew everybody's attention. Something made Phil leave in the middle of his narration."

"It's possible he received an urgent phone message," Cynthia suggested. "If Dalton has Phil's cell phone, he'd be able to see who called Phil last. Then again, if the bad guy was smart, he'd have taken Phil's phone."

"You're right. Let me see if Dalton has it." Marla sent him a text asking if he'd recovered Phil's phone. Her brow furrowed at the response.

"Phil's cell is missing," she told her cousin. "It wasn't on the body. Nor was it in his office or his townhouse."

"Maybe Phil's provider can do a cell phone triangulation to locate it, or whatever that thing is called that they do on TV."

"It's likely the killer turned off the phone. Phil's last location would be at the fishing shack in that event. Nonetheless, it's worth a follow-up." Marla added this item to her mental list of things to discuss with her husband.

Spotting the waitress, she signaled for the check. "On a happier note, I'd like to hold a retirement party for Dalton after this case is solved. His last day of work is in mid-September so I'm thinking of the eighteenth."

Cynthia's face brightened at the mention of a party. "I'll save the date. What did you have in mind? Do you already have a venue picked out?"

"Not yet. By the way, how are the kids?" she asked, realizing she'd been remiss in not asking about her cousin's family. Cynthia and Bruce, both ocean conservationists, had named their children Kelp and Anemone. Now grown, they were both personable young adults.

"They're doing well, thanks," Cynthia responded. "I can't

believe Annie is graduating college next year. Would you believe she's interested in selling real estate?"

"That must please your husband." A sparkler ignited in her brain. Aside from his interest in ocean conservation, Bruce was a property developer. He was respectful of the natural resources on the lands he purchased. Would he know anything about an outside offer on the village tract?

"Dalton discovered the fairground has received a proposal from a developer to buy the village," Marla told Cynthia. "Is there any way Bruce could ask around to learn the source?"

"Sure, I'll talk to him about it. We went to the history park years ago. Maybe we should make another visit. I could have Corbin show me his animals."

A flare of alarm hit her. "Nuh-uh. It's best to stay away. You don't want to stir up trouble. Where does Corbin live? He said his place is near the nature preserve."

"Marla, I've given you enough information. Dalton probably has a list of everyone's home addresses, so ask him about it."

She realized Cynthia didn't care to betray her brother's confidence any further. "Thanks, I'll do that. You've been very helpful, and I'm glad we were able to get together. If I need assistance in planning Dalton's party, I'll let you know."

Marla paid the bill since Cynthia had come at her invitation. They parted ways, and Marla hastened to get to the salon for her first appointment.

Along the way, she thought about their conversation. Did Simon's alleged crime have any bearing on what was going on now? Was that why he had acted so guarded about his herb garden? Could he be growing illegal marijuana plants there?

She had to meet Corbin again to ask him about Simon. Then again, Corbin might not be willing to talk against the man who got him this job. Maybe she'd have better luck approaching Uriah or Billy, assuming they both used herbs in their remedies.

A car cut in front of her, and she focused on driving. Finally reaching the salon, she barged inside and slung her purse into a drawer. She plugged in her implements, while aware her client could walk in at any moment. The familiar scents of shampoo and holding spray calmed her as did the splash of water in the background. Evidently, the water valve problem had been fixed.

Robyn sauntered over from the front desk and handed her a printed schedule. "Here you go," she said in a bubbly tone. "You're fully booked for today and the rest of the week."

"Great; just when I have people to see and things to do."

Robyn raised a darkened eyebrow. "Give me the word, and I'll cut back your hours. You know we've talked about it."

"I'm not ready yet. Is there something else?"

"When are you going to fill me in on the murder case?"

Marla's sleuthing exploits were well known amongst her staff. Nicole, at the next station, sidled closer. She'd just finished prepping foils for a highlights appointment.

"Yes, do tell." Nicole's warm brown skin glowed with the inner joy of an expectant mother. Her baby was due in October, only three months away. She'd been with Marla since the salon had first opened its doors almost fourteen years ago.

"We'll chat later. Here comes Babs." Marla pointed to the woman who'd just walked inside.

Her client hustled over, dressed in a lavender suit and wearing an impatient frown. A busy executive, Babs had come for a quick wash and style before catching a flight out of town.

Marla got through the next few customers before she finally had a break. She entered the back storeroom to gobble a container of yogurt she'd put there in the fridge. It was the only place other than outside where she could make a private call, and she had yet to return Tally and her mother's calls from Monday. She didn't want them to feel neglected.

She contacted her mother first. "Dalton picked up a case at the history park over the weekend," she explained. "I've been helping him by interviewing the cast members. Have you been to Pioneer Village? It's a living history park with costumed tour guides on the west side of town."

"I went there years ago," Ma replied in her singsong voice. "I hope you're not stressing yourself. You have enough going on between work and your son. Did you take Ryder to the July Fourth festivities on Sunday? I wish Reed and I could have joined you, but we'd signed up for things here."

Anita and Reed lived in a fifty-five plus community in Boynton Beach. Marla hadn't been happy when Ma had moved away just after Ryder was born. She would have liked her mother to live closer, but Ma had still been there for her whenever Marla needed her, despite the forty-five-minute drive.

"Dalton went to work on Sunday and Brianna came with us to the festival," she said. "We'll miss her when she goes to college. I can't believe she leaves next month."

"Time goes by too fast. Hopefully, Dalton will solve this case soon so he can enjoy his daughter's last few weeks here."

"She'll be home for vacations. Anyway, how was the concert at your senior center?"

"It was lovely, thanks. We could see the fireworks from the lawn."

"Nice. We're looking forward to seeing you guys at Michael's birthday brunch on Sunday. Speaking of celebrations, I'm planning a retirement party for Dalton. Do you have any anniversary plans I should know about for September?"

"Reed and I will probably play it low-key and go out to dinner ourselves somewhere."

"Okay. Then please reserve Saturday the eighteenth for us. Sorry, but duty calls. My next client will be arriving any minute." Marla glanced at her watch. After promising to call again when she had more time, she disconnected and dialed Tally. Guilt assailed her for having such little time to spend talking to her best friend.

"Hi Marla," Tally answered in a breathless voice. "I'm busy with a customer now. Can I call you later? Oh, and I've put aside an outfit for you from our fall line. We'll have to make a date when you can come into the shop."

"Sure," Marla said. "I'll check my calendar and get back to you."

She clicked off with a pang of regret. They'd been so close before kids and before Tally's husband had been killed. Now that Tally had reinvented herself and moved closer to her son Luke's school, they had less time available for getting together. Their widening friendship left Marla feeling bereft.

Robyn bustled into the back storeroom, her broad grin lifting Marla's mood. "Your customer isn't here yet. Spill the beans," the receptionist urged.

Realizing this chat was inevitable, Marla gave a quick review of her findings. She wished the hours would fly by faster. She wanted to be with Ryder and watch him play. His cute face would erase her concerns.

"I can save you time by researching Baffle House's history," Robyn offered. "Lizzy told you the county donated land for the fairground in 1956, right? Then her grandfather sold an additional hundred acres including the deed to Baffle House so he could pay off his debts."

"Yes, that's correct. Lizzy believes her grandfather might have been tricked into selling their property. See if you can find any records relevant to the sale. Dalton may be checking into this also, but he has a lot of avenues to follow."

"I'll get on it," Robyn promised, her face flushed with excitement.

"Dalton told me a developer has made an offer to buy the village tract," Marla confided. "I asked my cousin, Cynthia, to have her husband make inquiries. Maybe Bruce, who's also in the field, can find out who presented the deal. Both Lizzy and Phil, the tract's administrator, made bids to purchase the place, too. Now Phil is dead."

Robyn's brow wrinkled. "That's ominous. Have you asked Lizzy about this offer? Does she even know about it?"

"I have no idea. She owns a doll shop in Miami. I'll call now and schedule a visit with her for Thursday morning. Hopefully,

Lizzy will talk about the other village players more readily when we're off-site. Susan said she'd go with me." Robyn knew Susan from their same neighborhood and as a salon client.

Marla made the call while wishing she could leave right then to meet Lizzy. Impatience gnawed at her as the afternoon crawled by.

Wednesday wasn't much better. She jumped when her phone rang at midday. Dalton showed on the caller ID. What now? She answered amid eating an egg salad sandwich in the rear storeroom.

"I have news," he stated in a somber tone.

Uh-oh. It couldn't be about Ryder. The school would have called her first. She put down her sandwich on a paper plate. "What is it?"

"Do you remember Gilda Macintosh, the village guide who gave you and Susan a tour of the church? Apparently, she was a member of the fairground's board of directors. Nobody at the village knew this about her. I'm thinking she took the job as a cast member to scope out the staff's views on Phil's proposal."

"That's a possibility. River must have suspected something. She warned me to watch what I said around Gilda. Is Gilda involved in this real estate deal, do you think? Maybe she's hoping for a kickback if the sale goes through."

"Unfortunately, we can't ask her because the woman is dead."

Chapter Thirteen

Marla's heart jolted. "Gilda is dead? How is that possible?"

"Langley went to her apartment to question her about why the fairground directors wanted to sell the village," Dalton said. "She didn't answer the door, but it was partially open. He found her lying on the kitchen floor."

Marla clutched her cell phone in a tight grip. "Gilda collapsed at home alone?"

"It appears so. Langley noted a fresh bag of groceries on the counter. She must have just come in from food shopping. He also found a bottle of Pepto-Bismol by the sink, along with a box of chocolate chip cookies. It was open and looked as though she had dug in."

"Maybe she ate too many sweets, and it gave her a stomachache."

"The box had no label," Dalton pointed out. "It couldn't have come from the store."

"She might have baked them herself. Unless... do you think there was something in them?" Horrified by the notion, Marla clapped a hand to her cheek. Then again, Gilda could have choked on a piece. How did they know that wasn't the case?

"We'll do the preliminaries, and if it's warranted, I'll take over as lead investigator," Dalton told her. "Langley can handle it until we get more data."

"First Phil dies and then Gilda under strange circumstances? This can't be a coincidence, Dalton." Surely, he'd agree with her. There had to be a connection.

"I'll let you know when I learn more," he said in his noncommittal tone. She could picture him straightening his shoulders and resuming his professional demeanor.

Something must have alerted Sergeant Langley that Gilda hadn't been felled by natural causes, Marla figured. Dalton wasn't sharing the details, but it sounded as though they were treating this as a suspicious death. She could wrangle the facts from him later. Or not. All that mattered was the cause of death, which was up to the M.E. to determine.

Another issue came to mind. "Did you discover anything new regarding that private property located behind Baffle House?" she asked before Dalton hung up.

"Yes. It's owned by an individual named Greg Harris. He's on my list of people to contact. I've got to go, Marla."

"Okay. Thanks for the update." She rang off, considering what she'd learned.

Gilda was dead. She couldn't wrap her mind around that one yet.

And a man named Greg Harris owned the property adjacent to Baffle House.

She went online and did a quick search but didn't find anyone in Florida by that name who might be relevant. Then she accessed Google Earth and saw exactly what Susan had been saying about the fairground's irregular shape.

With the piece of private property next door, it formed a perfect rectangle. Forest surrounded the area as a natural border.

The adjacent land appeared laid out like a farm. Buildings dotted the parcel that had defined rows that might be crops. Would there be a mailbox by a hidden drive? She hadn't noticed one when she'd cruised by with Susan. A driveway would provide a better means of access than through the woods behind the village.

Robyn interrupted her thoughts by peeking inside the store-room. "Your next client is here, luv." Without a second glance, the receptionist rushed off to attend to her duty at the front desk.

Marla stuffed her phone in a skirt pocket and hastened to her station.

"What's wrong?" Nicole asked after Marla sent her customer to get shampooed. "You have that glassy look in your eyes that you get when you're upset."

"Dalton's team found another dead body related to his case."

Nicole's eyes rounded. "No way. Who was it?"

"Gilda Macintosh. She'd given me and Susan a tour of the church at the living history village. She seemed like a nice woman, although River said to be careful what we said around her. Apparently, Gilda was a member of the fairground's board of directors and was posing as a tour guide for unknown reasons."

"This puts a new spin on things. What will you do next?" Nicole knew very well that Marla wouldn't sit back while Dalton pursued the case.

"I'd like to sneak a look at the adjacent private property. We saw a man talking to Lizzy who didn't belong to the village. He disappeared in that direction. I'm wondering if it was her neighbor."

"Who's Lizzy again?" Nicole asked with a frown.

"She's the host at Baffle House, the mansion at the history park. Her ancestors used to own the property as part of a plantation. From what I overheard, she and the strange man are involved in something that includes Simon the farmer. I wonder if Gilda found out what they're messed up in."

"And one of them committed murder to silence her?"

"Gilda's death hasn't been ruled a homicide yet. I'm seeing Lizzy on Thursday morning and will sound her out on things. Meanwhile, I should stop by City Hall to ask about Greg Harris's property next door. Robyn offered to research Baffle House's last sale and my friend Susan is working on the story of lost Confederate gold."

"Sounds like you have things covered, girl. Let me know if I can help in any way."

Marla's customers consumed her attention for the rest of the day. By the time she left work, she barely had time to pick up Ryder and begin their evening routine. Once again, she had to get through his dinner, bath, and bedtime ritual without Dalton's help. It sure would be nice when he was home full-time.

She kissed her son goodnight, lay him in his crib, rubbed his back, and murmured endearments to him until he closed his eyes. Tiptoeing from his room, she shut the door in her wake and stuffed a towel across the threshold to block the light. He needed it pitch dark to sleep.

Dalton came home too late for them to talk. She was already in bed, the need for sleep making her eyelids heavy. The morning would come soon enough, assuming Ryder slept through the night. Reassured that Dalton was home safe, she murmured a greeting then shut her eyes.

She must have been exhausted because she didn't hear the toddler until dawn. After a quick bathroom break, she entered his room and lifted him in her arms. She'd let Dalton sleep in. They could catch up on their news later.

However, the morning rush left no time for business talk. Dalton wasn't even dressed when she whizzed out the door with Ryder to drop him off at day care. Then she headed toward City Hall. Susan wasn't expecting her until ten, so she had time to kill. She meant to learn what she could about Greg Harris's property.

"What's the address?" asked the lady behind a glass partition at the Tax Collector's office where the front desk clerk had sent her.

"I can show you on a map if you have one."

The woman's lips pursed. "I need the exact street number or parcel ID."

"Sorry, I don't have either."

"Then try the Property Appraiser's office a few doors down."

Same result. They couldn't look up the property without an address or parcel number. What else could she ask? Robyn had offered to research Baffle House's history, but Marla was already there. "How about this place?" she said, giving the address for the recreated village.

The brunette nodded. "Just one moment, please." She tapped on her computer and finally sat back with a puzzled frown. "There was a deed transfer in 1958 from Ian Winthrop to the country fairground. The only registered sale before that one was to Adam Canfield."

Lizzy's ancestor. "Is there a price listed for the exchange between Ian and the fairground, or does that go too far back?" Phil and Gilda's deaths may have had nothing to do with the past, but it helped to get the facts straight.

"I don't see anything. It's been over sixty years and not everything has been digitized," the lady said with an apologetic smile. "Or perhaps somebody screwed up and didn't make the proper entry. Nonetheless, the fairground holds the deed to the property."

Marla thanked her and left. On the way to Susan's house, she mulled over this information. She agreed with Lizzy that something didn't add up about the fairground's acquisition. Otherwise, the sale by her grandfather should have been recorded. The deed transfer had gone through. What had happened to the rest of the real estate transaction?

Maybe the mysterious Greg Harris was somehow involved. He'd held onto his portion of land that must have originally belonged to the Canfield family.

She told Susan what she knew on their way to the doll store. "We have to get Lizzy to talk. All of this might tie in with the developer's plans to buy the place."

"Is that why someone murdered Phil Pufferfish? Because they wanted to ensure the sale went through?" Susan looked comfortable in a pair of white Capris with a forest green top. Sparkly gold sandals covered her feet.

"Phil was in direct competition with the developer's bid to buy the place," Marla replied. "That might be reason enough. Then again, he'd offended several villagers. Billy, the shaman, wasn't happy about the Seminole village being eradicated if

Phil's plan had worked. He said it was another example of white people bumping the Native Americans off their land."

"Yes, but this is a pretend village. It's not as though it's real."

"Billy still felt strongly about it. Or maybe Phil hit on River, and Billy wanted to ensure he'd stop bothering her."

Susan cast her a shrewd glance. "You could say the same for the shopkeeper. Didn't you tell me Uriah is sweet on the schoolteacher?"

"That's right. Violet was the one who found the body. She could have axed Phil herself and then faked her reaction."

"What about the weapon? Would she be capable of hefting an axe that way?"

"Tomahawks aren't that heavy. They weigh less than two pounds, so weight isn't an issue. As for the skill, Angus, the blacksmith, competes in axe-throwing contests. He suspected Phil was on the take with village funds, but that wouldn't give him a strong personal reason to kill the man. If he had proof, he could have just exposed him."

"Maybe he did find evidence, but Phil blackmailed him into silence."

"On what grounds?" Marla asked, watching ahead as another driver changed lanes. "I'm still thinking the culprit is someone else. Uriah was the last person to possess the pearl button that Dalton's team found beneath Phil's body. Did I mention this to you? That button is like a hot potato. Henry, the village preacher, used to be in the garment business. He collects buttons and buys them at flea markets and local festivals. He'd loaned this one to Uriah to research with the possibility of selling similar buttons in the general store."

Paused at a stoplight, Marla showed Susan the photos.

Susan squinted at the small screen. "Then what? Uriah killed Phil, and the button ended up under his body?"

"Maybe Uriah showed it to Violet to impress her. Or he could have given it to Millie. She's in charge of the sewing circle." Marla pressed the accelerator when the light changed to green.

"So what? She had the button and murdered Phil? You're going out on a limb here."

"Remember, Millie wanted the chef position once Phil established a café on site. He might have gone back on his word. Or here's another idea. Maybe Lizzy found the Confederate gold, but she can't claim it until she owns the property. She got rid of Phil so his plan wouldn't win favor with the fairground. She wanted to buy the village herself."

"Then how did she get hold of the button? Moreover, does she know about the deal with the developer? That would have negated her and Phil's offers. If Gilda represented the fairground, Lizzy had the best motive for doing away with them both."

"We'll see what she says, but be careful. Somebody has already shot arrows at us."

Marla concentrated on driving, following the directions on her GPS to the shopping center that housed the doll shop. Palm trees and flowering shrubs landscaped the plaza.

"I haven't been to Papaya Corners in years," she said as she searched for a parking spot. "We try to avoid driving to Miami these days." Too much traffic and convoluted roads discouraged the forty-five-minute trip. She wouldn't have much time left when they finished here before heading to the salon.

After exiting the car, she and Susan strode along a winding concrete walkway past a gushing fountain. Elegantly dressed women strolled the outdoor oasis that held high-end shops and eateries. Caribbean music played from hidden speakers, while a floral scent filled the air.

They passed a bistro where the aroma of fresh-brewed coffee and cinnamon buns wafted out the open door. Lizzy's Doll Emporium was located between a jewelry store and a kitchenware place.

Marla's jaw dropped as she stepped inside the air-conditioned interior. Dolls in various sizes, modes of dress, and ethnicities met her eyes. She'd never seen so many in one shop. Lizzy's business must be brisk for her to afford the rent here. Right now, Marla and

Susan were the only customers for which Marla was grateful. They'd have the chance to talk to Lizzy in private.

"Marla, how lovely to see you again," Lizzy said, bustling forward from behind a counter. "You, too, Susan. I'm glad you called ahead. Millie is covering for me at the village. I would have asked Gilda, but she didn't answer her phone."

Marla exchanged a glance with Susan. Oh, dear. This would be awkward if Lizzy hadn't heard the news about Gilda. "Thanks for accommodating us, Lizzy. How do you staff the shop when you're playing your role at Pioneer Village?"

"I have a manager. She's here when I'm at the park. An assistant handles our online business. We're constantly getting orders."

"That's great. This place is amazing." The choices were truly dazzling, Marla thought, impressed by the displays.

"I love it," Susan said, roaming around to view the tiers of dolls grouped for different ages.

"Thanks. We have the largest inventory of collectible dolls in the area, if not the entire state. You'll find limited editions, premium brands and a large selection of teddy bears."

"I have an eight-year-old daughter," Susan said. "She likes the American Girl dolls."

"Right over here." Lizzy led Susan to the section indicated. "We have the books as well. You might also like the Madame Alexander collection."

Marla wandered to a nursery section with newborn dolls that looked so realistic she could swear they'd open their mouths and howl. Look at those cute dresses you could buy for the older babies, not to mention their pretty hair. Marla had fixed hairstyles on her Barbies. Lizzy had those in her store, too, along with strollers, carriages, car seats and other accessories.

Her mother and Kate would love this place if they had a granddaughter. Marla gave a wistful sigh. She and Dalton weren't planning on having a second child. Usually they took precautions, although there was that one time… she shook her head. Enough fanciful thinking. She had a purpose in coming here.

"Lizzy, I wanted to ask you more about Baffle House. Your grandfather Ian sold the place to the fairground in 1958, correct?"

"Yes, that was my understanding. Mom said the stress must have killed him because he keeled over before the ink was dry. She was only ten years old at the time. I always thought it terribly sad that she'd lost her father so young."

"Did she get a copy of the signed bill of sale? Is it in your files somewhere?"

"Why would I need it? That was so long ago. The deed belongs to the fairground now."

"Didn't you say you'd heard a rumor that your grandfather was tricked into selling the land? It would be helpful to see the actual document."

"Why do you care? Does this relate to Phil's murder?"

Marla fingered a frilly pink dress on the nearest doll. "Maybe. It worries me that there's been a second death."

Lizzy's eyes widened. "What? I hadn't heard. Is it anyone I know?"

Marla winced. "I'm sorry to be the bearer of bad news, but Gilda Macintosh has passed away." She watched for Lizzy's reaction, still unsure of the woman's role in recent events.

Lizzy clapped a hand to her chest. "Oh, no. Gilda? But how—?"

"My husband is investigating. There's been no evidence of foul play," she said quickly to reassure her. If this news truly came as a shock, Marla didn't want to cause undue alarm.

"Thank goodness." Lizzy sank onto a handy folding chair and stared blankly into space. "Then again, I wouldn't be surprised if someone had it in for her. That woman was a snake. Greg told me to steer clear of her, and he was right." Her expression changed from sorrow to a snarl in the blink of an eye.

Marla's heart pounded upon hearing the man's name. "Would that be Greg Harris by any chance?"

"Yes. What of it?"

"How do you know him?"

"He's my brother, not that it's any of your business."

141

Chapter Fourteen

Marla was taken aback by Lizzy's sudden hostility. Was it defensiveness toward her sibling that had closed her off? The man she'd seen talking to Lizzy at the side of Baffle House must have been her brother. They had discussed something involving Simon, if she recalled.

I'll find someone to cover for you, Lizzy had said.

Be sure to ask Simon about it when his assistant isn't around," the man had replied.

What was Greg doing that he needed someone to cover for him? And did Lizzy mean to ask Simon to do this job? Lizzy's revelation had just raised a host of new questions.

"I understand Greg owns the farm adjacent to the fairground," she said to Lizzy. "What is it that he grows there? I love to shop at farmer's markets if he sells his products to the public." She hoped this approach would elicit an explanation.

Lizzy's face turned to stone. "He raises corn and other vegetables."

Is that right? Then why are you so reluctant to talk about him?

"Is your brother acquainted with Simon?" she asked in a breezy tone. "They're both farmers and could give each other tips on growing crops." If Simon hadn't been as innocent as he'd claimed in cultivating marijuana, maybe he had reverted to his former activity. In that case, he might have recruited his neighbor to help expand the business.

"Simon is playing a role. He's only a pretend farmer."

"Perhaps, but he did study horticulture and seems very knowledgeable. His crops are doing well, from what I've seen. He could operate a real farm if he were so inclined."

Lizzy rose and adjusted her blouse. "Did you really come here to visit my shop or to interrogate me?" She had a hurt puppy dog look in her eyes. Then again, her expressions seemed to change as rapidly as the wind. Was she putting on an act?

"I told you I had more questions about Baffle House. And Susan is looking for a gift that her daughter might like." She pointed at her friend, deflecting the topic of conversation her way.

Lizzy approached Susan and lifted an infant doll. "These adoptable babies are popular with little girls. They come with a certificate."

Susan plastered a polite smile on her face as Lizzy described the brand. "Jess loves the American Girl line. Maybe it's the simplicity of the earlier eras or the stories that come with them." Susan indicated a collection of dolls wearing historical clothing.

A light bulb flared in Marla's mind. "Hey, that gives me an idea," she said to Lizzy. "Did you ever look inside those vintage dolls at Baffle House for the missing Confederate gold?"

"Not really. Those dolls were added later as part of the set decoration. I've looked everywhere and haven't discovered any treasure. I'm not sure I believe it exists, although tourists love the story."

"Wouldn't it belong to the property owners if found?" Susan asked, cocking her head.

"That's my assumption. It's a moot point until someone finds the stash. Historical accounts do seem to corroborate the tale."

Lizzy straightened a silicon infant that had fallen over. It had a hole in its mouth for a bottle. Marla wondered if it would need a diaper change as well.

"I believe Phil put in a bid for the village to buy the tract. Do you think he was hoping to find the treasure?" Susan persisted.

"In that case, it would belong to the newly formed nonprofit group." Lizzy thrust a strand of champagne blond hair behind her ear. "It's not the reason why I made an offer to buy the land. It should belong to my family. We'd owned it once and lost it through the stupidity of my grandfather."

"How did your brother retain his portion?"

Lizzy's maple eyes clouded. "Grandpa didn't sell all of it. I'm unclear on the details. It happened so long ago."

If it was my legacy, I'd want to know what happened, Marla thought. Maybe the records had been lost or the lawyer handling her grandfather's case had fumbled his job. That might be an avenue worth exploring. She'd suggest it to Dalton.

At any rate, it was in the past. Currently, three bids were made on the village tract. One was from Phil representing the villagers, one from Lizzy to regain her family's property, and the last from the unknown developer.

"Did you know Gilda was on the fairground's board of directors?" Marla asked Lizzy, following that last train of thought. The fairground would have favored the most lucrative deal.

"My brother found out. He received an offer to purchase his property as well. We figured Gilda had joined the village staff to influence our opinions."

Marla's gaze hardened. "You both knew about this deal? Was Gilda the swing vote needed to sway the rest of the directors?"

"How would I know? What are you getting at, Marla?"

"You have to admit, her death and Phil's have cleared the path for your offer to win."

Lizzy's eyes widened. "Are you implying Gilda was murdered same as Phil?" She seemed more alarmed than wary at Marla's innuendo.

"The cause of Gilda's death is yet to be determined. You'll have to agree it's suspicious, coming so soon after Phil's passing."

"Maybe she and Phil learned something that got them both

killed. If you're not careful, your questions could make you the next target."

Was that a subtle warning or a sincere concern? Marla wasn't yet convinced Lizzy was innocent. "I just want to help my husband bring Phil's murderer to justice." Marla retrieved her cell phone and accessed her photos. "By the way, do you recognize this button? Perhaps it goes with one of your vintage outfits at the village?"

Lizzy studied the images. "No, it doesn't look familiar. I have pearl buttons on some of my blouses, but they don't have gold shanks."

Marla glanced at the doll collections. "What about these? Any dolls have buttons like this one?"

"Nope, not even the antique dolls we use as set dressings in Baffle House. Where is it from?"

"Somebody found it on the village grounds. My husband was curious about it. Have you seen anything like this on anybody else's clothing?"

"No, Marla. Why? Is it related to the investigation?"

"Maybe." Marla moved over to a selection of accessories, where she pushed a baby carriage back and forth. Who used these in reality today? Strollers were expensive enough.

"How is your husband's case going? Has he narrowed down the suspects?" Lizzy asked, rearranging a stack of stuffed animals. Her tone betrayed only mild curiosity but her shoulders had tensed.

"He's working on it." Marla paused, detecting an opportunity to change her line of inquiry. "I am curious about one point, though. I noticed Millie glaring at Henry one day like she was resentful toward him for some reason. What might that have been about?"

Lizzy snorted. "She likes Henry, but he doesn't return her regard. He thinks her cooking stinks. He'll be glad she won't get the chef position now that Phil's gone."

"That's a shame. The place could use a restaurant. Henry

might have provided fresh fish since he manages the fishing shed. Would you happen to know what kind of bait he uses?" He'd rushed past her and Millie that day ostensibly to seal a container of live bait.

Lizzy grimaced. "I'm the wrong person to ask. I don't fish, so I've only been there on rare occasions. That place smells. Henry is lucky the odor doesn't stick to his preacher's robes."

"I imagine he chucks his outer garments when he holds fishing classes. Speaking of classes, does anyone at the village give archery lessons?"

Lizzy's lips pursed. "You can look up the workshop schedule online."

"The Native Americans in the battle scene used bows and arrows."

"Those arrows would have been blunted. And the actors didn't necessarily have to hit anything. They only had to look like they knew what they were doing. Where are you going with this?"

"Just curious," Marla said with a shrug. Except somebody had shot real arrows at her and Susan. She noticed Lizzy hadn't answered her question about who taught archery but let it go.

Lizzy moved behind the sales counter and shuffled some papers. "If you don't mind, I need to fill some mail orders. It was nice of you to visit."

Susan approached the cash register. She held an American Girl doll, a book to match, and a set of accessories. "Jess will adore this 1904 Samantha model. I'll have to take my kids to Pioneer Village. I think they would appreciate it at their ages."

Marla turned to Susan. "I should get one of those dolls for my niece. She's just turned seven last month, and I could give it to her as a belated birthday gift."

They made their purchases and left, promising to tour Baffle House again with their families. Marla could always take Brianna, who'd enjoy the experience.

"I still have some time left before I have to be at the salon,"

Marla told Susan in the parking lot. "Are you up for a drive? We could cruise by Greg Harris's farm again. If I can get his street address, I could look up the property records."

Susan's eyes sparkled. "Go for it, Marla. Clearly, Lizzy's brother is involved somehow. But we already drove around the perimeter. What else do you expect to find?"

"We'll look for a hidden driveway. He must have a mailbox somewhere." Lurking in her mind was the possibility that he used a post office box. Were properties required to have a mailbox out front? Or was that a personal choice?

Once they reached Broward County and headed west, Marla passed by the entrance to Pioneer Village. She cruised along the fairground's side, and then slowed as they met the grove of trees that bordered Greg's land.

It took a third pass for Marla to get lucky. She discerned a narrow road between the trees. "Look there," she cried, pointing. Her foot lifted off the accelerator. Traffic was light, and other cars whizzed by on their left. "We should see where it goes."

"It's a private road," Susan said with a thoughtful frown. "We can barely fit down it in your SUV. What if there's a dead end? We won't have enough space to turn around."

"You're right. I can park by the side of the road before it narrows. Are you up for a hike?"

The prospect didn't thrill her. It was steamy hot outside, but the lane was shaded at least. Neither she nor Susan were dressed for a long walk outdoors. She glanced down at the strapped sandals on her feet. Not the best for a dirty trek. Nonetheless, she was determined to see what lay at the end of the drive.

Cumulous clouds scudded overhead as they emerged from the car and headed down the tree-lined road. Humidity thickened the air that had an earthy scent.

"There's no mailbox, but this has to be the place," Marla said as they walked along a grassy swath. Shady branches from the bordering woods made the walk easier under dappled sunlight.

147

"This entire piece of land must have belonged to Lizzy's family in the past. It's a shame they had to divide up their plantation." Susan bent her head to watch her footing. Tree roots and rocks obstructed their path, making the trek hazardous.

"Her family didn't retain any of it except for the brother's farm. Maybe Lizzy's grandfather only sold the village tract to repay his debts," Marla suggested.

She increased her pace, aware that time was passing. Her sandals were caked with soil and grit had settled between her toes. Ugh, she'd need a shower after this adventure. "I wonder if Lizzy's brother lives on site. He could farm the land but have a place elsewhere."

"That's true." Susan, a few feet ahead, stopped abruptly. "Uh-oh. It's the end of the road."

Marla drew up beside her and gasped upon spying a blockade. "I might have expected the gate and the chain link fence, but why the barbed wire?"

"Greg must value his security. The fence might even be electrified. Better not to touch it."

Marla agreed and peered through the links. Beyond stretched rows and rows of shrubs that ended at a wooded border. The plants appeared well-tended with uniform heights.

"Look, there's a residence," Susan said, wagging her finger. "It's like a smaller version of Baffle House."

Sure enough, a two-story house sat on one side of the property. It was a mirror to the historic home in the living history park, albeit not as large.

Marla examined the gate. She didn't see a call box or any other way to gain entry. Greg probably had a remote device for his vehicle.

"There's something you should know," she told Susan. "Before Simon came to work at the village, he'd been in prison allegedly for cultivating marijuana. He claimed he was innocent. But if not, maybe he's doing it again and is in cahoots with Greg. That would account for this high level of security."

Susan squinted into the distance. "Those don't look like marijuana plants."

"No, but we can't see what's being grown beyond those buildings off to the side."

"Your cousin works with Simon, right? You should ask him about it."

"I need to talk to Corbin away from the history park. He rents a place near the nature preserve, but I don't know where. I've searched online and couldn't find an address. Nor do I have his phone number."

"You could check the vet offices and animal rescue places. Maybe he works at one of them in his spare time since he likes animals. Or if you want, I can call around for you."

"That would be great, thanks." Marla zeroed in on the crops stretching into the distance. "I should take some pictures before we leave. Dalton's team might be able to identify these shrubs." She snapped photos with her phone and then sent them to him.

"I'm not sure what we've gained by coming here," she said once they were back in the car. She started the engine and steered toward the main road. The heat had left her feeling deflated, or maybe it was the muddle in her mind that made her sluggish.

Susan adjusted her air-conditioning vent. "We've learned Greg Harris doesn't want visitors. Either he's afraid people from the village might trespass onto his property, or else he has another reason for keeping to himself."

"Do you think Phil discovered his secret? He might have demanded a cut of the action if Greg is growing something illegal."

"Or his crop might be perfectly legit," Susan reasoned. "Whatever he's doing, both Simon and Lizzy know about it. Lizzy lied when she said her brother grew corn and vegetables."

"That definitely makes her look suspicious."

"Let me know what you hear about Gilda's cause of death. It's one thing if someone murdered Phil over a personal grudge. It's scarier if a killer is targeting people who work at the park for another reason."

"I will. Please be careful. We've already made someone angry enough to shoot arrows at us." Marla glanced into the rearview mirror, aware they both needed to be more vigilant after asking so many questions. Lizzy had been right on that score.

"Despite the risks, this was fun." Susan grinned at her. "Jess is going to love the doll I bought her. I need to join you on your exploits more often."

Marla smiled in return. "We make a good team, and I appreciate the company."

After dropping her friend off, Marla headed to the salon. She washed up, getting rid of the grit from their impromptu hike. As she fell into her routine, she achieved a sense of comfort.

Her peace shattered later in the afternoon when a familiar figure strode through the front door. Marla's eyes widened as she glanced toward the entrance.

What was Violet, the village schoolteacher, doing there?

Chapter Fifteen

Marla bustled to the front of the shop. Her current client was getting shampooed, and she'd only have a few minutes. Was Violet there as a walk-in customer or merely to talk to her?

The former schoolteacher wore a shirtwaist dress and a natural hairstyle that made her look feminine yet vulnerable in an old-fashioned sense. Even her purse was a style the late Queen of England might have fancied. She carried herself with poise as she gave Marla a graceful wave. A pair of white gloves would have completed her image. She seemed more suited to period attire than to modern styles.

"Hello Marla," she said in her soft voice. "I hope I'm not interrupting, but I have some news to share. It won't take up much of your time." Her gaze flitted around the salon like a bird searching for a safe perch during an upcoming storm.

"Could you possibly wait twenty minutes or so?" Marla asked, wishing she could assign her client to someone else but dedicated to good service. "I have to finish a cut and blowout, and then I'll be free." She had finally asked Robyn to reduce her hours on Thursdays so she could leave earlier to get Ryder.

"All right, thanks." Violet claimed a seat in the waiting area, sitting stiffly on the edge. She gave a hasty glance outside. Was she nervous about being followed there?

Marla scanned the parking lot. No one was paying her salon any undue attention. She and Susan had reason to be cautious, but why was Violet concerned?

She completed her last client's appointment in record time.

151

Once she was done, she cleaned off the chair and signaled to Violet to come over. The salon assistant swept the floor and then moved out of earshot.

"Would you like a free consultation while you're here?" she asked Violet.

"Oh, um, sure." Violet took a seat as indicated.

She turned Violet toward the mirror and fluffed her natural honey-blond hair, then did a gentle scalp massage to relax her. "Your ends could use a trim. I can give you a complimentary cut if you have the time. That way, our talking together will seem natural."

"Good idea, thanks." Violet followed her instructions to get shampooed while Marla told Robyn to add their new client to the books.

Once Violet returned, Marla engaged her in small talk while she snipped and combed. "What is it you wanted to tell me?" she finally asked, giving up on eliciting more than monosyllables from the woman.

Violet's fearful eyes met hers in the mirror. "It's Uriah."

"What about him?" Marla asked, wondering why it was so hard for Violet to speak.

"I'm afraid he did it," Violet said in a barely audible voice. Marla had to lean forward to hear her.

"What do you mean?" she asked, holding off on using the blow-dryer until their discussion ended. She gently combed Violet's hair, hoping the motion would soothe her.

"This won't leave your salon, will it?" Violet said. "I don't want to get in trouble."

"My conversations with customers are always confidential. That is, unless it affects my husband's murder case. In that event, I'll have to share your information with him."

"I understand." Violet folded her hands in her lap. "In my last job, I'd accused the principal of sexual harassment. He denied it and I ended up getting fired. Phil knew about my history and hired me anyway. Later I realized he meant to use this knowledge to make me comply with his wishes. I didn't want to lose this job or be forced to quit, so I told Uriah." She glanced away, avoiding Marla's gaze in the mirror.

"Was hitting on women a habit of Phil's?" Marla asked, wishing to confirm her theories about him.

Violet shrugged. "I didn't see him make a pass at anyone else in the village. It's a good thing, too, or I couldn't have trusted my own reactions. After what happened with my mother and then to me at that school, I won't let another man abuse me or my friends."

Whoa, you've just admitted to a motive. Marla composed her face to hide her thoughts.

"What happened to your mom?" she asked in a gentle tone. It might help Violet to talk about the past since those events were still affecting her.

"My mother fell prey to a con man who stole her widow's pension. She had to struggle to make ends meet after he left her high and dry. I'll never forget her sobs when she learned she'd been duped. That louse had emptied her bank accounts and fled town."

"I'm so sorry. That must have been tough on you, too. But what does this have to do with Uriah?" Marla asked, unable to connect the dots.

Violet thrust a clump of cut hairs off her salon drape and onto the floor. "I know he cares for me, so I told him about Phil's unwanted advances. I'm afraid Uriah got rid of Phil to get him out of my hair." She gave a nervous cackle, darting a glance at Marla in the mirror.

Is she trying to slough suspicion onto someone else in her stead? It certainly seems that way with her casting blame on Uriah.

Marla put down her comb. "I appreciate you telling me this. Can you explain something else for me? What brought you to the fishing shed the day you found Phil's body?"

"Phil texted me and said he had something to relate about Uriah. When I went to meet him on the dock, he was already dead. Do you understand now why I'm afraid Uriah did it? Phil must have discovered a secret about him that he needed to protect. Phil knew things about us and used that information to his advantage."

Marla raised her eyebrows at this admission. Had Dalton found any files in Phil's office to corroborate this claim?

Then again, Violet might be lying. She'd just revealed a motive to do away with Phil and had found his body. Plus, her statements about Uriah were contradictory. Had he supposedly killed Phil to protect her from his advances or to guard his own secrets?

Her saving grace might be that text message from Phil. Perhaps she had met with him, and he'd revealed something detrimental to Uriah. Then Violet had killed Phil in a fit of fury to protect her beaux. Dalton should be able to verify her statement by accessing her cell phone records. Either way, these scenarios left several unanswered questions.

How did the tomahawk come to be there? Or the pearl button? And if Violet was the killer, would she have had time to wipe off the murder weapon, toss out any blood-spattered items, and look so fetching when Marla and Dalton arrived? Despite the woman's pallor, the male bystanders had clearly appreciated her looks.

"By the way, my husband found a vintage button on the deck," Marla remarked, observing Violet for a reaction. "Would you know who might have lost one like this?" She showed Violet the photos on her cell.

Violet coughed and covered her mouth. "Why would I know anything about a silly button?"

Marla's hackles rose. Violet was surely lying this time.

Henry had given the button to Uriah to research as a possible product for his store. Had Uriah held onto it, and the button dropped from his pocket when he murdered Phil?

If what Violet said was true, Phil had asked her to meet him by the pond. Why then? Unless the matter was urgent, he wouldn't interrupt his job of narrating the battle before he'd made a pitch for donations. The timing didn't make sense.

"Did Uriah give the button to you?" she asked Violet. "Maybe he thought you'd appreciate it as a token of his regard. Then when you went to meet Phil, you were so shocked by what you saw that it fell from your gown?"

She didn't understand how it would end up under the corpse otherwise. The button didn't have any shreds of fabric attached, so it couldn't have come off someone's costume, unless it had been loose. But according to Dalton, nobody's outfit had a button missing.

Violet pressed a fist to her mouth. "If you must know, he did give it to me."

Marla suppressed a smile of triumph. "Did you have it on you when you went to the boardwalk that day?"

Violet shook her head, damp tendrils of hair veiling her face. "No. I'd loaned it to Gilda. She said she'd look in the jars of buttons in the sewing room to see if there were any similar ones."

"Isn't Millie in charge of the sewing circle?"

"She and Gilda would cover for each other on occasion. Millie is the one with the actual skills as a seamstress, though."

Marla hefted the blow-dryer but didn't turn it on. "Is there anyone else you can think of who might have resented Phil enough to kill him?"

"I don't care to speculate. I just hope Uriah is innocent. I'd like to think better of him, but this whole thing has me scared."

You should be. Someone is murdering people from the village. Phil acted as administrator. Gilda represented the fairground's board of directors. If Gilda's death turned out to be unnatural, could someone be targeting authority figures there? If so, why? The only person who stood to gain from that scenario might be the developer.

"Does Uriah have any archery skills?" Marla asked, trying a different tack. "My friend is looking for someone who can teach her."

"We don't keep real bows and arrows on site. Even with blunted ends, they can be dangerous."

"What about Angus? He can throw an axe. Maybe he's taken up archery as well."

"Angus?" Violet chortled. "He may look fierce, but that man is a big teddy bear. Everyone knows he likes Lizzy."

Marla proceeded to dry Violet's hair while she thought about what to ask next. At least now she could tell Dalton the button had passed from Henry to Uriah to Violet. And she'd loaned it to Gilda. That still didn't explain how it had ended up under Phil's body. Of course, Violet could be lying. She might have placed it there herself to frame Uriah.

Marla stood back upon finishing her work. Honeyed waves caressed Violet's shoulders with an inward bent. She could still twist her hair into a schoolmarm's bun for her role at the village, but this softened her appearance and brought out the violet hue of her eyes.

"One more thing," Marla said, after letting Violet view the back of her head with a handheld mirror. "Have you ever seen Billy's herb garden? I visited the farm, but he wouldn't take me there. I'm thinking that herbs would be useful in several ways to the village."

Violet plucked at her dress once Marla had removed the drape. "You're right. Uriah and Billy both use herbs in their homeopathic remedies. Millie and River use them in their recipes. As for where Simon keeps his herb garden, I don't like tromping around in the dirt, so I haven't been over that way."

"I see. We're all done, Violet. I appreciate you coming in today and sharing your concerns. I hope you like the way your hair turned out."

"It's lovely, thanks." She stood and fumbled in her purse for her wallet.

Marla stayed her hand. "No need for that. I'm glad we had this chat."

Violet closed her bag and regarded Marla. "Please be

careful. You've been asking a lot of questions at the village, and it's been noticed."

"You, too. It's best for you to stay in the schoolhouse to be safe until the culprit is caught."

After Marla was alone, she collected her thoughts. Either Violet was innocent, or she'd been lying the entire visit. Now was not the time to sort things out, however. She had to retrieve her son from day care. She grabbed her purse, said goodbye to the staff, and texted Dalton that she was leaving to pick up Ryder.

At home, she took care of the dogs, fed and bathed her son, and put together a quick dinner for the rest of the family. She and Brianna ate together while Ryder slept in his crib and the pets in their doggie beds. Dalton hadn't come home yet. Marla appreciated this quiet time with her stepdaughter.

The teen's inquisitive nature surfaced, and she asked about the murder case. Marla gave her a quick summary of recent events.

"Have you searched for a way into the neighboring farm from the fairground side?" Brianna asked, rising to help Marla with the dishes.

"Are you suggesting I trespass onto private property?" Marla asked in a teasing tone. She turned on the sink to wash the plates while Brianna picked up a dishtowel.

"Why not? That's never stopped you before."

"True. Maybe there's an opening farther along the fairground's perimeter. A loose piece of fence could do the trick." She'd like to get a closer look at the plants Greg was growing. They looked more like bushes, but that way, she could get some actual leaf samples.

"Did you ever learn where Lizzy lives?" Brianna asked. "She could be staying in that farmhouse with her brother."

"She didn't say."

"Is Dad looking into this guy?"

"He doesn't have a valid reason to include Greg Harris in his investigation. We know Lizzy's brother is connected to

Simon but not much else. Maybe those photos I sent your dad will prove relevant." Marla resumed her chores, her shoulders sagging. She still had to pack Ryder's lunch for the next day before she could relax.

"How about alibis? Has Dad eliminated anyone yet?"

She'd make a great amateur detective, Marla thought. Then again, Brie could use those instincts for the medical research she wanted to do.

Marla washed Ryder's water cup. "Uriah was in the general store during the reenactment. Angus was at the blacksmith shop. Henry stayed in the church, and Lizzy was at Baffle House. They didn't have any guests coming by who might verify their statements. River was at the encampment, while Billy took part in the battle. Millie manned a booth at the exhibition. Any one of them could have left their station while the battle was going on."

"How about the farmer? Didn't your cousin say he'd run off on an errand?"

"Yes, and Violet claimed she went to the boardwalk because Phil called her."

"Maybe she killed him because he harassed her. He could have threatened to fire her if she didn't do what he wanted."

"She hinted that Phil had the dirt on others at the village. Dalton hasn't found any indications of blackmail, though. He has access to Phil's office and his home."

"Phil could have kept the files on his computer. It's interesting how many of the staff fled to the village as a sanctuary from their troubles."

"Yes, it is." Had Dalton sent Phil's computer to forensics? She should ask him, although he'd probably covered that angle.

When he finally came home, his face was haggard and dark circles ringed his eyes. She hated to add to his burdens, but had to tell him about Violet's visit to the salon. After heating his dinner and sitting at the table with him, she related her story.

"Violet and Uriah are definitely suspect," Dalton said upon her conclusion. "So is Henry the preacher. His excuse for rushing to the fishing shack that day doesn't hold water. He'd said he left a container of bait open and was hurrying over to seal it. I didn't see any live bait in the place unless he'd dumped it in the pond."

This confirmed what Marla had been thinking. "He could have been hiding the tomahawk under his robes and stashed it on the boardwalk. Why else would he have needed to go there?"

Dalton shoved a forkful of pecan-crusted tilapia into his mouth. "Henry had more of a motive than he let on. He orders the staff's costumes from his wholesale connections and supplies them at retail prices. Angus told me that Phil had proposed to get their outfits directly from the manufacturer. This would have cut out the middleman and saved the village money."

"Then Henry would have lost this source of income. He couldn't have been happy about the proposed changes. This gives him another motive to get rid of Phil."

"I can think of less drastic means," Dalton said in his wry tone.

"How so?"

"Phil's bank accounts show a number of regular deposits that don't relate to his salary. I've requested the village records from the fairground. It's possible Angus was right about Phil being on the take. He may have been siphoning money meant for the village. Henry could have gotten him fired if he'd discovered evidence."

"That would more likely be in Angus's purview. With his accounting background, he'd be a good candidate to replace Phil as administrator."

Dalton put down his fork. "Uriah has been appointed as a temp replacement. It appears his business abilities have impressed the fairground's directors. He's made the general store into a profitable venture."

"Maybe Uriah was after Phil's job all along. That would give him another reason to get rid of Phil, in addition to getting him off Violet's back."

"There's no indication he was vying for the post."

"Then maybe Violet was right that Phil had found some dirt on him. Did you confiscate Phil's files and the computers in his office?"

"We took whatever we felt was relevant."

"How did the fairground's directors react to Gilda's loss? Her death must have put a crimp in their plans to sell the property."

"They're worried about the staff's safety. This latest incident gives them an excuse to shut the village's doors."

"Lizzy's brother is unhappy about the deal with the developer. What do you know about him?" Marla had told Dalton earlier about her visit to the doll shop.

"Not much. It's only conjecture on our part that Greg Harris is involved. We'll need to see what the report is on Gilda's death. From the looks of things, she may have been murdered. I'm suspecting she was poisoned by eating those chocolate chip cookies. We won't know exactly what they contained until we receive the toxicology reports."

Chapter Sixteen

Marla didn't sleep well, tossing and turning while imagining Gilda eating poisoned cookies. What did they contain to make them lethal? Gilda couldn't have eaten that many.

"Poisoning is often a method favored by women," Dalton said in the kitchen when she brought up the subject in the morning. He was gobbling down a quick breakfast of scrambled eggs and toast while she got Ryder ready for day care.

"Were those cookies home-baked or store-bought? If the former, River and Millie come to mind with their culinary skills."

"If not, anyone could have bought a bag at the store and put them into a generic bakery box," Dalton pointed out. "You're getting ahead of things, Marla. We don't have the M.E.'s report back yet."

"Regardless of how she died, I'm sad for Gilda's family. She wasn't married with kids, was she?"

"Divorced, no children. The ex-spouse lives out of state. Gilda's sister is planning a memorial service once the body is released. I'll send Langley to cover it."

"It'll help when you get a definitive cause of death. Could the same person have killed Phil Pufferfish? The method in his case was much more violent." Marla cringed at the mental image of someone swinging an axe into flesh and bone.

"Speaking of Phil, what was it you overheard Simon saying to him the day of the battle?"

"'I can bring you down like an avalanche if you don't leave this alone.' But this implies Simon had something on Phil to influence him. In that case, Simon would have been the one to end up dead."

Dalton rose to refill his coffee mug. "It's more likely Phil discovered what Simon is doing and demanded a piece of the pie. Blackmail would certainly be a motive for murder. Either way, we need evidence, and I don't have enough reason to get a warrant for the brother's property without further indication that he's involved."

Marla finished packing Ryder's lunch and zipped the bag. Ryder, who'd finished eating, played with his toys on the family room floor.

"With his experience in horticulture, Simon might be advising Lizzy's brother on how to get the best yield for his crops," she ventured. "Or maybe Greg is using Simon for his black-market connections to sell the stuff if it's anything illegal."

The brackets by Dalton's eyes deepened like they did when he was hard at thought. "That's an interesting idea. The brother is still a wild card, though."

"It would help if we got an ID on those plant photos I sent. By the way, did you ever recover Phil's cell phone or obtain the records from his provider? We need to verify what Violet said about getting a text message from him."

"I'm working on it. I'll let you know when I have an update."

Marla glanced at Brianna, who had plans with friends for the day. She was refilling the dog dishes while listening in on their conversation. Spooks and Lucky bounded over to eat their meals.

A momentary wave of nausea washed over Marla as she sniffed their dog food. *What's this?* She pressed a hand to her stomach. Maybe she should change back to their previous brand. Those pellets hadn't affected her, but they had gotten too expensive.

"What's the matter?" Dalton said as he brought his empty plate to the sink.

"I'm thinking of those poisoned cookies, that's all," she

replied to deflect his concern. She must be overdoing things and it was getting to her.

"You're stressing yourself out, Marla. You need to relax more and let me handle the case."

"No way. I want the bad guy behind bars so you can move on. It's too close to your retirement. I do need to cut back on my hours at the salon, though. I plan to eliminate Saturdays and Thursdays altogether."

That meant she would work three days a week on Tuesday, Wednesday, and Friday. Her regular customers wouldn't be happy, but her family took precedence. Her staff could handle the overflow.

"It'll be nice to have weekends together when I'm retired," Dalton said, tickling her back where she stood by the sink.

"I know." His proximity sent a zing of awareness along her nerves. She glanced at her watch. It was almost eight-thirty. "I have to leave if I want to make it to the salon by nine."

She strode over to where Ryder played at his toy garden with its flashing lights and cheery music. "Come on, sweetie, let's check your diaper before we go."

Dalton left for work while Marla finished getting Ryder ready. She waved goodbye to Brianna on their way out and headed to her car.

After dropping Ryder off at day care, she aimed for the salon. At the front desk, she broached the subject on her mind to Robyn.

"Hey, I'm ready to cut back my hours more drastically starting in August. No more Saturdays, and I'd like Thursdays off as well. I need more time at home."

Robyn shoveled a strand of pink highlighted hair off her face. "Good move, Marla. You've been looking tired lately. I'll reschedule your customers booked for those days." She leaned forward, elbows on the counter. "Any progress on the case?"

Marla gave her a brief summary. "We'll talk more later. I need to get ready before my first appointment."

Robyn rolled her eyes. "Like you don't want to talk about it. Did you ever tell Dalton someone shot at you and Susan with arrows?"

"I finally confessed, and he wasn't pleased. I should visit Billy at his casino. He's more likely to be knowledgeable about bows and arrows if he uses them during the reenactments. Can you call the gift shop and see when he'll be there?"

"Sure. I'm glad to help," Robyn said, turning back to her scheduling.

Marla greeted the other stylists as she walked to her station. Several customers later, she got a call from her cousin. Her brows raised at seeing Cynthia's name on the caller ID.

"Bruce found out the developer is Sandicott Corporation," Cynthia said. "In return for buying the village, they've promised to keep Baffle House as a museum."

What? Did Lizzy know about this offer to preserve the mansion? She felt it should belong to her family. That bargaining chip would be like a slap in the face to her.

"Thanks, this is useful," she told her cousin.

"How is the case progressing? Has Dalton narrowed the suspects yet?"

"He's getting there." She didn't mention Gilda's death. Had Lizzy been so angry at Gilda for her role in the real estate deal that she'd murdered her? Maybe she'd hoped the deal would fall apart with Gilda out of the way.

"Anyway, I have to run," Cynthia said. "I've a meeting this morning with Ocean Guard's volunteer corps. We have a beach cleanup coming up if you'd like to join us."

"No, thanks. Ryder might like to participate when he's older, though." Marla disconnected and went back to work. The door chimes rang on and off as clients and delivery men came and went during the day.

Later in the afternoon, Robyn sauntered toward her holding a square gold box.

"This is for you," she said, handing it over.

Marla peered at the familiar logo. "Who is it from?" She undid the bow and removed the lid. Nestled inside was a delectable selection of artisan chocolates.

"Some guy delivered it. He drove a white van. There's no card inside?"

"Nope. That's odd." She stared at the contents. The sweet aroma tempted her to try one.

"Maybe Dalton sent you a gift. Is this a special occasion?"

"Our anniversary is in December. Besides, he wouldn't be so mysterious."

Her cell phone rang before she could contemplate who else might have sent it. "Uh-oh. It's Ryder's school. What do they want?"

Her day crashed at the teacher's response. "Ryder has a strange rash. You'll have to come pick him up. Here, I'm sending pictures."

Marla winced at the photos. Her child had welts on his face, back, and buttocks. "These look like hives. Has he come into contact with any vegetation outside? Or eaten anything unusual?" It wasn't a heat rash. What else could it be?

The teacher answered in the negative. Marla hung up and dialed the doctor's office. They gave her an appointment at four o'clock.

At least she'd finished her latest client. She stopped by the front desk to explain her reason for rushing out the door.

"I hope Ryder will be okay," Robyn said with a sympathetic smile. "I'll see if Nicole or Jen can handle your last two clients."

Marla texted Dalton what was happening and fled outside.

At the day care center, she lifted Ryder in her arms. He fussed a bit, but his skin didn't feel warm and his eyes didn't glaze over like they did when he had a fever. It seemed more like an allergic reaction, but what did she know? She took him home, where he ran to play right away. He didn't act as though he were sick.

Marla retrieved the box of chocolates from the car and stuck them in the fridge. She'd brought them home so Dalton could examine them. A chill skittered up her spine as she remembered an incident in the past where she'd received a gift of tainted marzipans. And coming on the heels of Gilda's suspicious cookies, it paid to be extra cautious.

The appointed hour came for the doctor visit. Soon she was in the waiting room with Ryder. The antiseptic smell was all too familiar to her by now. Ryder played with the toys available while she worried about all the germs he was touching.

"It's a viral rash," the pediatrician announced after examining him. "Has he been ill?"

"His nose has been a little sniffly, but nothing significant. A couple of other kids in his class are out sick. But he hasn't had a fever or any other signs."

The doctor gave a wise nod. "He probably has a mild case. The rash will show up and go away spontaneously and can appear on any part of his body. It's nothing contagious. There's no reason why he can't return to school."

Marla heaved a sigh of relief. She'd notify Robyn that she'd be back at work tomorrow.

Dalton made it home earlier than expected, anxious to see his son. Ryder appeared well, other than the peculiar rash.

They sat for dinner in the kitchen. Marla savored her husband's presence, glad to have him there to share her concerns. Brianna was still out, so Marla had taken care of the dogs in her absence. Lucky and Spooks sniffed around Marla and Dalton's ankles, hoping for morsels.

Marla dove into her meatloaf, mac and cheese and broccoli. It was a basic meal but easy to prepare. Ryder ate with his fingers in his child seat attached to the table.

"Did you send me a box of chocolates?" she asked Dalton after she'd eaten enough to satisfy her appetite. "I received one at work today. It didn't have a card or any package wrap. The delivery man didn't know who'd sent the candy, but had orders to deliver the box to me."

"I didn't send it. Let me see the thing."

Marla got up to retrieve it. "It looks legit but I'm not touching these chocolates without knowing who sent them." Her hands shook. What if Robyn at the salon had tried one, or Brianna had come home earlier and dug into them?

Dalton lifted the lid and sniffed the contents. "They look normal. Nobody took a bite, did they?"

"Thankfully, no. After what happened to Gilda, I'm not taking any chances."

"I'll take these into the lab. Can you describe the delivery guy?"

"I didn't see him. Robyn said he drove a white van."

"That could be anyone. You need to be more cautious. Somebody has already shot arrows at you. You'd better warn Susan to be on the lookout."

Marla felt her face drain of color. "I hope she hasn't had any issues."

Dalton stuck the chocolates in a bag and put them in the spare fridge in the garage. Meanwhile, Ryder was done eating and Marla let him go play. She made a call to Susan to fill her in.

"Omigod. First Gilda eats cookies and dies, and then you get a box of unlabeled chocolates? That's scary, Marla. The killer may be targeting you now."

"I know, although we only suspect Gilda ate something bad. The tox reports aren't back yet."

"Still, it's alarming. I'll be extra careful, and you'd better watch your back even more so with this development."

Marla promised to touch base with Susan early next week and went to get her son's bath ready. She came back to retrieve him, smiling as she noted the adoring look on Dalton's face while he played with Ryder. It would be good to have him around more when he retired.

First, they had a murder or two to solve. After Ryder was asleep, she told Dalton about Cynthia's news. "The developer means to preserve Baffle House," she concluded. "Do you think this was a concession to get Lizzy on board? I'd think she would be more offended than pleased."

"Perhaps. They might have hoped to gain her support so she'd convince her brother to sell. He's more likely to be the sticking point. I finally heard from the lab regarding your photos. Those aren't marijuana plants. They're not sure what it is without an actual physical sample."

He'd already removed his belt and secured his weapons and other police gadgets. Now, moving into their bedroom, he took off his shirt and tossed it on the bed. Marla trailed him and took off her earrings by the dresser.

"What about blueberry bushes? They're more like shrubs than plants. They don't look like olive trees. We've seen what those were like when we toured that grove. And peach trees would be taller, I'd think." If only she could get her boots on the ground, so to speak, she could snitch a branch for closer analysis.

"Whatever Greg Harris is growing, he doesn't want visitors," Dalton stated. "That's clear from the barbed wire and gated fence. But it still could be something innocuous."

Marla drew a mental picture of the property lines. "Simon's herb garden must be located by the rear border between the village and Greg's land. I haven't tried to find it from the fairground side. Maybe there's a way onto Greg's farm from that direction."

Dalton's pants landed on the bed after his shirt. "Let it go," he said. "You've done enough, and someone is watching you. You can't put yourself in harm's way again."

Unsure how to proceed, Marla refocused her thoughts on their immediate plans. Tomorrow was a workday. Sunday was Michael's birthday lunch. Marla looked forward to seeing her brother's kids and showing off Ryder.

By the next morning, his rash had mostly cleared. She'd offered to call a babysitter so Dalton could go into the office, but he had said he could work from home. Langley and his team would do the footwork over the weekend while he watched Ryder.

Marla entered the salon at nine on Saturday. Her feet dragged. It was getting harder to leave her son, especially on weekends. She couldn't wait until her schedule lightened, although her clients wouldn't be happy about the change.

She gave a half-hearted wave to Robyn, picked up her list of appointments, and headed to her station. After stashing her purse in a drawer, she nodded to Nicole. The other stylist had come in early for a client. Nicole had already announced her intention of taking weekends off once her first child was born in October.

"What's the matter, Marla? You look down," Nicole said. She wore her hair in a high ponytail. Her maternity clothes showed off her baby bump.

Marla plugged in her curling irons and blow dryer. "I want more free time, but I also want to be here for my clients. Brianna will be leaving for college soon. I haven't gotten together with Tally in a while. I owe my mother a visit. I'm neglecting the people I love, and for what?"

Nicole's eyes glistened with sympathy. She paused, comb in one hand and shears in the other. "You have too many responsibilities. It'll be better once you lessen your load. Is Dalton watching Ryder today or is your stepdaughter there?"

"Dalton is staying home. I feel guilty about that, too. He has a case to solve, and here I am at the salon."

"You have customers who depend on you and you're a business owner. He understands and is proud of you."

"I know. I wish I could be more helpful to him, though."

Nicole resumed cutting her client's glossy chestnut hair. It was similar to Marla's natural color. The woman had dark brown eyes same as her. She was about twenty years younger, however. Marla felt her age today as a bone-weary fatigue set in. At forty, she wasn't any youngster. And Dalton was eight years older. She should cherish their time together.

She drowned her doubts in work as her first customer arrived and she shoved aside any thoughts about the murders until her friend Jill called.

"Hey, Marla, sorry it's taken me so long to get back to you. Things have been crazy busy."

Marla hadn't seen Jill or Arnie since she'd run into them at the park. Robyn retrieved their daily order of bagels for customers from Arnie's deli each morning. And Jill was busy at her job in public relations. Marla remembered Jill had promised to look into local ads for Pioneer Village.

"That's okay," she said, vowing to be a better friend. "Did you learn anything interesting?"

"Nobody I asked has seen any advertising materials for the living history park. How do they expect people to know about the place? The fairground only mentions their own events."

"I think the fairground is hoping to divest themselves of the property. I'll tell you more about it later. We'll have to make a date to get together after Dalton solves this latest case."

"Let's do that. I've got to go. The kids are about to jump in the pool."

Marla hung up and mulled over the possible reasons for the lack of advertising. If Phil received the funds for the village, he might have pocketed the money meant for publicity.

From the fairground side, perhaps Gilda had been responsible for doling out funds to the different tracts. Phil found out she'd been embezzling money and blackmailed her. She got rid of him to avoid exposure. But then who had killed her, if she'd died from unnatural causes?

Marla discarded the blackmail scenario. Phil was the one who had unexplained deposits in his personal bank account. Dalton said he'd track the source by corroborating the village's financial records with the fairground's reports. Had Phil been falsifying the books?

Angus, a former accountant, suspected as much. But murdering Phil due to his pilfering didn't seem like a strong enough reason, especially from the violent way he'd died.

Regarding other motives in Phil's case, she counted them on her fingers.

Phil's proposal to buy the village could have obstructed the sale to the developer.

Phil had collected information on people that they didn't want exposed, such as Uriah.

He'd made unwanted advances to Violet and River.

He had promised Millie the chef position at a café, but maybe he'd changed his mind.

He meant to eliminate the Seminole camp if his secession plan had succeeded.

And he might have demanded a cut of whatever Simon, Lizzy, and Greg had going together.

In other words, almost everyone in the village could be considered a potential murderer.

Chapter Seventeen

"Marla, I have news about Billy Cypress for you," Robyn said during a break in Marla's appointments. She'd come over to where Marla was cleaning her counter before her next client arrived.

Marla glanced at the brunette, whose streak of pink hair stood out like a patriot's flag on enemy territory. "What's that?" she asked, forgetting what she'd asked Robyn to do.

"Billy will be at the casino on Monday. Do you want me to go with you?"

Marla's pulse accelerated. This would be a great opportunity to sound him out about his alibi for Phil's death and to get him talking about the other characters in the village. While Uriah and Simon topped her suspect list, she hadn't ruled anyone else out just yet.

"Sure, that would be great," she responded, unable to keep the glee from her tone. "What hours will he be there?"

"Nine to five. I guess he'll be absent from his job at the village. I'm going to visit the history park on Sunday to see what the hullabaloo is all about."

"Be careful what you say to the cast members. It's bad enough someone shot arrows at me and Susan. That box of chocolates could also be dangerous. I gave it to Dalton for analysis." She reminded Robyn about the marzipan incident.

"You're right. I should have recognized right away that the delivery was strange. You said the village offers various workshops, correct? I could always say I'm interested in taking archery lessons there."

"Good idea. If you visit the Seminole camp, talk to River. She plays Billy's wife and may be helpful in that regard."

Marla didn't really consider River a suspect, but she could be one. She had reason to resent Phil, who'd intended to eliminate the Seminole site. And if she used herbs in her cooking, she might know something about Simon's secretive garden.

Robyn nodded. "I'll check her out if I can do so without running into Billy. He'll think it suspicious if I turn up twice."

"Okay. How about if I pick you up at eleven on Monday? We can talk to Billy at the casino and then have lunch in their themed restaurant."

"Sounds like a plan. What are you guys doing tomorrow?"

"It's my brother's birthday. His wife is hosting a party at their house."

"Will Dalton be able to go? I know he gets his nose to the ground when he's on a case."

"I'm hoping he can pop in. I wish I could think of some more ways to help him."

"If you're not busy Sunday morning, why not check out the farmer's market? Didn't you say Millie from the village attends craft fairs?"

"Yes, although I think she only rents space at bigger festivals. I suppose it couldn't hurt to take a look, though."

Later that evening, Marla asked Dalton if he'd care to go with her, but he declined. He wanted to go into work early on Sunday before Michael's party. Instead, Brianna offered to accompany her. Her stepdaughter was too keen on helping solve murders for Marla's comfort, but she appreciated the support.

****

Sunday dawned bright and clear. Live oaks shaded the park where the farmer's market set up every weekend. Enticing aromas came from the food booths, while colorful glass globes twirled on poles meant for lawn decorations.

As they strolled past a French pastry tent, Marla's mouth watered. She moved on past, aware she'd eat later at Michael's party. The scent of brewed coffee mingled with spices further along. Brianna stopped at the Cuban tent to get a spinach and cheese empanada.

"Is Dad any closer to an arrest?" she asked, biting into the savory pastry. They both wore dark glasses as the July sun blazed in the sky.

"Not really. He has his suspicions but nothing solid."

"Did you ever talk to your cousin Corbin again? Maybe he'll spill the beans."

"I don't know how to contact him away from the village. Susan offered to check the local animal shelters to see if he volunteers there. I need to follow up with her."

Marla pushed Ryder's stroller ahead. The air was dryer than usual, making the morning pleasant. Later would be a scorcher, however. She'd been smart to apply sunscreen.

Her eyes widened as she spied a familiar face poking out from one of the tents. "Look, Millie is here after all."

Eager to chat up the seamstress, Marla hastened forward to her tent. Aprons and sundresses swung on racks in the breeze, while tables holding scarves and gloves filled the interior. A hat rack held frothy creations in all hues of color.

"Hi Millie, it's good to see you again."

Millie gave her a startled glance. "Marla… What are you doing here?"

"This is my son, Ryder, and my daughter, Brianna. We came out for a walk and to take Ryder to the playground. I'm surprised you're not at the history park today."

Millie waved a hand. "I don't have any demos there until this afternoon. And the sewing ladies love it when I sell their products at these shows."

"Do they ever join you?"

"They'd rather do the sewing and leave the selling to me. We make more money this way than through the village general store."

"I'd expect so. Has Gilda ever covered for you so you could attend more weekend events?" Marla asked to gauge their relationship.

Millie's face fell. "Haven't you heard the news? Gilda is dead. I still can't believe it."

"Yes, my husband told me." Marla was momentarily distracted by Brianna who offered to take Ryder to the playground. She handed over the stroller. "Who notified you?" she asked once she was hands-free. Now she could focus solely on Millie.

"The fairground told Uriah, who passed on the news to the rest of us. Apparently, Gilda had been a member of their board of directors. We'd never realized she was a wolf in sheep's clothing," Millie said with a bitter undertone.

"That's rather harsh. Why would you say that about her?"

"It's clear what her purpose was in being at the village," Millie snapped.

Marla stepped into a patch of shade to cool off. "How so? I don't get it." She purposefully pretended ignorance to see what she could learn.

"Uriah also told us the fairground was considering an offer by a developer to buy our village. I suspect Gilda was snooping into our affairs to make sure no one sabotaged the deal. She may have been instrumental in finding a buyer."

"If that's true, she would have opposed Phil's plan for the villagers to buy the tract."

Millie's eyes narrowed. "Either way, she's not a problem anymore."

That wasn't the reaction Marla had expected. Millie didn't seem in the least sorrowful about Gilda's loss. Even if she'd resented the woman's role at the village, she should feel some sadness that Gilda had died too soon.

"What do you think happened to her?" Marla asked, keeping her tone mildly curious. She adjusted her sunglasses, glad they hid her expressions.

"I figure Gilda must have had a medical condition no one noticed," Millie said. "Why are you asking all these questions, anyway? Did your husband send you?"

"No, I came here to buy some vegetables. I had no idea you'd be present," Marla lied. "Dalton is doing a preliminary investigation as a routine matter. I'm wondering if Gilda's death is related to Phil's case."

"Poor Phil. I'd supported his plans, you know. He would have made me the chef at our new on-site café once we took control of the property."

The blithe way she spoke made Marla glance at her. Was there something untruthful in what she'd said?

"Who do you think killed him?" Marla asked in a blunt tone.

"I'm not fond of tattling, you understand. But if your husband wants to find the culprit, tell him to examine Violet's actions more closely. She's the one who found the body."

"What could possibly be Violet's motive?" Marla knew Violet's workshops were about to be eliminated due to lack of funding. That might give her a reason to get rid of Phil if she believed he was responsible for their shortage. But was it reason enough to murder the man?

"Violet had a personal issue against Phil," Millie said, adjusting a display of socks on one of the tables. "She resented predatory men because she'd been let go from her previous job due to a lecherous principal. She'd made a complaint about him, and he saw that she got fired."

"Poor thing. That happens too often in the workplace," Marla replied in a sympathetic tone.

"You may not have been aware, but Phil hit on several women at the village. He might have incited Violet one time too many."

"Phil never approached you that way?"

"I never struck his fancy. Nor am I a youngster like Violet and River. He tried with Lizzy, too, but she set him in his place."

Here was an opening Marla couldn't resist. "Speaking of

River, I tasted her stew. It got me thinking that she could use some fresh herbs from Simon's garden. They'd be helpful for your cooking demos, too. I'd love to see his herb garden, but he's shy about showing it to people."

"Simon is a skilled farmer. I would have loved to helm a café on site and could have used his vegetables for my dishes. If only Phil hadn't... well, that's water under the bridge."

Marla figured she'd been about to say if only Phil hadn't died. Or was that not what she'd meant?

She hadn't considered Millie as a suspect up until then because she didn't appear to have a clear motive. She'd supported Phil's plan, and he hadn't made unwanted advances her way. So that seemed a dead end as a lead. As for Gilda's case, poisoning someone might be within Millie's abilities. But again, why do it? Just because Gilda had worked for the fairground?

Marla glanced down the path. The lanes were becoming more congested. She might only have a few more minutes before Millie got engaged by a customer, plus she needed to rejoin Brianna and Ryder. What else did she need to know since Millie was willing to talk?

"Do you think the real estate deal will fall apart now that Gilda is gone?" she asked.

"I would hope so, but who knows?" Millie smiled at a woman who stopped by to lift a scarf, only to put it back down and move on.

"I hope you'll be careful," Marla told her. "Two of your colleagues have died within the past few weeks. If it were me, I'd be nervous."

"Why should I be? I've done nothing to attract attention if there is a killer lurking around."

"Maybe it's the work of a vigilante. I understand you'd been fired from your last job. An arsonist burnt the restaurant down where you had been chef," she said to provoke Millie.

Millie stiffened. "The owners accused me of having a hand in it, but why would I do something so stupid?"

Because you wanted revenge? Marla thought but didn't voice aloud. "Was Phil aware of these accusations when he hired you?"

"He knew a lot of things about all of us. Now if you don't mind, you're blocking my booth."

It seemed everyone at the village had secrets to hide, and Millie was no exception. Had Phil been hiring these people with shady pasts so he could blackmail them? If so, perhaps the deposits to his bank account were payoffs from his victims rather than embezzlement of village funds. Hopefully, Dalton could figure it out.

Marla headed for the vegetable stand. She purchased a couple of glossy purple eggplants along with some tomatoes before rejoining Brianna and Ryder. She'd make eggplant parmesan for dinner tomorrow night.

She waved off Brianna's questions, knowing the teen would want to rehash the case. Marla wasn't in the mood. It was a beautiful day and she wanted to enjoy her family. She'd taken enough time away from them already.

"We'll talk about it later," she promised, retrieving Ryder from the baby swing. She unhooked his harness and scooped him into her arms. His warm body felt like heaven. Thankfully, the rash had completely disappeared along with his brief bout of the sniffles.

They left the farmer's market at ten a.m., so Marla could refrigerate her purchases and change into a nicer outfit for her brother's party. Brianna kept on her tank top, shorts and flip flops. She packed a swimsuit in case she decided to use the pool at Michael's house.

Marla would be busy watching Ryder. He was already slated for swimming lessons. Kids in Florida had to learn pool survival skills early. The thought of him in the water made her heart race as painful memories surfaced to haunt her.

By the time Marla was ready, Dalton had barreled in the door. He'd come home in time so they could drive together.

Brianna left in a separate car since she planned to meet friends later.

"I have news," Dalton said during the drive north. He kept his eyes focused on the road.

"What's that?" Marla had already related her conversation with Millie to him. In the backseat, Ryder was singing to himself, perhaps one of tunes he'd learned at day care.

"Henry, the village preacher, used to own a garment company. He's the one who obtains costumes for the cast."

"That's right, and Phil planned to eliminate his position as middleman and go directly to the manufacturer. What about it?"

"Henry's firm outsources their labor overseas so they can charge low prices. But it seems they use sweatshop labor to produce the fabric, and that's illegal in this country."

"Why would it matter? Henry sold his interest, didn't he?"

"No, he's still a silent partner. Perhaps Phil used this information to blackmail Henry. He'd lose more than his job at the village if the authorities found out."

"Did you ever ask Henry about his real purpose at the fishing shack? You've established it wasn't to seal a container of live bait. So why did he lie about it?"

"That remains to be seen."

"No word on Gilda's cause of death yet?"

He grimaced. "Still waiting on it. If she was poisoned, it's clearly a premeditated act. So was Phil's death. Someone had to hide or carry the tomahawk to the boardwalk. But the two methods of murder are completely disparate."

"Maybe two different people are involved."

"I doubt it. It may have been a matter of opportunity. The battle scene was the perfect distraction for getting rid of Phil. Gilda's manner of death is only a guess until we get confirmation. Anyway, enough shop talk for now. Let's have a pleasant afternoon."

Dalton hauled their baby supplies and Michael's gift inside her brother's house, while Marla carried Ryder. They were

179

greeted with a flurry of hugs and kisses. Marla got tired of standing and found a seat on the family room sofa. The morning's excursion in the heat had left her feeling wilted.

While Ryder's grandmothers watched him play, Marla slumped bonelessly back on the cushions. A delicious aroma that smelled like cinnamon buns emanated from the kitchen.

"Can I help you with anything?" she called to Charlene.

"No, thanks. I'll have the food ready shortly," her sister-in-law replied. "I can't believe how big Ryder has grown since we'd seen him last." She wore her natural golden-oak hair straight down her back and had on minimal makeup to cover her freckles.

"I could say the same about your kids." Marla's niece and nephew sat on the play mat along with Ryder. They occupied the toddler, handing him colorful blocks that fit together at either end. Jacob was ten and Rebecca had just turned seven last month. They had their mother's refined features and their dad's dark brown eyes.

Michael entered along with Marla's stepdad. He and Reed had been chatting while setting up a highchair at the dining room table. Reed went over to the bookshelves where he studied the titles on display. A retired literature professor, he always gravitated toward books. They were Charlene's collection more than her brother's. As a financial advisor, Michael was more into watching stock market changes on TV rather than reading.

Her brother's gaze zeroed in on her. "Marla, you look tired. Why don't you let Ryder nap here instead of rushing home? We can open our temporary crib."

"We'll see." She'd like to crash later but wouldn't be able to rest if they stayed.

"Are you eating enough?" her mother asked, sitting next to Marla. She smoothed the turquoise pants she wore along with a patterned top.

"Yes, Ma. We went to the farmer's market and playground this morning. The heat sapped my energy, that's all."

Ship's bells chimed in the background as the hour struck

noon. Familiar with Michael's timepiece collection, the sound didn't startle her. She hoped Charlene would serve the meal soon or Ryder would get off schedule.

"Dalton, how is your case going?" his mom asked with a frown of concern. Kate had twisted her auburn hair atop her head with a clip and looked cool in Capris and a silky blouse. She sat in an armchair opposite her husband, John.

Marla's father-in-law still appeared tall and dignified, despite wearing a pair of shorts and a Cuban shirt. The former attorney had foresworn dress clothes once he'd retired.

"We have several leads to follow," Dalton replied. He summarized the case, only sharing items that had been released to the press. Marla was glad her cousins weren't there in case Corbin's name surfaced. Thankfully, Dalton didn't mention him during his terse explanation.

"The food is ready," Charlene announced, saving him from further inquiries.

Dalton prepared a dish for Ryder at the buffet-style spread on the granite countertop before getting his own plate. Marla went over after she'd settled Ryder in his highchair. She wasn't that hungry and only took a dab of Charlene's baked egg and zucchini dish. The cheesy hash brown potatoes only mildly tempted her, too. Her sweet tooth zeroed in on the French toast casserole and the ginger cake. She cut herself generous helpings, wondering why she craved sugar all of a sudden. She chose orange juice for a drink.

"Marla, you'd said Millie and River do cooking demonstrations," Charlene said in a soft voice that reminded Marla of Violet at the park. The two of them would get along as schoolteachers. "Have you been by the city museum to ask Becky more about them?"

"No, but that's a great idea," Marla said, her pulse thrumming. The museum curator was the one who'd informed her about the reenactment. Becky had done a cookbook signing at the general store, where she'd met Uriah. She might know things about these people that would reveal more about them.

"Have you ever encountered Violet Honeycomb?" Marla asked Charlene. "She's a former teacher who gives tours at the schoolhouse in Pioneer Village."

Charlene's tawny eyes met hers from across the table. "Sorry, her name isn't familiar."

"You haven't heard any rumors about a teacher who got fired after she accused the principal at her school of sexual harassment?"

"No, but I can believe it." Charlene's mouth turned down. "It's typical that a man gets excused for bad behavior, while the woman bears the brunt of shame. Don't get me started on the lack of women's rights in this country. It's a *shandeh*," she said, using a Yiddish word meaning a shame or disgrace.

"Violet must have known the risks in accusing him," Marla stated.

"True, but she still exposed herself. She was lucky to find employment elsewhere." Charlene passed the coffee carafe down the table.

Marla exchanged glances with Dalton. *Possibly Violet jumped from the frying pan into the fire with Phil making advances toward her.* How had she reacted to his overture? Did she tell Uriah as she'd claimed, or did she plant an axe firmly in Phil's head to even the score?

One thing was clear. Charlene had a good idea about Marla talking to Becky.

Marla added a visit to the local history museum on her agenda for the next day.

Chapter Eighteen

Marla woke up bright and early on Monday to Ryder's cries. For once, she didn't miss sleeping in as she had so much to do that day. She rolled out of bed, leaving Dalton still asleep, and padded into her son's room. His big brown eyes stared up at her from his crib.

"What's the matter, sweetie? Are you hungry? Do you need a new diaper? Come here to mama." She picked him up and snuggled his warm body before commencing her morning routine.

As she went through her automated motions, she let her thoughts drift back to yesterday's events. Charlene had given her a new direction to follow. She'd run over to the museum this morning to talk to Becky. The curator might be able to fill her in on the players from the village. Then she'd pick up Robyn at eleven to interview Billy at the casino.

One thing at a time, hon. Take care of your family first.

Marla served their son breakfast and ate some of the scrambled eggs she'd prepared. Dalton appeared in the kitchen doorway, his pajama bottoms ruffled and his chest bare. His jaw looked scruffy and his hair mussed. A fond smile curved her lips at his unkempt appearance.

"It's late. You should have woken me," he said, stretching his arms with a yawn.

"You needed the extra sleep, and I was getting up anyway." Still in her night clothes, she sipped her coffee at the table.

"Hey, buddy," he greeted his son, who warbled happily back at him. "Drink your milk."

183

Ryder responded by throwing bits of egg on the floor and laughing.

"Go get dressed," Marla said. "I'll get Ryder ready this morning."

"Okay, thanks." He left for the bedroom while she attended to Ryder's needs.

Dalton reappeared a short while later to watch the child. In the master suite, Marla tossed on a pair of royal blue Capri pants with a comfortable top. She did quick work of applying makeup and fixing her hair.

When she returned to the kitchen, she noted Dalton had washed the dishes. He snatched his keys from a set of hooks on the wall.

"I'm leaving. I may be home late today," he said with an apologetic glance.

"What are you hoping to get done?" she asked, curious about his to-do list related to the murder case.

"I want to stop by the lab first to hound them for results on those chocolates you'd received. Then I'll track the fairground's transfer of funds to the village and correlate them with Phil's receipts as administrator. That's where things get fuzzy and where he may have been cooking the books. If there is a discrepancy, it might explain the source of deposits into his personal bank account."

"Don't forget to ask the M.E. for the report on Gilda's death."

"What are your plans for the day?" Dalton asked, patting his pockets to make sure he had everything he needed. It was a habit of his before he left the house.

"I'm heading to the city history museum to talk to Becky, as Charlene suggested. Then Robyn and I are going to the casino gift shop to meet Billy."

"It's good you're not going alone. Be careful, you hear?"

"Aren't I always?" She didn't wait for an answer and turned to the fridge to retrieve Ryder's lunch kit. Dalton left for work while she collected her son's gear. Brianna had promised to take the dogs for a walk after she got up.

Once Marla had dropped Ryder off, she headed to the museum. The single-story brick building stood amidst stately live oaks, mahogany trees and graceful palms.

The door was still locked as it wasn't quite nine, so she returned to her car and checked email on her phone. Drat, she'd forgotten to ask Dalton about Phil's cell phone. Had they found it yet? What about Gilda's device?

She sent Dalton a text, then put her phone away as the front door cracked open and a gray-haired woman peeked her head out.

Marla filed inside, the sole visitor at this early hour. The foyer held a ticket desk and a rack of brochures listing local events. A stone statue of a Native American woman holding an infant stood in the lobby's center. Signs pointed to different sections. Currently, they had a model train exhibit, an Everglades diorama, memorabilia from the local fire department, and a display on the Tequesta tribe. Dalton might enjoy the trains, she thought, resolving to mention it to him.

The gray-haired lady—a volunteer from her logo smock and nametag—greeted Marla with a friendly smile. "Welcome to our museum. Is this your first time here?"

"Not really. I was hoping to speak to Becky. I'm Marla Vail, a friend of hers. Is she in yet?" Marla realized she should have called ahead. With so many things on her mind, she hadn't thought about it. However, she had remembered to bring along the copy of Becky's cookbook that she'd purchased at the village store.

"Ms. Forest is in her office, but she has a meeting at nine-thirty. I'll see if she's available now." A few minutes later, the volunteer returned. "Go ahead but be aware Ms. Forest's time is limited."

"Thanks so much." Marla hurried down a short corridor where fossils and artifacts decorated the walls along with various educational posters.

Becky's door stood open. The curator, seated behind her desk, glanced up at Marla's entrance. Dusty books, photos of relics and scribbled notes covered every available surface along with various knickknacks. Sunlight streamed in through the lone window in the room.

"Good morning. What brings you here so bright and early?" Becky said with a grin. Her teeth shone white against her caramel complexion. She wore a coral blazer with a bone shell and cocoa brown pants that matched her eyes. Her silver-streaked hair added to her professorial air as she folded her hands on the desktop.

Marla retrieved the cookbook from her tote. "First, I'd like you to personalize this signed copy if you don't mind. I bought it at Pioneer Village. We went on Saturday for the reenactment. I'm sorry we missed your signing."

"No problem. I'm happy to add your name." Becky scribbled on the title page and then handed the book back to Marla with a flourish. "Now, why else are you here? You wouldn't have come all this way just to butter me up for nothing."

"How well you know me," Marla said with a chuckle, tucking the book back into her bag. "Dalton and I enjoyed the show but not the aftermath. Have you heard anything about it?" It was possible Becky had heard the news on TV about Phil's death.

"I haven't been in touch with anyone there since my event. What's going on?"

"Two people who'd worked at the park are dead. Their deaths may or may not be related."

Becky's eyes rounded. "Oh, no. Who were they?"

"One of them was Phil Pufferfish, the administrator and town marshal. The other was Gilda, a volunteer tour guide. She was also on the fairground's board of directors."

"What happened to them?" Becky asked, shaking her head in disbelief.

"Phil was murdered. Gilda's cause of death is yet to be determined, but it's suspicious."

"Good heavens. Is that why you're here? I assume your husband is on the case."

"Yes, he's in charge of the investigation. He found out that a real estate developer has made an offer to buy the village."

Becky pushed herself from the desk and stood. "No way! That's awful news. It would be a deep loss to the community if the living history park got eliminated. Do we need to raise a petition to prevent this deal?"

"I don't know if that would help. Uriah, the shopkeeper, might know more about it. He's been appointed temporary admin in Phil's absence. What did you think of him when you met for the signing? Had you known each other before? Is that how you got the gig at the village?"

Becky sank back into her seat with a disconsolate expression. "I'd approached Phil first about carrying my cookbooks in the store. He told me to ask Uriah who ordered their inventory. My publisher doesn't do returns, so this makes my books harder to place."

"Returns? What's that?"

"Bookstores can return unsold books for a credit. These returned books count against an author's royalties. Most major publishers offer a discount plus returns. Small presses can't always compete."

"So how did you get Uriah to agree to your request?"

"I offered my books on consignment. He agreed a signing might help to spur sales."

"Uriah didn't actually purchase any stock?"

"He said they didn't have the funds, although he seemed hopeful about the future. Uriah said next year they might be able to expand the shop. He seemed excited by the prospect."

That confirmed what he'd told Marla. Uriah supported Phil's plan because then he could add an apothecary section to the store. It didn't make sense that he would kill Phil. That might have made her eliminate him as a suspect if not for the things Violet had told her.

She tried a different approach to sound out Becky on the village women.

"Since your specialty is ancient Florida food practices, I'm wondering what you know about Millie and River. Millie does baking demos at the history park, and River offers samples of Native American dishes. River said you'd modified several of her recipes for your latest book. She was thrilled to be included in the acknowledgements."

Becky's eyes warmed. "I love listening to her stories. River has been very helpful to me. Millie, not as much. She's less willing to share, so we've mainly discussed cooking in general."

"Are you acquainted with Violet, the schoolteacher?"

"Not really. I've toured the schoolhouse, but that's it."

"How about Simon, the farmer? I understand he keeps an herb garden. Millie and River could both use fresh herbs for cooking."

Becky's brow furrowed. "I had a nice conversation with Simon after mentioning I'm a paleoethnobotanist. I asked him if he grew any of the early Florida food sources like cocoplum, pond apple, saw palmetto, or cabbage palm. He said those native plants were part of the original habitat. I spotted some of them in the forested area."

"River makes flour from coontie roots. We sampled her cakes. Where does she get the plants?"

"Simon grows it for her in a corner of his farm. Did you know that many plants were raised by the Native Americans for their fibers in addition to being a food source? These fibers were used in construction, clothing, rope-making and basket weaving."

Marla wasn't interested in a history lesson unless it pertained to the case. "Did Simon share what else he grows in addition to corn and such?" she asked, aware that her time there was limited.

"He cultivates indigo for Millie to use as a dye for her fabrics. Otherwise, he rambled on about how large tracts of land were being plowed down for commercial usage. He'd hate the idea of a developer razing the land."

"I'd agree with him on that point." Did Simon hate the idea so much that he did away with Gilda, hoping her demise would sour the deal? Then he should have been in favor of Phil's proposal that would have kept the village intact. He had no motive to get rid of Phil unless the administrator had found out something about him that Simon didn't want aired.

"There's one more thing," Becky mentioned. "Simon said, 'This land is far richer than anyone realizes.' I thought he was referring to the soil's fertility and let it go. But when I expressed interest in viewing his crops at the far edge of the property, he shut down."

"Really? That's where I'm thinking his herb garden is located." What was going on that made Simon guard this piece of land so carefully?

Becky checked her watch. "I hate to cut this short, but I have an appointment at nine-thirty."

"No problem. I appreciate your information. It's been great seeing you again. I'll have to bring Dalton by to see the model train exhibit."

As she left, Marla tightened her resolve to get a glimpse of Simon's pet project, and she didn't mean his animals. Simon's remark about riches made her even more determined to see his distant plot of land. Maybe Billy would offer a tip on how to view the farmer's secret garden.

She reviewed the questions she wanted to ask the village shaman on her way to get Robyn. Marla picked her friend up at the assigned time and they headed to the casino. Marla had only been there once before and cringed at the memory. The loud noises and flashing lights produced stimulus overload.

Robyn looked fresh and cool in khakis and a popover top. She'd made up her eyes and had on rose lipstick that comple-mented the pink streak in her hair.

"I loved the village when I visited yesterday," Robyn said after fastening her seatbelt. "You were right that it takes more than one day to see everything."

189

Marla flicked a glance her way. "Who did you meet?"

"Henry, the pastor, was in the church. He gave a long spiel on the building's history. When I asked if they rented out space for special events, he became less friendly."

"That's because Phil wanted to bring in a real minister, in which case Henry would have lost his role. Did Henry say anything else that might be relevant to the case?"

"Not really. I went to the schoolhouse next. Violet seemed very sweet. She explained how kids of different ages shared the schoolroom in the old days. Children must have had more stamina back then to sit on those hard chairs all day."

"Did you ask about archery lessons?" Marla focused on the road as another driver cut in front of them.

"The shopkeeper said Angus, Millie and Lizzy offered workshops."

"Really? It's interesting how neither Millie nor Lizzy have mentioned those skills. What else did you learn?"

Robyn peered out the window at the passing scenery. "I toured the big house but couldn't speak to Lizzy privately. When the group tour was over, she went back inside."

"She didn't say anything about Simon? Lizzy and her brother are entangled with the farmer in some way."

"No, sorry. And I avoided the Seminole camp, so I didn't get to meet the folks there."

Marla nodded. "It's best that Billy didn't see you before today."

"Is Dalton any closer to nailing a suspect?"

"He's still tracking various leads. By the way, it's a good thing you didn't taste any of those chocolates I received at the salon. He sent them to his lab to be tested for poison."

Robyn gaped at her. "Omigosh, I might have eaten one!"

"We need to be careful what we say to Billy today. Somebody is pissed off at my interference."

"Obviously. Oh, my. Let's hope Billy isn't the guilty party."

"For sure. How about if you soften him up by admiring the

goods in his store, and I'll ask the harder hitting questions. That way, we won't be putting your safety at risk."

"Sounds good to me. Do you have any other trails to follow?"

Marla thought about her next move. "I still want to have a chat with my cousin Corbin. He works with Simon at the village farm. He could be a good source if I can get him to talk."

"He might be more willing to spill the beans if you're not at the village." Robyn's eyes glimmered. She enjoyed being a participant in Marla's exploits.

"I know, but he didn't give me his contact info," Marla said. "Susan is checking into animal rescue places in the vicinity to see if he volunteers at any of them."

"That's a great idea."

Robyn fell silent, while Marla's body sagged. She should be planning Dalton's party, taking her mother to lunch, and visiting Tally's shop. Guilt weighed her down, but she and Dalton had to catch the killer before life could return to normal.

Once at the casino, she found a parking space in the already crowded lot. Gamblers didn't have a favorite time of day. They were present at all hours to spend their money.

Her ears protested the dings and clangs from gaming machines as they entered through a set of double-wide doors into a huge space surrounding a central bar. Corridors branched off from this circle like spokes on a wheel. Off to the side, cashiers exchanged vouchers for money at a series of windows.

Marla stepped forward, noting the ocean blue carpet underfoot that depicted the sea along with dolphins and fish and other creatures of the deep. Art works on the walls continued the theme, with a cascading fountain in one corner where gamblers could toss in coins for luck—another way to lose more of their money.

Marla's nose wrinkled from the smell of whiskey and cigarette smoke. Waitresses circulated around carrying trays laden with cocktails.

"I hope this shaman is friendlier than the last one we met,"

Robyn said, her steps slowing. "Remember Herb Poltice and his protest at our clubhouse? Have you asked Billy if he knows the guy?"

"It hasn't come up in conversation. Besides, Herb works at a different casino." Marla recalled the palatial exterior of his place. It was much more elaborate than this smaller building.

"Still, shamans might know each other, especially if they're in the same tribe." Robyn resumed her pace toward the gift shop at the opposite end of the central atrium. Naturally, it would be situated within the highly trafficked concourse.

"We'll see. I have other questions to ask. I don't want to dig up old dirt." Marla recalled the murder case where their homeowners' association president had died. She had enough on her mind without raising that subject.

They stopped in front of the gift shop. Beaded jewelry, woven blankets and feathered dreamcatchers gleamed in the window display along with tacky Florida souvenirs such as plastic alligators and plush flamingos.

Inside, Marla almost didn't recognize Billy without his headdress and native garb. Standing at the cashier's desk, he wore a dress shirt tucked into a pair of belted jeans. His longish black hair and chiseled features exuded sensuality. Marla saw Robyn stare at him as though mesmerized.

"Marla, isn't it? What are you doing here?" He glanced from her to Robyn and gave her friend a speculative once-over.

"This is my friend, Robyn Piper. She wanted to see the casino, and I remembered that you worked here part-time. I was hoping to say hello. Robyn visited Pioneer Village yesterday. She must have missed your exhibit."

Robyn came to her senses and gave a tinkling laugh. "There was so much to see. I'll have to return another time. What role do you play at the village?"

He puffed out his chest. "I'm the village shaman."

"Is that for real or part of your job?" Robyn asked, batting her lashes.

"I have the proper certifications. It's regrettable you missed my performance. You'll have to return when I'm demonstrating my skills."

"What would those be? Fixing thatched roofs? Or maybe archery?"

He raised his arms like a prize fighter and bunched his muscles. "I'll have you know that I wrestle alligators with my bare hands."

"Is that so?" Marla cut in, figuring she should say something. "I didn't see any listing for that activity in the brochure. Simon said you perform the green corn dance."

"What's that?" Robyn asked. "Is it similar to a hot dog eating contest?"

He stiffened at her teasing tone. "I should say not. It's an annual celebration of spiritual renewal dedicated to the Creator for blessing us with food."

"Why is the corn green? Is it picked before it's ripened?"

"That's correct. The ritual takes place prior to harvesting, usually in the spring."

Robyn gave him a coy glance. "Do you have to take your shirt off for this dance?"

"That depends on the audience." His voice took on a husky quality. "I could give you a private demo if you're really interested."

All right, that's enough, Robyn. You're supposed to be admiring his merchandise and not his physique. Or are you flirting for real?

Either way, it was time to start asking more direct questions related to Phil's murder.

Chapter Nineteen

"I understand you use medicinal remedies in your role as shaman," Marla said to Billy. "Does Simon grow the herbs you need, or do you get them from a commercial source?"

Billy's mood sobered. "Why do you care?"

"I'm interested in Simon's herb garden. Would you happen to know what he grows there aside from the usual plants?"

"That's his business. Those of us with assigned roles usually stick to our sectors. I've only seen the farm on a few occasions."

"Then Simon doesn't supply herbs to either you or River for her stews?"

"Did your husband send you to grill me again? I've already told him what I know."

Marla realized he hadn't answered her question about getting herbs from Simon. "I'm just trying to help him solve his case. Don't you want the victims to get justice?"

"Victims? There's only one." Doubt filtered into his voice.

"Gilda's death is suspicious. My husband is waiting on test results to determine how she died." Marla stepped closer. Focusing on their conversation, she was able to block out the muted slot machine sounds from outside the shop. Gentle flute music played from hidden speakers inside Billy's domain, where the scent of sage pervaded the air.

"Why would someone want to harm Gilda?" Billy asked with a puzzled frown. "I can see how Phil's plan would upset people, but Gilda played a minor role at the park."

"Phil's proposal would have eliminated the Seminole

exhibit. I know you opposed his bid to secede from the fairground," Marla said to expand upon his statement.

She glanced at Robyn, who'd wandered over to a selection of woven baskets. Her friend gave a small nod in return as though content to let Marla take the lead. Had her coy behavior earlier been a ploy to soften Billy up? If so, Robyn's acting skills could land her a part at the village.

The creases deepened beside Billy's eyes. "If Phil wanted to add a café, he could have chosen another site. Once we had become independent, I would have convinced him to keep our camp." He jabbed a finger at Marla, whose expression must have betrayed her thoughts. "It wasn't me who killed him. I'm just sorry my prized tomahawk was used to do the deed. Poor fellow. That was a bad way to die."

A surge of sympathy hit her at Billy's predicament. He had motive, means, and possibly opportunity, and yet his words rang true to her ears.

"Why keep a real weapon instead of a prop?" she asked, curious.

He stared into the distance. "The tomahawk was a gift from my father. It was decorated with our clan colors. However, it didn't do any good sitting in my closet at home." A look of sadness washed over his face as he spoke.

"Where did you store it on-site?"

His gaze met hers and held no hidden nuances. "In the central meeting hut at the encampment."

"In plain sight or hidden away from prying eyes?"

"It was included in our display. That was a mistake on my part."

"That means anyone could have come by and stolen it," Marla said, realizing Dalton had probably asked Billy the same questions. However, the man might recall something new that could help them. "How would this person have gotten past you and River?"

He gazed at her askance. "Are you kidding? Any one of the

costumed characters could have stashed it under their outfit. One of my beaded lanyards was missing, too. The guilty party could have tied the axe to their leg under a long dress or robe."

"Such as Henry? I saw you talking to him at the chickee hut before my friend Susan and I met you. What was that about?"

His face reddened. "You'll have to ask the preacher. It's his story to tell."

That gives me another reason to visit Henry besides his button collection.

"Do you definitely believe one of your colleagues is involved in Phil's murder as opposed to a visitor, then?"

"That's right. I don't like to consider what it means for the rest of us."

"It means you need to watch your backs," Marla advised. Likely the reenactors had come a day or two before to rehearse their roles, and exhibitors would have been setting up their booths. However, these people would have been noticed if they'd strayed from their posts.

Marla conceded that Billy wasn't high on her suspect list. For some reason, she believed him. He'd freely admitted he opposed Phil's plan. If the village had succeeded in gaining control of their tract, he probably could have convinced Phil to add a café elsewhere.

As for Phil hitting on River, the former model could handle herself from what Marla had seen. Unless River had some other grudge, she didn't score a spot on Marla's list at all.

"I hope you'll warn River to be careful," she told Billy. "Do you have any ideas about who might have stolen your tomahawk?"

"Whoever it was meant to frame me. I noticed it missing when I got to work that day and was gathering my equipment for the battle. I assumed it had been stolen the day before, but now I'm not so sure."

"Who locks up the place each night?"

"The fairground secures the perimeter after hours."

"Really? I would have thought the village took care of their own property. Did Gilda have access to a key?" Maybe she'd stolen the tomahawk and killed Phil to eliminate the competition for the real estate deal. But then who had done away with her, if she'd been murdered?

"Gilda may have had one," Billy said, stacking receipts into a pile on the counter. He paused to meet Marla's gaze. "I can't believe she was on the board of directors for the fairground this entire time. If it wasn't her, she could have let someone else inside."

Like whom—the developer? That exalted person wouldn't want to get his hands dirty by being directly involved. "Could your weapon have been stolen the morning of the battle instead?" Marla asked, needing to get a clear timeframe of events.

"It's possible. I was late in getting to work that day. I had to collect my horse before going to work."

"Oh, you ride a horse, too?" Robyn said, rejoining them. She held a few souvenirs in her hands. "I'd love to see you astride."

"Robyn!" Marla couldn't believe her friend's impudence. She turned back to Billy, who had a dumbstruck look on his face. It made his high cheekbones stand out and pulled his skin taut. Surely with his good looks, he was used to come-ons from women. Could he really be affected that much by Robyn's boldness?

She'd never seen Robyn act this way, either. Did she genuinely like the man?

"Do you own the horse?" Robyn asked. "If so, I'm wondering if you give lessons. Does it come from a stable nearby?"

What's she getting at now? Does it matter where the horse originated?

"We rent the horses from a local ranch."

"Who covers the cost? I mean, who pays for the reenactors and all the props needed for the battle? I'm so sorry I missed it. I imagine the scene was glorious." Robyn's expression indicated she thought Billy's part in the drama would be glorious.

"In truth, the real event was a massacre. There was no glory in it, even for our ancestors. They were merely defending their land. But to answer your question, the fairground pays for everything. They're the ones who gain the profit."

"Doesn't the village get a percentage? Those funds could be used for repairs," Marla said, following Robyn's line of reasoning.

Billy snorted. "As administrator, Phil received our share. Has your husband checked the records to see how much the fairground transferred over, compared to what Phil recorded in his ledger? It would be nice to know the fairground didn't stiff us."

"What are you saying?" She didn't mention that Dalton was already following the paper trail. Standing at her side, Robyn plopped the items she held down on the counter.

"The village isn't getting our due. Somebody is cheating us." Billy's voice held a hint of anger. "Angus implied the same thing at our town meetings, but he never had proof."

"If it's the fairground, they could have a reason," Marla suggested, the idea just now popping into her head. "They could mean for the village to fall into disrepair so attendance would drop. Then it would seem more logical for a developer to buy the tract."

Robyn tapped her arm. "You're forgetting something. In addition to Phil's offer, the fairground also received a bid to buy the village from Lizzy."

"This is true." And it implied Lizzy had a motive to do away with both Gilda and Phil so her bid would be the only one left. That applied only if Gilda's participation was crucial to the developer's interest. Once Dalton ruled her death a homicide, he should look into this angle.

Marla addressed Billy. "Speaking of Lizzy, have you ever met her brother? He owns the adjacent property. He has a farm, but he doesn't grow corn there."

Billy glanced at the outside corridor where a noisy crowd had gathered. "I can't say we've met. Nor has Lizzy ever mentioned a sibling before. It's odd she wouldn't tell us about him."

Marla made one last-ditch effort to gain new information.

She showed him the button photos on her phone. "Have you seen this object before? Like, is it used on anyone's costume at the village?"

Billy frowned as he studied the photos. "Nope, I've not seen anything like it. Now if you'll excuse me, ladies, I need to get back to work." He threw Robyn a regretful glance.

Robyn made her purchases then scribbled something on a scrap of paper and handed it over. "Here's my number if you think of anything else," she said, her tone making it clear she didn't only mean the murder case.

He grinned and tucked the paper inside his pocket. "Thanks. I'll be in touch."

As the group from the outer hallway entered the shop, Marla and Robyn headed toward the Old West themed restaurant.

Inside the darkened interior, cozy booths invited quiet conversation. Marla's gaze swept the paintings of western landscapes that adorned the walls and the pine-scented candles that sat on the wood tables. Subtle drumbeats played in the background.

"What were you thinking?" she asked Robyn once they were seated and had ordered drinks. "Billy is a murder suspect and you gave him your phone number. Are you nuts?"

"He's a hunk," Robyn replied with an adoring expression. "Did you see his muscles? He must work out in his spare time."

"Yeah, maybe he throws axes for sport like Angus." Marla calmed down as she sipped her iced coffee with cream. "I don't think Billy is guilty, though. As he said, someone meant to frame him or to deflect attention in another direction. Dalton didn't get any prints off the murder weapon. Either the killer wiped it clean, or they wore gloves."

"That's an interesting notion." Robyn took a few gulps of her unsweetened iced tea. "I noticed handmade gloves for sale in the village gift shop. They had gardening gloves, too. It wouldn't have to be those blue Nitrile things."

"You're right. It makes more sense that any gloves used would fit in with someone's costume. I'll ask Dalton if he found a pair discarded anywhere near the body. Most likely, the killer filled them with rocks and tossed them in the pond." Marla drummed her fingers on the table, matching the beat on the speaker system.

"What do you know about the button so far?" Robyn's clear brown eyes regarded Marla. Her face was more expressive since she'd started wearing contact lenses.

"Henry gave the button to Uriah who gave it to Violet. The schoolteacher said Gilda borrowed it to check for similar ones in the sewing room. I need to talk to Henry again. He offered to show me his button collection."

"Don't go alone. He's still on the suspect list."

"I know. Henry had a motive to do away with Phil. If Phil's plan had succeeded, he would have lost his role as minister and his position as middleman in supplying costumes. However, he'd still run the fishing shack."

"True, but has he admitted why he went to the shed the day you and Millie saw him?"

"He said he went there to seal a container of live bait, but Dalton didn't find any on site."

"Who else do you believe might have done it?" Robyn fiddled with her spoon.

"Lizzy puzzles me. I can't help wondering what she's involved in with her brother and Simon. It would help if I could snip a branch from Greg's farm next door to the village. And before you say anything, don't worry. I won't go alone."

"I was going to say, if you need company, let me know."

Their lunch arrived, and they fell to discussing more mundane things about the salon and a fundraiser Robyn suggested to benefit a local charity. Those were always popular. They gained new customers through discounted services and the nonprofit gained a generous donation. This subject kept them chatting all the way home.

After dropping Robyn off at her place, Marla headed to her garage in the same community.

Grateful to be home, she freshened up inside, checked her email, and called her friend Tally. They were long overdue to get caught up on each other's lives.

After inquiring about Tally's son and her recent activities, Marla dove into the subject at hand. "I'm planning to hold a retirement party for Dalton on September eighteenth, so please reserve the date. I'll need a new dress if you see anything suitable."

"Awesome," Tally said in her bubbly voice. "I told you I'd already put aside an outfit from our fall line for you. When do you think you can stop by?"

"I'm not sure. Things have been hectic with Dalton's new case."

"How's that going? I try to keep up by watching the local news."

"It's progressing." Marla didn't feel like explaining the details. "Anyway, I'll let you know when I can come over." They spoke a few minutes more before breaking off.

Marla needed to give her brain a rest. She was tired of thinking about suspects and motives. She was about to throw a batch of laundry in the washer when her cell rang with a text message.

Your cousin Corbin works at Friends for Life Animal Rescue off the Sawgrass Expressway just north of Oakland Park Blvd, Susan wrote. *I hope this helps.*

Thanks, I appreciate the info, Marla typed back. *We'll touch base later.*

So much for her peace of mind.

After tossing the dirty clothes into the washing machine, she took a seat at her computer to look up the phone number for the animal shelter. She wouldn't go there without knowing if Corbin would be present.

"Hi, is Corbin there today? I'm Marla Vail, his cousin," she said when a woman answered her call. "I have some questions about my dogs and was hoping to stop by to see him."

Lucky and Spooks sniffed the floor at her ankles as though

they knew she was talking about them. She'd let them outdoors earlier and given them treats upon their return inside.

"He's not in right now, but he'll be here Tuesday morning," the lady responded. "Shall I tell him you'll be coming?"

Marla did a mental review of her schedule. "Please do me a favor and don't mention it to him. I'd like my visit to be a surprise."

Marla disconnected and ruminated over her plans. She also needed to set a date to view Henry's button collection, but barely had any spare time.

Eager to discuss her findings with Dalton, she suppressed her news until after he'd come home, eaten his dinner and looked more relaxed. Ryder was already asleep by the time he got home. She suspected he'd timed his arrival that way on purpose so the house would be quiet. Brianna was in her bedroom reading a book, and the dogs had settled onto their cushions.

She prattled on about her events of the day before hitting him with a question.

"Where can I find Henry outside of the village? He's offered to show me his buttons."

Dalton pulled out his cell phone, looked an item up, and sent it to her device. *Bingo!* Henry's home address. He lived in Davie, the next town over.

Marla gaped at Dalton. "That's it? You're handing me his contact info without any warnings to be cautious?"

"Just take someone with you for backup. We know Henry lied about his reason for going to the fishing shed the day of the murder. Maybe you'll have better luck in getting an explanation from him."

"Any lab results yet?" she asked, aware this had been his first stop earlier in the day.

"They know the chocolates contain an additive but are having a hard time identifying it. Nor have I received the M.E.'s report. It's frustrating." He scraped a hand through his hair. "Tell me again about your conversation with Billy."

Marla sank into a kitchen chair. She'd put away the last of their dishes. "We talked about his tomahawk and who might have stolen it and how they'd have access. I couldn't get much else out of him, because Robyn flirted outrageously and then a crowd of tourists came into the shop."

He smiled at her words. It eased the lines on his face and relaxed his posture. "Robyn likes Billy? That's something I didn't expect to hear."

"I know. She practically threw herself at the guy. I've never seen her act like that before."

"She'd better not go out with him until this case is solved."

"I told her the same thing, and I hope she listens. I'm going to see Corbin tomorrow. Susan found out where he volunteers at an animal shelter. Don't you have his home address in your files? Cynthia wouldn't give it to me."

"His sister respects his privacy. So do I."

"All right." At least Corbin wouldn't feel Dalton had betrayed him. "Have you eliminated anyone from your suspect list?"

He nodded, ignoring a lock of peppery hair that had fallen onto his forehead. More silver streaks had infiltrated his natural black hair over the past couple of weeks. It wasn't fair that men appeared more distinguished as they aged while women just looked older. Covering gray roots was a large part of her business.

"I've narrowed things down to Millie, Violet and Lizzy for the women," Dalton said, a furrow creasing his brow. "As for the men, Angus, Uriah, Henry and Simon are still viable suspects."

"And Billy?"

"I'm on the shelf about Billy. I want to believe him, but he had a strong reason to get rid of Phil. River vouches for his claim that the tomahawk must have been stolen, but she's his friend. And, it would have been easy for him to disappear during the smoky battle scene to meet up with Phil."

"The same could be said for the rest of the cast. I imagine

the village emptied out during the reenactment. Nobody could vouch for each other's movements."

Dalton stood and pushed his chair back in place. "My brain is too tired to debate the subject. Let's shelve this discussion until tomorrow."

She rose and studied his worn face. "Sorry, I should let you get your rest. We don't want you to get sick before your big retirement party."

"What party?"

Her mind scrambled for a logical response. "Surely, the boys at work must be having a sendoff for you." Her skin heated. Did he suspect she was formulating her own plans?

"Nobody has said a word to me. Do you know something I don't?" he asked with a coaxing smile.

"Nuh-uh. I just assumed they wouldn't let you go without a proper celebration."

"We'll see. I'll take Ryder in the morning so you can interview Corbin at the animal shelter. What do you intend to ask him?"

"I want the scoop on Simon. Maybe Corbin has seen his herb garden. Then there's the issue of Simon, Lizzy and her brother. If possible, I'd like to obtain a sample of Greg's plants so we can determine what he's growing. Corbin might know a way inside."

She wouldn't have to do this if Dalton could get a warrant to search the brother's farm, but he didn't have a reasonable cause.

Marla saw the words forming on his lips. "I know," she said, raising a hand to forestall him. "Don't trespass onto private property. At least, not without backup. I've learned my lesson and won't go alone."

His eyes turned to molten steel. "Good, because Greg Harris could be dangerous. For all we know, he might be involved in something that he would kill to protect."

Chapter Twenty

Tuesday morning found Marla bright and early at the animal rescue place where Corbin volunteered. It was seven o'clock, and she didn't have to be at work until nine. Hopefully her cousin could settle her questions about his mentor at the history village.

She faced a modest house that had been converted into a pet shelter. Other residences along this street had also been commercialized. A locksmith, a real estate office, and a cell phone repair place had set up shop there.

Marla imagined herself operating a salon this way. She'd convert the living and dining rooms up front into hair and nail stations. Extra bedrooms could become waxing suites. That would leave the master bedroom, kitchen, and family room for her family's private use.

No, thanks. She'd rather be in a modern setting and live away from her work environment. However, this arrangement could work for folks who wanted to save money on rent. They wouldn't need a separate storefront for their place of business.

She rang the bell, eliciting a series of barks from the interior. She thought of Lucky and Spooks with an affectionate smile. They had a loving home, unlike these poor creatures. Corbin was doing a good deed by working here.

"I'm coming," called a muffled voice from within.

Marla bided her time by examining the Adirondack chairs on the front porch and the thriving potted plants. Somebody had a green thumb. The exterior paint seemed well-maintained, as were the shingle roof and the gutters, telling her the owner took pride in the place.

"Oh. It's you!" she exclaimed when her cousin threw open the door. She'd expected the lady from the phone call.

Corbin looked disheveled with his plaid shirt half tucked into his jeans and his hair uncombed. Gray nestled in his strands that she hadn't noticed before, and he needed a shave.

Wait, was he living here? When he'd said he lived near the nature preserve, she assumed he had his own place. Or was this a room and board arrangement where he worked for his keep?

"Marla, what are you doing here?" he said with a scowl.

"Can I come inside? I need to talk to you."

His eyes narrowed. "How did you find me?"

"If you're wondering, Cynthia didn't give me your address. I knew you liked animals and called around. It's wonderful that you volunteer at a shelter." She spoke in a gushy tone, focusing on his work with animals so he'd invite her in.

To her relief, he gestured her inside. "You can follow me around as I do my chores."

She trailed him into a large, sunny room that must have been a living room in its previous incarnation. It had wide windows, worn couches, and children's drawings tacked to the walls.

He noticed the direction of her glance. "We hold workshops for school kids. They like learning about the animals and take our flyers home. Once a year, we have a big fundraiser and get lots of adoptions. All our pets need permanent homes."

"Where do they sleep?" she asked, thinking it was too hot in the summer to house them outdoors.

"We've converted the Florida room at the back of the house. If we can raise the funds, we'd like to expand and add more facilities."

"You do know that we participate in fundraisers at my salon, yes? We'd be happy to support your events."

He flashed her a quick grin. "That's generous of you, Marla. I'll keep it in mind. Come this way. I have to refill the food bowls."

She followed him to the rear where he distributed the feed

and refreshed the water dishes. Various pens in the large, sunny room held smaller dogs and a variety of cats.

"Who owns this place?" she asked, wondering at her cousin's arrangement.

"I do," a woman from behind said in a raspy voice.

Marla whirled to face a sleepy-headed woman in a shift dress and sandals. She had luxurious black hair that cascaded over her shoulders and cornflower blue eyes. Her gaze was curious as she regarded Marla.

"I'm sorry to disturb you this early," Marla said, embarrassed by her intrusion.

"This is Iliana Mendez," Corbin stated. "Iliana, meet my cousin, Marla Vail. She's married to the homicide detective I told you about."

The woman's eyes widened. "Ah, yes, we spoke on the phone."

"It's nice to meet you in person," Marla told her. "You're the owner?"

"*Si.* These dogs and cats are my children. I want them to be happy."

"They must keep you busy. How did you get started in the business?"

"I worked as a pet groomer in Boca Raton at a shop that catered to the elite. A stray dog hung out in the parking lot. I felt sorry for the fellow and took him in. Soon I found myself with more strays. My apartment manager said either they had to go or I did, so I bought this place."

"She's great with animals," Corbin said. "They all love her." From the adoring look in his eyes, he felt the same way.

Marla glanced between them. "Forgive me for asking, but are you two together?"

Iliana lifted her chin. "*Si*, we are. I've been urging Corbin to go back to school to get trained as a vet technician, but he's stubborn about it."

"He can be difficult," Marla agreed, remembering Cynthia

had offered him money for school that he'd refused. What was holding him back—his pride? "Anyway, I won't keep him long. I know he has more chores to do."

Iliana pointed to a set of sliding glass doors that led to a screened patio and a large backyard. "If you'll excuse me, I need to check on our newest resident. Spangles was abandoned on the roadside, poor fellow. He has a limp from a leg injury. He's outside doing his business."

Marla glanced outdoors and spied the shaggy dog exploring a far corner of the fenced yard. They'd have plenty of space for additional structures when they were ready to expand.

She handed the woman a business card. "I own a salon in town. We participate in fundraisers. Let me know when you plan your next event, and we can help."

"Thanks; that would be great." Iliana took the card and left with a wave. A remnant of her sunny presence remained to warm the room.

Marla turned her attention back to her cousin who gazed after Iliana with a puppy dog expression. *Oh, dear, he has it bad.*

"I like her," she told him. "How long have you known each other?"

"It's been nine months. We ran into each other at the vet's office."

"Does she know about your past history?"

"Yes, and it doesn't matter to her. Iliana has a big heart and a generous soul."

Aware she'd be on her feet for the rest of the day at work, Marla took a seat at the kitchen table. "It can't be easy to run a nonprofit shelter," she said in a sympathetic tone. "Are there grants for funding available?" If not, they'd have to rely on large donations and constantly strive to find ways to raise money. Feeding and housing pets, along with their grooming and medical needs, were expensive responsibilities.

He shook his head. "We do fundraisers, and we have several patrons who contribute. Iliana handles the business angle."

"I'm glad you found someone, Corbin. Have you told your sister about her?"

"Cynthia knows." Corbin yanked out a chair and sat opposite her. "Why are you really here, Marla?"

"I'm planning a retirement party for Dalton and would like to send you an invite," she said, mentioning the date. "Now that I know about Iliana, I'll include her as well. I didn't have any way to contact you aside from the history park."

"All right, but that's not the only reason for your visit."

"True. I'm curious as to why you took a position as Simon's assistant at Pioneer Village."

"I needed a job and Simon told me there was an opening. It was hard getting a position with my history."

"Was Phil aware of your background when he hired you?"

Corbin hesitated, his gaze troubled. "That man was a sly actor. He knew about all of us and said he supported people who needed fresh starts in life. But a few weeks after I'd been working there, he offered to lend me money to become a licensed vet technician. In return, I needed to alter the village ledger for him."

"In what way?" Marla barely breathed, afraid to say something wrong that would shut Corbin down.

"I should show that the income from the fairground was less than it actually was. Phil said my skills in the financial sector would be useful to him." Corbin spoke in a bitter tone as though he should have known the job offer came with strings attached.

Marla stared at him. "He admitted his embezzlement scheme? Wasn't he afraid you'd tell someone?"

Corbin snorted. "Who would believe an ex-con? Phil would make sure the finger pointed my way rather than at him. At any rate, I refused his offer. I said I didn't want his dirty money."

"How did he react?" she asked, stunned by this revelation. It certainly confirmed their theories about Phil's source of bank deposits.

"Phil laughed at me and said I'd better keep my mouth shut if I wanted to keep my job. I noticed he increased my pay, though. That was his way of ensuring my silence."

"I'm surprised you stayed under such awkward circumstances," she said with a surge of sympathy. The poor guy couldn't seem to get a break.

"I stayed out of loyalty to Simon. He's been good to me." Corbin leaned inward, his elbows on the table. "I'm the one who put a bug in Angus's ear about the village funds. He's an honest chap and I knew he wouldn't let things slide."

"Too bad he never got proof." Marla was glad to have her opinion confirmed about the blacksmith's integrity. "I understand Angus clashed with Phil at the town meetings. Did you attend those events?"

"Nah. Simon would go to represent our sector."

"Regarding Phil, how come you didn't mention his request to Dalton? His misuse of village funds may have factored into his death."

"Are you kidding? The cops would suspect me. I don't want to get in trouble again."

She could understand his reaction. "Who do you think killed the guy? We know about Phil's proposal to buy the village tract from the fairground. Some people supported his plan and others opposed him."

"I heard rumors about a development deal. Phil would have fought it when he found out."

"So would Lizzy. She'd put in a bid to buy the property herself."

He gave a bark of laughter. "Lizzy believes in those ghost stories and the legend of the missing gold. If you ask me, she's off her rocker."

"Or she knows something we don't. Are you aware her brother owns the adjacent farm? I overheard the two of them talking and they mentioned Simon. Would you know anything about that? What would they have in common?"

Corbin glanced at her as though she had marbles missing upstairs. "They're farmers. They could have been discussing the soil quality or which fertilizers are best."

Marla shook her head. "I don't believe it was anything innocuous. Simon is doing something fishy in his herb garden. He wouldn't let me see it when I visited his site."

Corbin scraped his chair back and stood. "I mind my own business. Whatever Simon is doing, that's his privilege."

"I'm aware he was a prison mate of yours and that he'd been convicted for cultivating pot. Is that what he's growing back by the fence?"

"I seriously doubt it. He told me he's gone straight, and I believe him."

"Prove it and show me his private garden. If he is involved in something illegal, you could be considered an accessory."

"And I'm telling you he's innocent. You're sniffing up the wrong tree if you think he murdered Phil." Corbin's tense posture indicated his adamancy on the topic.

"I'm only concerned that you're not drawn into this. If Simon and Lizzy's brother have got something going on, Phil might have found out and demanded a cut of the pie. That would give them a motive for murder."

Corbin ran stiff fingers through his spiky black hair, while Marla noticed his paunch had grown. Iliana must be a good cook as well as a kind-hearted caretaker for lost pets.

"Fine, I'll take you there so you can see for yourself Simon has nothing to hide. You'll have to pay admission and come in through the front gate, but then head over to the petting zoo. Simon has an appointment in town, so he won't be there."

"I'm sorry to impose upon you, but we have to eliminate him as a suspect." Marla glanced at her watch. "It's eight-thirty already. I have to be at the salon by nine."

"The village doesn't open until then. I need to clean out the litter boxes and then I'll be free. We can do this now or not at all."

"Okay. I really appreciate it, Corbin."

Inside her car, she texted Robyn that she'd be late to work. As long as she was on the edge of the farm, she could search for a means of entry into Greg's land. Simon might have a proper herb garden himself, but he could be helping the neighbor grow something shady. A fresh sample was the only way to get answers.

She considered what Corbin had said about Phil fighting the development deal. However, his stance would have had nothing to do with Gilda's death. Phil was already gone when she died. It seemed more likely Lizzy, Simon and Greg had conspired together to do away with both victims. That would clear the path for Lizzy's bid to win favor with the directors.

Clearing her thoughts, she drove to the living history park and pulled into a space in the nearly empty lot. The gates hadn't opened yet, and several visitors hovered by the ticket booth. Marla waited in her car and accessed the browser on her cell phone. While the bushes she'd seen on Greg's property were not marijuana plants, that didn't exclude it from being grown elsewhere on his site.

According to what she researched, marijuana was an annual herb with two main strains. These each contained different levels of the psychoactive substance, tetrahydrocannabinol also known as THC, and of the medicinal substance, cannabidiol also known as CBD. The plant fibers were valued for hemp production.

The fan-like leaves had serrated edges. While Greg's crop didn't look anything like these pictures, he could grow pot in between the taller shrubs or even in a far corner of his land. She'd only know for certain if she could get a closer look.

She bought a ticket as soon as the booth opened. Her steps veered to the right where the farm was located along with the Seminole camp and Baffle House. The sewing room was around there, too, on a divergent path.

The tourists must have headed toward the initial exhibits on the other side of the town square. Marla hurried along the concrete path, her strapped sandals tapping out a rhythm. Shady branches let in dappled sunlight while the humidity lent a veil of mist to the place. Birds twittered from overhead, breaking the stillness.

Corbin waited for her by the entrance to the petting zoo. "This way," he said without preamble. He set a quick pace toward the rear of the farm.

She followed him past the zoo with its animal smells and beyond past the corn fields. At the far corner of the property, he stopped.

"The herb garden is inside that hedge border. You'll see there's nothing unusual. The plants are labeled. I guess before Simon's arrival, this was part of a self-guided tour."

"Thanks so much. I know you have your chores with the chickens and such. I'll see myself back to the main path when I'm done."

"Don't stay too long. Simon is due back after lunch. See you around, Marla." With a wave, he turned and left.

Marla suppressed her joy. She thought it would be harder to get into the herb garden, like the neighbor's fenced property next door. But only a hedge bordered this plot of land.

She moved inside, the warm air redolent with basil, thyme and sage. As Corbin had said, each bed was labeled. The rows looked well-tended, with weeds absent and the soil rich. Simon's horticultural training must come in handy here, she decided, impressed by the garden. Too bad tourists couldn't see this portion, but perhaps Simon didn't want it to be contaminated by visitors tramping through.

Her gaze scanned the leafy rows. These herbs would be perfect for an on-site restaurant. It seemed likely that Simon shared them with Millie and River for their cooking demos.

Nothing looked like Cannabis plants.

Exiting the herb garden, Marla strode along the outer edge of the village until it ended at the woods. If Simon came through here to help Greg with whatever they had going on, where did he enter the adjacent property? She tramped through the trees to follow the fence. Her shoes crushed pine needles underfoot as she proceeded along the perimeter.

Wait, what's this? She stopped abruptly upon spying a hinged gate hidden behind a wall of bamboo. Not believing her luck, she pushed the gate open and walked through. No audible alarms rang to sound an intrusion.

Inside, rows of waist-high shrubs stretched into the distance. Their alternating-patterned leaves had an elliptical shape, slightly serrated edges, and tapered ends. These weren't marijuana plants, nor did she see any evidence of them having been planted elsewhere.

She broke off some branches and cringed as she touched the leaves. Their undersides had a hairy feel. Being careful to keep hold of the wood, she placed the branches into a paper evidence bag she kept in her cross-body purse. Then she crept along the border, hoping there weren't any security cameras monitoring her movements. She took photos along the way. Her breath came in pants, either from nerves or from the heat. Sand irritated her toes, rubbing against her skin.

A greenhouse, a large squat concrete building, and several smaller structures bordered the field. Wishing she had a pair of binoculars, she squinted at the residence in the distance. No one was visible but that didn't mean the owner wasn't around.

Hoping she wasn't under surveillance, she retraced her steps and left the way she'd come.

Marla located her cousin, thanked him for his assistance, and told him he'd been immensely helpful. Then she made a beeline for the park exit.

Before turning on the ignition inside her car, she used hand sanitizer to cleanse her skin. Then she sent Dalton her photos and mentioned that she had a sample of Greg's plants.

He called her back immediately. "What were you doing going there by yourself?" he shouted when she explained her foray next door. "Are you crazy? Somebody shot arrows at you last time you visited the park."

"Nobody posed a threat, and Corbin knew where I'd gone. He would have summoned help if I hadn't reappeared."

"You were foolish, Marla. We're not dealing with pranks here," Dalton said in a gruff tone. "We got the analysis back on the cookies Gilda ate. They were laced with nicotine, a highly toxic substance in its pure form. Only a few drops can kill a person."

Chapter Twenty-One

"Nicotine? Like in tobacco? Do you think that's what Greg is growing?" Marla doubted it. He wouldn't be so guarded for a common crop that was widely grown throughout the Southeast.

"Pure nicotine can be sourced from various products," Dalton explained. "You can probably find instructions on the Internet. It doesn't take much. Symptoms can begin within minutes of ingestion leading to death within hours. Nicotine is a potent neurotoxin that causes respiratory paralysis. Those chocolates you'd received were poisoned with the same substance."

Icy water washed through Marla's veins. "Dear Lord. To think Brianna or I might have eaten one." Her knees weakened and her heart beat a rapid staccato. "Does this mean anyone could be guilty and not just a cigarette smoker?"

"Correct. Your actions are a threat to someone, Marla. I'm concerned for your safety. And now you've gone off to trespass onto private property. How can I protect you when you act so rashly?"

"I'm sorry. I'll be more cautious." With a guilty flush, she glanced out the window to be sure no one was watching her as she switched on the ignition.

Dalton snorted. "I've heard that before."

"If nicotine killed Gilda, does that mean somebody baked it into those cookies?" she asked. "Or were they store bought? I suppose the substance could have been injected as well."

"Either way, it has the same effect," Dalton said. "I'll know more details when I get the written report. Can you stop by the station to drop off those leaves?"

215

"Sure. I'm already late to work so what's another few minutes?"

She swung by the police department, greeting people she knew as she got a visitor pass and proceeded inside. A restroom stop allowed her to thoroughly scrub her hands to get any residue from the leaves off her skin. She didn't want to risk contamination through skin absorption. She should have thought to wear gloves at Greg's farm.

Upstairs, Dalton's division smelled of freshly brewed coffee. His glass-enclosed space separated him from the other members of his bureau. Papers lay randomly strewn about his desk and countertops. She didn't know how he could find anything, but he claimed it was organized chaos.

"Can you rush this analysis since you know nicotine killed Gilda?" she asked, handing over the package. "If these are tobacco leaves, would that be enough to get a warrant for Greg's property?"

Dalton peeked inside the bag and frowned. "We'll see. These leaves don't look as broad as tobacco, but I'm no expert. And while Lizzy and Simon might be involved in something that involves the brother's farm, you should still be diligent around the other villagers. Have you made plans yet to interview Henry about his button collection?"

"I'm not sure when I can squeeze it in."

"Wait until I can go with you. Henry doesn't have a clear alibi and he lied about the bait. He's hiding something from us."

"I'll have to see when he's available." Marla appreciated Dalton's concern, but she wasn't one to back down from a case, especially if she was getting closer to the truth.

If necessary, she'd take a friend with her.

She suppressed a grin as the perfect person came to mind. Outside the police station, she paused under a queen palm and phoned Susan.

"Hey, it's Marla. I've another lead on an article for you. Remember Henry, the preacher from Pioneer Village? He collects buttons and has offered to show me his collection. Your women readers might be interested to learn more about the subject."

"I'll go with you to interview him, if that's what you're asking," Susan said with a chuckle.

Marla smiled. "You have me figured out. What's your schedule like? I need to call him for an appointment."

Henry agreed to see them on Thursday morning. He'd delay his departure for the village so they could view his collection at home. He seemed thrilled by the offer of publicity in Susan's magazine.

Would a killer want to be viewed in the public eye that way? Marla supposed it would depend upon their personality. A narcissist might delight in the attention. Henry didn't strike her as the boastful type, however. His passion for history seemed genuine in that he wanted to share his knowledge.

She could barely wait for the days to pass. She got through her clients that afternoon, while Wednesday's routine seemed to crawl by at a tedious pace.

Finally, Thursday arrived with a pink tinge on the horizon heralding late thunderstorms. Dalton hadn't been able to accompany her, so he was glad Susan would be going. He let Marla go with a word of advice. She should mention to Henry that her detective husband knew about her visit and that she would report to him when she left.

Marla picked up Susan and they headed over to Henry's house. He lived in a modest ranch-style home with a shingle roof and a white-columned front porch. The yard needed a trim and the house's paint needed a fresh coat. Whatever his goal was in making money off the costumes he sold to the village staff, it wasn't to upstage his neighbors.

Henry answered the door, and Marla scanned his button-down shirt tucked into a pair of tan pants. Even without his ecclesiastical robes, he appeared dignified. He'd brushed his blond hair with graying edges back from his broad forehead. A vision of Peter O'Toole from the classic film, *Lawrence of*

Arabia, filtered into her mind. Henry reminded her of that actor, albeit an aging version but no less handsome.

She introduced Susan. "We're excited to see your button collection," Marla said. "My husband is interested in hearing about it, too. I'll be briefing him about our visit afterward."

"I get it," Henry said with a twinkle in his blue eyes. He must suspect her true purpose in coming, but he didn't seem perturbed by the thought of another interrogation. Maybe he just looked forward to having an audience for his button lore.

They followed him into a cozy living room. Slipcovers protected the sofa and two armchairs. A coffee table, bookshelves, and end tables completed the furnishings. One corner held a scratching post.

"I have a cat," he explained with a diffident smile. "Bubbles is hiding."

"We have two dogs," Marla said to ease into their conversation. "Cats are a lot easier on visitors. Our pets would be sniffing at your feet."

She scanned the dusty knickknacks and framed family photos on his shelves. She didn't note any evidence of a wife and kids. These must have been from his earlier days.

"Please ignore the mess," he said with a sweeping gesture. His usual stentorian tones seemed subdued. "I don't have time to straighten up these days. I manage my mom's care in my spare time. It would be easier if she'd move in with me, but she wants to stay in her condo."

"You're her primary caregiver?"

"That's right. We have aides coming in during the daytime, but it's too expensive to hire them around the clock."

"It's not easy when your parents get old," Marla said in a sympathetic tone.

"No, it's not. Please have a seat. Can I get you ladies something to drink?"

"I'm good, thanks." Marla settled onto the sofa and crossed her ankles.

Susan declined his offer and roamed to the bookshelf while Marla glanced at the trophies there. Did Henry engage in sports? His lean figure didn't strike her as the athletic type.

"You were kind to allow us into your home to view your button collection," she began, anxious to ask more direct questions but needing to soften him up first. "Can you tell us how you got started in this hobby? Was it from your fabric business?"

He didn't sit but paced the room. "Yes; I got bitten by the bug when I was in the garment industry. Did you know the word 'button' comes from the French word *bouton*, meaning bud or knob? The earliest button surfaced in the Pakistan region. It was made from a curved shell, its purpose more ornamental than useful. The ancient Romans also had buttons made from wood, horn and bronze. However, it wasn't until the thirteenth century that buttonholes were invented."

"Are any buttons valuable?" Susan asked, claiming a seat beside Marla. She withdrew her notepad and began scribbling notes.

"Not really," Henry replied as he regarded her. "Some buttons can fetch a fair price among collectors but it's nothing like jewelry. Buttons became widespread throughout Europe and then button-maker guilds were formed. The guilds regulated the manufacture and use of buttons. In those days, they were signs of prosperity. By the eighteenth century, steel and ivory buttons replaced ones made by fabric. Then pewter and brass came into play."

Marla wanted to steer their conversation to pearl buttons but had to be subtle in her approach. Meanwhile, she hoped this info would prove useful for her friend's magazine article.

"What about the costumes for the battle scene at Pioneer Village?" Marla asked, meaning to eliminate the reenactors from the suspect list.

"The army outfits use U.S. Eagle buttons made from brass or pewter. Those were prevalent during the Indian wars," Henry explained. "By the mid-eighteenth century, gilded brass buttons also came into use. These were dipped in a mixture of mercury and gold."

"Mercury is toxic. Wasn't that dangerous?"

Henry paused and spread his hands. "Possibly. At any rate, fabric-covered buttons started being made mechanically in the middle of the next century."

"What about pearl buttons?" Marla asked, finally getting around to the desired topic.

He shot her a sharp glance. "If you're referring to the history, early pearl buttons in the U.S. were produced from imported sources. Then an American manufacturer discovered that a bend in the Mississippi River near Muscatine, Iowa, caused mussel shells to accumulate there. He began using this source to manufacture buttons. By the turn of the twentieth century, over one-third of the world's pearl shell buttons came from this region. The industry declined when plastic buttons were introduced. Depletion of the source and the high cost of labor contributed to its demise."

"Did women use pearl buttons on their clothing?" Susan asked, her pen poised. Marla cast her a grateful glance. She knew where this was going.

Henry shook his head. "Not right away. Until the nineteenth century, most buttons were used for men's clothing. Women's clothes were fastened by hooks and laces. Then women became the primary consumers."

Marla leaned forward. "What about identifying stamps or marks?" Perhaps the button Dalton found had a mark on it, although she didn't recall one from the pictures.

"Some buttons may be stamped but it's not a requirement like for sterling silver." Henry resumed his pacing. "Would you believe there's a fear of buttons called Koumpounophobia?"

"Is there really?" Susan said. "That's something I never knew. Can you spell it for me?" She wrote down the info while Marla noted she'd filled several pages already.

Henry's eyes glowed with fervor. "Here's something that

will interest your readers," he told Susan. "Do you know why men and women button their clothes from opposite sides?"

"No, why?" Susan asked as expected.

"Men's clothes wrap from left to right with the button on the right side. That's because most men were right-handed and dressed themselves. Wealthy women, on the other hand, were often dressed by maids. Placing buttons on the left side made it possible for servants to face their ladies to complete the task. Also, most women held their babies in their left arms to nurse the infant, so this made access easier."

"That is interesting," Marla admitted. Despite her focus on the pearl button, she appreciated learning something new.

Henry signaled for them to rise. "Come, I'll show you my collection. It's in the guest bedroom."

Marla's eyes goggled at the array of buttons. He pointed out how early buttons were hand-sewn onto cards to be sold to the public. His collection seemed to include every shape and source possible. He'd meticulously labeled each item and catalogued them into a series of journals.

"I'm the founder of the Anachronistic Button Society," he stated with a huff of pride. "It's expanded nationally, although I am no longer in charge. We hold monthly meetings at our local branch."

"That's wonderful," Marla said, impressed by the passion he had for his hobby. Was he equally enthused about fishing? Why else would he run the bait and tackle shed at the village and give fishing lessons? "Besides collecting buttons, what else do you do in your free time? Do you like to go fishing? I noticed some trophies on your shelves."

"I used to compete in fishing tournaments. It was challenging and fun. I don't do it anymore since my mother occupies my time, and I need the money for her care."

"How about the pond at the village?" Marla asked as he stashed his goods back into a closet fitted with custom shelves. "I imagine it was a peaceful place to fish until Phil died there."

Henry's expression sobered. "It relaxed me to cast a line in the water, and I enjoyed giving lessons. Tell me, how is your husband's investigation going? Is he any closer to nailing the culprit? I can't believe Phil died in such a heinous manner."

"Dalton has some leads to follow," she responded in a noncommittal tone. "Why were you really headed to the fishing shack earlier that day? You told me when I met you at the Seminole camp that you'd gone there to seal a container of live bait. My husband didn't find any evidence that you used this type of lure. Were you concealing something under your robe, perhaps?"

"What, like an axe?" he scoffed. Henry led them back to the living room but didn't indicate they should sit. "I resented Phil's plans but wouldn't kill him to save my hide. I might lose my post as minister, but I'd still have the fishing shed to manage."

"How about your profitable scheme of acting as middleman for the costume sales? Don't you need the extra money for your mother's care?"

He winced. "I'll admit, her situation is taking a gouge out of my savings. I've been trying to get power of attorney to access her accounts. She's refused to do any sort of estate planning other than a basic will. It's been difficult."

If Henry was telling the truth, his possible motives had just gone up in smoke. He wouldn't have to pay for his mother's health aides once he had access to her money.

"You still didn't explain why you went to the fishing shack that morning," Susan reminded him in a gentle tone. "Had something distressed you that you needed to unwind with a fishing pole? Or were you meeting someone for a lesson?"

His gaze swung her way. "If you must know, Billy called me. He was upset over what he termed a betrayal. We met at the shed so he could explain what he'd learned. He had just heard about the plans to sell the property to a developer."

"Billy was there at the shed with you?" Marla asked.

Henry twisted his hands together. "I didn't want to mention it before, since it wouldn't look good for him. He got the news from a real estate friend of his. He put two and two together and figured out Gilda's role."

"I don't understand," Marla said, adjusting her purse strap over one shoulder. "Billy asked to meet you at the fishing shack. Why not the Seminole camp or the church?"

"He didn't want River or Lizzy to spot us. He knew Lizzy especially would be upset by the news. She had made a bid herself to buy the land."

"Is this what you were discussing with Billy in the chickee hut the next day?" Marla sent Susan a subtle smile. At last, they'd gotten around to discussing the murder.

"That's correct," Henry replied. "We'd rather Lizzy won the sale if the fairground truly meant to divest themselves of us. We were brainstorming ways to support her."

"Why her and not Phil? He was dedicated to keeping the village intact. They shared the same goal."

Henry's brow furrowed, and he stuck his hands in his pockets. "Angus got us thinking about why we never seemed to have the funds for repairs. And where did Phil get the money to pay for his fancy Lexus? We trusted Lizzy more than him. She has a family history with the place. It means a lot more to her."

Marla exulted inwardly. She'd have lots of new info to share with Dalton from this interview. It's why they worked well as a team. If Dalton had come along, Henry might have been far less chatty. A police detective's presence could be intimidating.

"Do you think Lizzy got rid of Phil to eliminate the competition?" she asked.

"Certainly not! Lizzy cares about the village. She wouldn't do anything to stain our reputation. Besides, getting Phil out of the way wouldn't have helped to discourage the developer's proposal."

"What about Gilda? She acted as a liaison to the fairground. With her gone, the deal might fall through."

He sucked in a breath of air. "Do you know something I don't? I thought she had collapsed, like from a heart attack."

"I'm sorry to be the one to inform you, but Dalton suspects foul play in her death."

"Gilda was killed? Same as Phil?"

"Not with an axe, but somebody killed her."

He sank into a chair and covered his face with his hands. "What's happening to us? Is it all a ploy for the fairground to get rid of the village?"

"That's an interesting theory." Marla wondered if Henry's idea held merit. "Forgive my questions, but it will help my husband narrow the suspects. Where were you during the reenactment?" From his reactions, she didn't believe the man was guilty, but Dalton had taught her not to make assumptions.

"I had offered to play one of the soldiers but was told they had enough actors. So I hung out in the church in case any tourists came by."

"And did they?"

"No, it was quiet. Sadly, as I told the detective, nobody can vouch for my alibi." His face flushed in a manner that made her doubt his statement. What was he hiding?

"How come the village doesn't have security cameras? That would help to keep track of everyone." It sure would have made Dalton's job easier.

"Why do you think? They cost money, especially for the monitoring service."

Susan spoke up. "Did you notice anyone outside the fishing shack around the time Phil was killed?"

Good question. Marla cast her a grateful glance.

"No, I was, um, occupied."

"Didn't you see Violet headed that way?" Marla asked. "How come I didn't notice you in the crowd after she'd screamed? You would have heard the commotion from the church."

He shuffled his feet and didn't look their way.

"Something is bothering you, Henry. It would help to get it off your chest."

"Fine. If you must know, I'd asked Billy to stop by the

church during the reenactment, and that's when I made a pass at him."

"What?" Had Marla heard him correctly?

Henry's face reddened. "Billy worked with River every day and yet he never seemed attracted to her. I thought maybe it was because he was... of a different persuasion. I'd asked him to meet me during the battle scene so I could see him in his Indian chief outfit. His costumes turned me on."

Speechless, Marla stared at him. No wonder he wasn't interested in Millie. He had other preferences. "How did Billy react?"

"He was shocked at my proposition and quickly set me straight. River was only a friend. Otherwise, he was interested in women. I'd made a gross mistake."

Marla sank onto the couch as did Susan. Beside her, Susan stayed mute. Marla gave her a questioning glance. Susan shrugged as though to say, what now?

"Let me clarify the sequence of events," Marla said. "On the day Phil died, you went to the fishing shack in the morning. Billy had called and asked to meet you. That's when he told you about the developer's bid to buy the property."

"That's right. I asked him to stop by the church later when he was dressed in his regalia."

Marla nodded. "He took a break during the battle and came over. The two of you were in the chapel while Phil was being murdered. Are you sure Billy didn't stop by the fishing shack first? He had a clear motive to get rid of Phil."

"No, he came directly to the church. He didn't have all that much time before the smoke cleared from the fight scene. As for Phil's plans, Billy had some ideas about where else they could establish a café if we'd obtained control of the tract."

"And after you'd finished your conversation?"

"Billy headed back to where he'd left his horse to resume his role in the reenactment. I stayed inside the church, too embarrassed to be seen by anyone."

Marla sympathized with him. Coming out and then being rebuffed must have been painful.

"Why did you go see Billy the next day? Was it to discuss ways of helping Lizzy win the bid or for some other reason?"

Henry's voice softened. "I wanted to apologize for my unwanted advance. Billy said he was flattered I'd thought so highly of him, and that was the end of it."

"After he'd left you at the church the day before, weren't you curious to see what was happening when Violet screamed?"

"The church walls are thick, and I was in the back office. I didn't hear anything. Millie told me about it later. She was beside herself. I've never seen her so distraught. She'd even forgotten to put on her apron, and usually she's meticulous about her costume."

Too bad you couldn't provide her with the comfort she craved. "Phil's death must have dashed her hopes of running an on-site restaurant. Did she tell you where she'd been during the skirmish?"

Henry appeared bewildered. "I imagine in the sewing room. She might have been hanging out there in case any tourists stopped in. I didn't think to ask since she was so upset."

Marla felt she had enough information for now and didn't care to press her luck any further. "If it's okay with you, I'll share your news with my husband so he can verify your alibi with Billy. This has been very helpful."

Henry stood with an air of dismissal. "I'm glad you came by. It felt good to tell my story." He turned to Susan. "I hope you'll leave anything personal out of your article."

"Don't worry. My focus is on your collection. Our readers will love the button history, especially the part about men's and women's fashions. It'll be a popular piece." She stood, stashing her notebook and pen in her purse. "I'll be sure to send you a copy of the magazine when the print issue comes out."

"Thanks again for taking the time to see us," Marla said, rising.

This would help Dalton narrow the suspects once he

confirmed the men's alibis, she thought as Henry led them toward the exit. Oh, that reminded her to ask another question.

She paused in the foyer. "One more thing. Have you ever met Lizzy's brother? He owns the farm adjacent to the village. The developer made a similar offer on his land, too."

Henry swung open the front door. "He might be the stranger I've seen at the village from time to time. Simon gets into intense discussions with him. I don't know what's going on between them, but it isn't my business to find out. I'd suggest you steer clear of the fellow. He struck me as being a dangerous man to cross."

Chapter Twenty-Two

"What do you think?" Marla asked Susan during the drive home. "If Henry is telling the truth, he and Billy have an alibi for Phil's murder."

"You're right. Then who does that leave as suspects?"

Marla glanced into the rearview mirror to make sure they weren't being followed. "Regarding the men, not too many. With Henry and Billy out of the picture, that passes the baton to Angus, Simon and Uriah. Angus wouldn't kill Phil because he was embezzling money. All Angus had to do was find proof. And he likes Lizzy, so he would be concerned about protecting her and not ending up in jail."

"Unless Angus murdered Phil because he hit on Lizzy."

Marla stopped at a red light and surveyed the palm trees and flowering shrubs by the roadside. "Lizzy hasn't mentioned that Phil bothered her. I think she could have handled him on her own if that was the case. Uriah, on the other hand, cares about Violet. If he knew about her background with the school principal, he might have done away with Phil to save her from further pain."

"Except he wanted Phil's plan to succeed so he could expand his shop."

"Right. His motive seems weak unless Violet's story was true." Marla bit her lower lip, thinking hard as pieces of the puzzle tumbled through her brain. The light changed, and she pressed the accelerator. "Billy and Henry have alibis. Simon doesn't appear to be growing anything unusual in his herb garden. He might be involved in something shady with Greg next door, but we've no proof Greg is doing anything illegal."

"Dalton hasn't gotten the lab report on those leaf samples yet?"

"No, it's too soon. My instincts have me looking at the women. River seems too serene to commit murder, although looks can be deceiving. However, she has no viable motive. She wasn't worried about Phil's plan, because Billy would have persuaded him to find another site for the café. That leaves Lizzy, Violet and Millie."

"Go on," Susan said when Marla paused.

She passed a busy intersection, her attention focused on the drive until they got safely across. "Violet found Phil's body, so that puts her directly at the scene of the crime. She claimed Phil had texted her to meet him there to reveal something about Uriah. When Violet reached the boardwalk, Phil was already dead. This assumes she's telling the truth."

"Has Dalton confirmed her statement with her cell phone records?"

"He's requested them. Meanwhile, Lizzy said she was at Baffle House, but nobody can vouch for her. And Millie flits around the park, so who knows where she'd been. Henry figured she'd stayed in the sewing room."

"Let's look at means, motive, and opportunity. Could one of them have stolen the tomahawk from Billy's chickee hut?"

"It would have been more difficult for Violet." Marla drew a mental map of Pioneer Village. "The schoolhouse is across the square. She would be spotted too easily, and where would she have hidden it? Under her skirts?"

"Why not? Any one of the women could have stolen it."

"It seems as though Phil mainly hit on River and Violet," Marla said. "This wasn't a crime of passion, however. His death was premeditated. It's more likely Phil knew something that got him killed."

"Like what?"

"He'd demanded a cut of the operation from Simon, who's in cahoots with Lizzy and her brother. The trio are hiding something, if not on village land than on the brother's turf. That may have given Lizzy a motive. As for Millie, I don't know what she'd have to gain by Phil's death."

"He'd promised she could be chef at the café he would establish. Maybe he went back on his word."

"Then she'd have killed him in the heat of the moment, not coldly planned it out. And what about Gilda's death? The method was different, but it was also planned in advance. That suggests the killer took advantage of the opportunities in each instance."

"Regarding a motive for getting rid of Gilda, the bad guy could have figured the real estate deal would fall through without her involvement."

Marla agreed with her friend's logic. "Gilda's death meant Lizzy's bid would be the only one left on the table."

"She's one of the villagers who gives archery lessons," Susan reminded Marla. "And she's passionate about her family history. How far would she go to claim her heritage?"

"Lizzy didn't plan to purchase the tract for personal use. Like Phil, she wanted to preserve the village. So that motive doesn't work for me. It's more likely Phil and then Gilda found out what she has going on with her brother. Anyway, we're almost home. Thanks so much for coming with me today."

"It was fun, Marla. Call me anytime you want to go sleuthing."

"I'm hoping to put that hat away once Dalton retires."

After dropping Susan off, Marla stopped quickly at her house to freshen up and let the dogs out before heading to the salon.

She entered to the familiar sounds of blow-dryers whirring and water splashing. Holding spray scented the air. Robyn waved to her from the front desk. She wore big gold hoop earrings that contrasted against her freshly tinted dark brown hair. Tired of her pink strand, she'd done an overall rinse and a shorter cut that looked cute with her heart-shaped face.

"Hey, Marla, what's up? Anything new on the case?" she asked with a grin.

"You'll be happy to hear Billy and Henry have alibis." Marla related what she'd learned.

"Awesome. Does that mean I'm free to date Billy if he calls?"

"I'd wait until Dalton has the culprit behind bars."

"I knew you'd say that." Robyn gave a resigned sigh. "What's your next move?"

"To take care of my clients." Marla signaled to her customer, seated in the waiting area and wearing an impatient frown. "Tammy, you can come on back."

Marla pushed aside all thoughts about the case as the afternoon wore on. She went home in time to give Ryder his dinner. Dalton had picked him up from day care.

Her husband wanted to hear the details of her interview with Henry. She'd only skimmed over it earlier during a quick text message. She waited until they were in the bedroom getting ready for bed to describe what she'd learned.

"Henry never told me all this stuff. You did good." Standing by the dresser, Dalton pulled a clean tee shirt from a drawer.

Marla sat on the side of the bed. "You'll have to verify his story with Billy. If it correlates, then they're eliminated as suspects."

"I still need to get Violet's phone records to corroborate her claims. As for Phil's cell, we did get a last location at the village. We're still waiting on the rest of his data."

"That's not too helpful. You already know Phil was at the fishing shed." She yawned. "Let's get some rest. My brain is too foggy to think straight anymore."

When Friday morning arrived, they resumed their discussion in between chores. Marla stood in the kitchen serving breakfast.

"Judging from the arrows shot at me and Susan and the poisoned box of chocolates, we must be getting closer to the truth. Now if only we could get a definitive answer about those plants on Greg Harris's farm. Can you push the lab for a response?" she asked Dalton, who sat next to his son at the table. Ryder threw a crumb on the floor and gurgled with laughter.

"I'll stop by there today," Dalton said, his mouth set into determined lines. "It's still a longshot that he's the killer, though. Oh, and I have other news. Langley got the fire inspection report from the incident at the restaurant where Millie had worked."

"What did it say?"

"Investigators found evidence of chemicals that may have been used as an accelerant. The ingredients can be found in paint thinners."

"That means anybody could have done it."

"Magnesium residue was also found on site. That's unusual."

Marla had no idea what that meant. "Where was Millie when this fire started?"

"She was having dinner with her boyfriend at a place across the street. Langley interviewed the guy. He said she left the table briefly for a restroom visit. When she returned, Millie told the boyfriend she wasn't feeling well and needed to leave."

"That doesn't prove anything. Millie said the owners were trying to frame her."

"Just so. But it's something to consider."

"What other leads do you have? Lizzy is still on my list, and Simon is a strong possibility if he's colluding with Lizzy and her brother about something they want to stay hidden. Nor should we eliminate Violet. She could have been lying about how things went down that day. She seemed reluctant to cast blame on Uriah but that could have been an act."

"Let's not discount the developer," Dalton said, taking a sip of coffee. He'd already finished the scrambled eggs and toast Marla had made. "This person might have paid Gilda to sabotage the village so the fairground would be justified in selling it."

"How? By setting the villagers against each other? I doubt the developer would resort to murder if the trail could lead back to him. That brings us back to the cast members as the main suspects." Motives swirled in Marla's mind, creating a kaleidoscope of possibilities.

Ryder whined in his highchair, demanding her attention.

She finished getting him dressed while Dalton left for the day. Brianna meandered into the kitchen and offered to take the dogs for a walk.

Marla finally dropped her son off at day care and headed to the salon. Ryder had clung to her this morning and cried when she pried him off. Maybe he was teething again. She felt guilty walking away, but knew he'd soon join his classmates to play.

Aware she'd been remiss with her other loved ones, she returned phone calls during breaks at work. She spoke to her mother and caught up with Tally, who'd found a dress for her to wear to Dalton's party. She also located a restaurant with a private room available for that date and reserved the space. Then she reviewed Robyn's inventory list and placed some orders.

At lunchtime, she ran home to pick up the dogs and take them to their grooming appointment. Brianna would fetch them when they'd finished.

She was in her car when a text from Dalton came through.

I got the lab results from the leaf samples. They're from a camellia sinensis plant.

Paused at a red light, Marla called him on her speaker phone. "What kind of a plant is that?" she asked.

"They're tea leaves," Dalton said in his wry tone. "If that's what Greg Harris is growing, it's a dead end as far as the case is concerned."

Marla's heart sank. Had they been looking in the wrong corner? Was Greg's operation purely as innocent as growing tea? But then, why all the security? And why had Simon threatened Phil the day she'd overheard their conversation?

There had to be something they were missing.

"Why have a barbed wire fence to keep out trespassers if all he's growing is tea?" Marla said. "It must be a cover for something else going on in those buildings or inside the greenhouse. We should talk to Lizzy and ask her to take us there."

"Oh, that reminds me," Dalton cut in. "I've located the lawyer's office that handled the real estate transaction for the

233

village tract. Sadly, the senior member has passed away. His staff is looking into their archives for a signed bill of sale."

"I asked Lizzy to find the original document, but she hasn't gotten back to me. We can always use that as an excuse to see her."

"Good idea. Sergeant Langley is following the paper trail. We're hoping Phil's phone records will come in soon. Meanwhile, we received the financials from the fairground, so that will be helpful in comparing them to Phil's ledgers."

"That's great. I'll talk to you later."

The latest news hovered on her tongue as she greeted Robyn at the front desk. Marla wanted to tell her about the lab report, as well as text Susan. The two of them had been following the case with her and would be interested in the results, but she held back until she learned more. Work became a balm that calmed her mind and restored her balance.

As the weekend crawled by, Marla couldn't wait for Sunday when she and Dalton would be free. They'd visit the village and stop by Baffle House to see Lizzy. One way or another, they'd gain access to Greg's facilities. Brianna had offered to babysit for a few hours, so they couldn't take too long.

Finally, the allotted day arrived. Marla and Dalton gained entry to the village amid a crowd of tourists. At this rate, they should buy annual passes... not that she'd want to come back here so fast after this case was solved.

Lizzy, dressed in a long skirt and blouse, greeted them at Baffle House. This corner of the park remained quiet, most of the visitors crowding the exhibits near the entrance.

"Marla, it's nice to see you again. And Detective Vail. What brings you by today?"

"We have some more questions to ask," Dalton said in a casual tone.

"Sure, how can I help?"

Marla glanced at the buttons on Lizzy's outfit. They looked to be manufactured ones. The puzzle of the pearl button continued to elude her. So did the missing gold. Lizzy claimed she'd never found the stash, but was she telling the truth?

"Tell us about your brother, Greg Harris." Dalton folded his arms across his chest as he regarded the shorter woman.

Marla studied Lizzy in a new light. She had asked Dalton if the angle of the axe planted in Phil's head might tell them anything about the killer's height. He'd said no, although it had indicated the culprit was right-handed. She would think, if it was a shorter person, hefting an axe to strike upward would require more force.

Considering the women, only Millie, River and Gilda matched or exceeded Phil's height. As for muscle power, Dalton had said Billy's tomahawk weighed less than a pound, so strength wasn't an issue.

"What is it you want to learn about him?" Lizzy asked.

"We understand he owns the adjacent farm. How well did he know Phil Pufferfish?"

"Greg ran into him a few times, but he had nothing to do with Phil's murder. Is that why you're here, to cast out a net and see what you catch?"

"That depends. Why don't you take us on a tour of Greg's farm? We'd like to see what he grows there. Or would you prefer I get a warrant?"

Lizzy heaved a sigh. "I'd rather do this peacefully. Greg has nothing to hide."

"Should we drive around to the main entrance?" Marla asked in a soothing tone. Dalton wouldn't get far by antagonizing the woman. Besides, he would have gotten a warrant already if he'd had reasonable cause.

"No, we'll take a shortcut through the woods. By the way, I've looked for that document you'd asked me to find. I can't locate it among the papers we inherited. I told Greg to search for it. His farm is the only piece of property that our family retained."

"You have joint ownership?" Dalton asked.

"That's right. You'll see his house is almost an exact replica of this one, only it's smaller. We both live there now. I moved in after my husband died."

"I'm sorry. Do you have children?" Marla asked.

"I've a daughter and two grandchildren. They're my lifeline."

Before they left, Lizzy hung a sign in front indicating the time for the next tour. Then she locked the door and led them through a stand of woods toward the adjacent fenced property. Marla was surprised she didn't head toward the secret entrance by Simon's herb garden. Instead, Lizzy took them to the locked rear gate where she entered a code.

Once inside the perimeter, they skirted rows of bushes to reach the house.

Lizzy rang the bell to alert her brother before retrieving a key from her skirt pocket. Before they could enter, a man flung open the door. He had a clean-shaven jaw, golden oak eyes, and sandy hair.

Lizzy introduced them as they stood on the front porch. Marla's gaze roamed over the guy's broad shoulders and muscled arms. Farming must keep him fit.

"I know who you are. Lizzy has told me about you," he said in a smooth voice. He regarded his sister. "I've found a bill of sale, but it lacks a signature. We've been remiss in not looking for a signed copy earlier."

"Didn't Ian Winthrop die on the eve of the transaction?" Marla asked.

"True. His debts forced him to sell our family estate. The shame must have caused his heart attack. At least he held on to this piece of property."

Ian must have signed the document before he dropped dead, Marla figured. She assumed the lawyer had found it and filed the papers since the deed had been duly transferred.

"Who survived Ian?" she asked. Perhaps the widow had handed the document over to their lawyer along with her husband's other estate papers.

"Our grandmother Carole," Lizzy said. "Carole and Ian had

two daughters. My mother was Sarah. She married Randolph Harris, our father."

Dalton addressed Greg. "This family history is fascinating, but I'd like to learn more about your crops. In case you haven't heard, two deaths occurred among the villagers next door. Phil Pufferfish was murdered with a tomahawk, and Gilda Macintosh was poisoned with nicotine. You're not growing tobacco, are you?"

Marla glanced at him. Was he purposefully trying to provoke the man?

"Certainly not." Greg swept his arm toward the field of green plants that lay under the scorching sun. "I run an artisan tea plantation."

"Isn't most of the world's tea grown in Southeast Asia?" Marla asked.

"That's so. China, Sri Lanka, India, and Kenya are the four major sources. The tea plant grows best in places with high heat and humidity, good rainfall, and acidic soil. What do you know about American-grown teas?"

"Not much," Marla admitted.

Greg indicated they should step into a shadier spot. "Tea bushes first arrived in the United States from China in the 1700s. Attempts to cultivate the plant in this country failed until Dr. Charles Shepard founded a plantation in South Carolina in the late 1880s. He produced award-winning teas until he died, after which his land lapsed into neglect.

"In 1963, the Lipton Company purchased a farm on Wadmalaw Island in South Carolina. They relocated Shepard's plants there. William Barclay Hall bought the land in 1987. He'd received formal training as a tea taster in London."

Lizzy cut in, her voice laced with enthusiasm. "Hall converted the farm to a commercial operation, and the Charleston Tea Plantation was born. Their American Classic tea was the first brand made from leaves grown solely in America. Eventually, Bigelow bought the property and changed its name to the Charleston Tea Garden. They give tours if you're interested."

"Is this why your place is so well guarded?" Dalton asked. "Because tea is a rare plant in this country?"

Greg shook his head. "I'll explain in a minute. You need to hear this first to gain some perspective. Black, green and oolong teas are the most popular. For green tea, we pick only the top two leaves and a bud from one stem. This is called the flush. During harvesting season, the plant produces a new flush every seven to fifteen days. For black and oolong tea, we pick two to four leaves down from the top. White tea, which is less common, is made from the buds of a plant."

"Do you use machines to do this work?" Marla inquired. It seemed like a delicate job.

"No. We prefer to harvest by hand. Lizzy, Simon, and I do all the work, including weeding and pruning. Tea plants can grow into a tree if not properly maintained."

"Simon works for you? In what capacity?"

"He's our horticultural expert. Lizzy introduced us and suggested we bring him on to help. The guy really knows his plants. We're lucky to have him as a consultant."

"What's in the greenhouse?" Marla wondered if Simon plied his old schemes there.

"Come and see for yourself. We can go there first." Greg led them inside the humid structure where rows of young plants grew in cultivated beds. "Simon uses the greenhouse for his experiments. He tests different strains to see what might grow well here. It's also where he raises new seedlings. It takes three to four years for a bush to reach maturity."

"What are those flowers?" Marla pointed to a colorful array of purple, white, and lavender blossoms in a far corner.

Greg beamed with pride. "That's my orchid collection. It's a personal hobby. Now let me show you our tea production facility."

Marla didn't see a single marijuana plant anywhere in the greenhouse. Nor were there any broad-leafed tobacco plants that she could tell. She gave Dalton a significant glance as they trailed Greg to the next building. So far, so good. But if Greg grew nothing illegal, why the security features? He still hadn't answered that question.

Greg walked over to the first piece of equipment. "After water, tea is the most consumed beverage in the world. Each type of tea requires a different process. You can't just pluck leaves off a plant and brew a pot. Green tea leaves are steamed on arrival to halt oxidation and to preserve their freshness. Black tea requires withering, rolling, and oxidizing. Oolong, which means black dragon in Chinese, is a semi-oxidized tea that falls in between the other two."

"You'd mentioned white tea," Marla said, while Lizzy leaned against a wall with a bored expression.

"White tea isn't steamed like green tea, nor is it oxidized like black tea. The only step is drying to reduce moisture and achieve the desired flavor. Then there's yellow tea. This variety is similar to green tea in the initial processing, but it requires an additional procedure called sealed yellowing. This removes the grassy scent we associate with green tea."

He led them around the interior, pointing out the purpose of each machine.

Marla had no idea the tea production process was so complex. "I suppose you have an area for packaging, labeling, and shipping?"

Greg pointed to a far corner. "That takes place over there."

Dalton strolled over for a closer inspection, and Marla joined him. Observing the colorfully labeled tins of tea packed into cartons, she figured it would be hard to hide any illicit goods inside.

"Who buys your teas?" Dalton asked, returning to where Greg waited with a patient air.

"We sell to private consumers. Our product is not available to the public. Let's go back to the house and I'll explain why we need such tight security."

Chapter Twenty-Three

"In this country, we face certain obstacles for producing artisan teas," Greg continued as they walked outside to retrace their steps back toward the house. "These include high shelf prices, a belief that specialty teas can only be grown in equatorial regions, and steep labor costs."

He gestured broadly, while Marla noticed his sinewy arm muscles. It must be backbreaking work to pluck the tea leaves by hand during harvest season. Nor had she noticed a forklift around, meaning he must lift those cartons himself to stack them for shipping.

"I don't understand," Dalton said to Greg. "What are you saying about your product?"

"When we inherited this estate, the citrus trees weren't thriving, and I didn't know what else to plant or even if I wanted to become a farmer. I joined the army, thinking I could use the educational benefits to study architectural design. Then I was stationed overseas. That's where I learned about rare teas and had the brilliant idea to bring cuttings over here."

"You didn't consider raising corn or blueberries instead?" Marla asked, thinking that would have been easier.

"Making artisan tea appealed to me. It would involve crafting something special, almost like creating art. After I left the service, I stayed abroad to study with a local tea farmer in India and then took a certified tea master course. Lizzy helped me transform the farm here once I got back. She had money saved up from her doll store and we used some of those funds to get started."

"How did you feel about her plan to buy back the village?" Reaching the porch, they stood under the roof. "Why bother when you have this fertile land to cultivate? Do you plan to expand your operation?"

"No. Lizzy means to preserve the village. That's more about sharing our heritage."

"Would you sell your teas in the gift shop? I imagine they'd be popular with guests."

"We don't sell to the public."

He seemed vehement on this point, making Marla wonder what was so special about his products.

"Why not? And why the tight security measures? You still haven't answered our questions in that regard."

Greg's face flushed. "What I'm about to tell you is in strict confidence, okay?"

"That depends on how it affects my case." Dalton swiped a line of sweat from his brow. He looked as hot as Marla felt.

"Certain rare teas are worth a lot of money," Greg explained in a low tone. "And I mean, a fortune's worth. For example, a kilogram of genuine Da-Hong Pao tea is more expensive than gold. One cup of Panda Dung tea costs two hundred dollars. The Tieguanyin variety we produce here isn't that valuable, but it still fetches up to three thousand dollars per kilogram. It's a type of oolong tea and is also the name of the tea cultivar."

Marla gave him a startled glance. His crop was worth that much money? No wonder he guarded his farm so diligently. If someone stole cuttings and produced it more widely, the value might drop.

Had Phil found out what was going on here? Is this the operation he meant in his conversation with Simon? If he'd demanded a cut of the pie, that would be enough grounds for murder with so much money at stake.

"Are these teas processed the same way as other types?" Marla asked, thinking the production must be more difficult to make it so rare. Or perhaps the plant itself was a sparse commodity.

Greg stuck his hands in his jeans pockets and leaned against a wall. "The techniques vary depending on the varietal we want to produce. For example, if we want a stronger flavor, we'll bake the leaves longer. For our lighter teas, we'll use a less intense process."

"How does Simon fit in? He's not trained in tea-making, is he?" Dalton asked.

"No, but as a horticulturalist, he's working on an Anxi Tieguanyin for us. It's a lightly oxidized tea with a delicate aroma. Then there's the Muzha one, which requires more roasting. It has a stronger taste with a nutty quality. We're hoping to increase our product line with these varietals."

"How did you get your original plants through customs?" Marla asked, curious. Were they full-grown plants, seeds, cuttings, or seedlings? Her knowledge of botany was as comprehensive as a worm. She ate what was in front of her without worrying about its source.

"I used another route to bring them into the country." Greg glanced away, avoiding their scrutiny.

From his dodgy response, Marla surmised he'd smuggled them in. It didn't matter now. His enterprise had been successful, and he had a thriving tea farm.

"Where do you sell your product if it's so expensive?" she asked. She tried to imagine how much it would cost for a tin of his specialty tea and couldn't do the calculations. If he made such good money, maybe he'd been the one paying for repairs on Baffle House. That would account for the house's upkeep while other buildings needed renovations.

"We have a roster of select customers. Would you like to come inside the house? You both look wilted from the heat."

"Sure, that would be welcome." Dalton stepped inside with a keen expression, while Marla wondered which he wanted more—to get cooled off or to scope out their house.

They moved past a foyer cluttered with accent pieces and into a living room with traditional furnishings. Gone were the lacy curtains, like in Baffle House, replaced with custom shutters.

Indicating Marla and Dalton should be seated, Greg said, "Lizzy, why don't you get our guests some iced tea? They can taste one of our varieties."

Dalton waved a hand. "No, thanks. We can't stay much longer."

Marla figured he was thinking the same thing as she. They hadn't yet determined who'd sent her the tainted chocolates. This would give Lizzy the perfect opportunity to poison them. Or to leave the room and get a gun. How far would they go to protect their secret from getting out?

She perched on the edge of the couch, debating how to proceed. What else did they need to know?

"Where were you during the battle reenactment at the village?" Dalton asked, folding one leg across his other knee. "You must have heard the gunshots from over here."

Greg gave him a level glance. "I was in town that Saturday. I volunteer at the veteran's center twice a month."

"What hours were you there?"

"From twelve to four."

Dalton got out his notebook and scribbled notes. This should be easy to verify, Marla thought. If true, it would eliminate Greg from their suspect list. But not Simon.

"I overheard Phil, the village administrator, talking to Simon at the park one day," she said. "Phil mentioned your operation and Simon threatened him. Did Phil learn what you were growing here and demand a percentage for himself?"

Greg shook his head. "Phil knew Simon was working with me and figured he was up to his old tricks of cultivating pot. He didn't believe Simon's claims of innocence. Simon couldn't disprove him without exposing our crop. He got angry when Phil demanded a portion of the profits in exchange for keeping silent."

"Do you think Simon got angry enough to kill Phil?" Marla said. "I understand Simon left the farm around the time of Phil's murder."

Greg's gaze darkened. "Simon wouldn't do anything to

jeopardize his position. I'd asked him to cover for me at the production facility while I did my stint in town. I was in the middle of processing a batch of leaves and needed him to stop the oxidation. It's in our logs if you want to see for yourself."

"I may take a look later," Dalton said. "What about Gilda? Did she pressure you to sell your land to the developer?"

"I didn't have any personal contact with her, but she harassed Lizzy."

"Gilda tried to convince me to drop my bid for the village tract," Lizzy explained. She'd taken a seat across from Marla and Dalton. "I got upset when I learned she'd been working for the fairground all along. Her death took me by surprise. You said she was poisoned?"

"That's right. She was poisoned with nicotine. This substance can be an ingredient in insecticides," Dalton remarked, his expression impassive.

"We don't use synthetic pesticides," Greg said. "We practice organic farming and sustainability on our farm."

Lizzy faced them with a look of hurt in her eyes. "Are you implying we did Gilda in to get her off our backs? We didn't murder anyone, Detective. You know all our secrets now. What more do you want?"

"What about the legend of the hidden treasure?" Marla asked. "Have you found it? Is that why you really want to buy the land from the fairground?"

"I want to preserve the village without a corrupt administrator in charge. I've no idea where the Confederate gold is, assuming it even exists."

"Stop implicating my sister in this mess," Greg said, his voice turning hostile. "If you must know, we've made a counteroffer to the fairground that tops the developer's bid. They're considering it. This village has been a thorn in their side. They'd rather spend their dollars on the annual fair and other events. Pioneer Village should have been an independent enterprise from the start."

"I hope you win," Marla responded, surprised that she did favor their proposal.

If they eliminated Simon, Greg, and Lizzy as suspects, who did that leave? Uriah and Violet? Only one other person came to mind, and that was Millie. She had no apparent alibi for Phil's death but no visible motive, either.

Why would she have murdered Gilda? Maybe they'd both discovered the treasure and had fought over it. But the gold would rightfully belong to the fairground as the current property owner. So that couldn't have been a point of contention between them.

Then there was the issue of the pearl button. Who had placed it under Phil's body and why? Was it to implicate Uriah or Violet?

"What is Millie's viewpoint on all this?" Marla asked Lizzy. "Didn't she support Phil's proposal? He'd promised to let her run the kitchen in his proposed café."

Lizzy made a face. "Have you tasted her food? I wouldn't be surprised if Phil reneged on his offer. She can be an odd duck. Mostly she sticks to the sewing room in between her other duties. Are you aware she's the sole person in their so-called sewing circle?"

"What? How do you know this?"

"Phil commented on it once, and then I realized he was right. There aren't any other women that I've ever seen there. Millie talks about it as though it's a group, and she even has Uriah believing the goods she gives him to sell are produced by them, but she's the lone seamstress."

"I've met Daisy there," Marla said, mentioning the schoolgirl. "She must help out."

"She's only a volunteer and comes on certain days. Millie keeps the sewing room locked, otherwise. It's supposed to be open for self-guided tours."

"It wasn't locked when I visited. What would she have to guard in there?"

"I'd stashed a lot of items from Baffle House in the backroom for storage prior to opening day. Some of those vintage jars are quite old and fragile. I told Millie not to touch them or to let Henry inside. He'd want to riffle through the buttons."

Marla remembered her glimpse of those jars. What if...? A sudden urge compelled her to revisit the sewing room. She waggled her brows at Dalton, indicating they should move on.

"Thanks so much for the tour," Marla said as she and Dalton stood. "It was an education. I'd no idea tea-making was such a production. If you'd sell your private label tea in the village store, I would be your first customer."

"Thanks, but our Tieguanyin tea is too expensive for the average consumer," Lizzy responded. "However, I have been urging Greg to make some yellow tea. We could offer that variety to the general public. We'll see what happens with my bid to buy the place."

"That sounds like a great idea."

Lizzy rose and escorted them to the door. Her smile seemed genuine as she waved them off.

"I did not expect their operation to involve rare teas," Marla said to Dalton, once they were out of earshot.

"Me neither. Logic led me to believe they must be engaged in unlawful activities. I think we can remove them from our suspect list once I verify Greg's stint at the veterans' center and Simon's log entry."

Just then, Dalton got a text message. He stopped walking, read it, and typed in a reply.

"That's Langley. He received Violet's cell phone records. They confirm that she received a call from Phil Pufferfish in the time frame before his murder."

"Then Violet was telling the truth. What about her fears on Uriah's behalf?"

"He's still a possibility, but he had no reason to kill Gilda. The differences between the two deaths still puzzles me, yet the cases must be related. The burning question remains the motive."

His words simmered and ignited in Marla's brain.

She grabbed his arm. "That's it! You've just said the key word. We've been looking at this all wrong."

Chapter Twenty-Four

"We need to check out the sewing room again," Marla said. "Your mention of the word 'burning' tipped me off. I believe Millie's past may have come back to haunt her."

Dalton held open the rear gate for her to pass through. "You think she's responsible for the murders?" He followed on her heels, careful to latch the gate behind them.

"That's right. Concerning a possible motive, we've been thinking Phil may have backed out of his promise regarding the chef position. In her rage, Millie killed him. But his death wasn't done in the heat of the moment. The killer coldly planned it. If Millie murdered him, his betrayal may have triggered the event, but I don't believe it was her main reason."

"So what was it?" Dalton's face reflected his skepticism as they re-entered the history park and strode toward Baffle House.

"I believe it relates to her prior job at the restaurant that had the fire."

"She had an alibi, remember? Millie was eating dinner with her boyfriend at the time."

Chills ran up Marla's spine as her theories gelled. "When Sergeant Langley interviewed the boyfriend, he said Millie left for a brief interval to go to the restroom. Think about it. Millie knows archery and could have been the one who shot arrows at me and Susan. She could easily have baked the cookies that Gilda ate and spiked those chocolates I received."

"I don't know. What about her motive?"

"I need to look something up." Marla paused under a tree to

access the browser on her phone. She searched for fire starter kits. Sure enough, the information she sought was readily available.

She opened her mouth to share this tidbit with Dalton when a glint of white caught her eye. She glanced toward the front yard at Baffle House.

An image seemed to coalesce and then disappear.

Her skin crawled. Was that the ghost of the White Lady? What did it mean to tell her?

Sloughing off the vision, she moved ahead to the building housing the sewing room as a plan of action formed in her mind.

"I think you should stay out of sight," she told Dalton. "If Millie is inside, you might spook her. Here, I'll leave my phone on." She took her cell from her cross-body purse, dialed his number, and put it in her pants pocket.

Marla twisted the knob, but the door was locked. A moment of dismay hit her. What if Millie wasn't there?

She rapped her knuckles loudly on the wooden door. A flicker of movement showed in a nearby window. Several moments later, the door swung open.

Millie stood in the doorway, her hair knotted in a bun and her face registering surprise. "Marla, what are you doing here?"

Marla hoped Dalton was out of sight. "I missed some exhibits last time I was here so thought I'd return for another visit. I'd love to see the collection of vintage button jars. Lizzy told me about them. She said she'd stored them here to reduce clutter at Baffle House."

"Why the sudden interest in old jars?"

"I might start collecting vintage glass. It would be a fun hobby."

Millie looked as though she'd sucked a lemon. "Uriah has some good reproductions in the general store," she said with a lift of her chin.

"I'd rather see the real thing." Marla elbowed her way inside to avoid having the door shut in her face. "Where are they? In the storeroom?" She'd remembered the door hidden behind the hanging quilt. Daisy had said that space was off-limits to guests.

She breezed past the quilt and noticed the storeroom door was partially open. Millie must have been in there when Marla had knocked. She stepped inside. Shelves lined the walls while a single overhead bulb lit the space. Several jars lay open, their contents on the counter.

Staring at the disarray, she heard the front door closing and the latch snicking. Uh-oh. How would Dalton get inside if she needed help?

As for the lone window, it was in the front section, and Millie blocked the path. With her old-fashioned blouse and long skirt, she looked the image of a pioneer woman except for the malicious expression on her face.

"Why are you really here, Marla?" Millie asked, advancing toward her.

Marla stood her ground, ready to lay her cards on the table. She needed to wrestle a confession from Millie. "I remembered you had a campfire burning at your baking demo. You showed me how to get a spark going with flint and steel. Is that how you started the fire at the restaurant where you'd worked?"

Millie's eyes glittered. "What did you say?"

"According to the inspection report, investigators found evidence of chemicals that may have been used as an accelerant. The ingredients can be found in paint thinners."

"What's your point?"

"Henry said you'd helped him put a fresh coat of paint on the church. That means you know how to handle a paintbrush. I'll bet you use a thinner solution to clean your brushes." Marla hadn't the least idea how to paint or to clean a brush. She was hoping her bluff worked.

"Lots of people do their own painting. Lizzy is always touching up Baffle House."

Marla ignored Millie's attempt to transfer suspicion onto someone else. "You like Henry, don't you? You'd probably hoped to gain his favor by helping him fix the church."

"How dare you make presumptions about my regard for him. Where did you hear such a preposterous thing?"

"From the horse's mouth himself. He's not interested in you, Millie. You'd best pin your hopes on someone else. Henry favors his own sex for amorous entanglements."

"You're lying! He appreciates my efforts on his behalf."

"I'm sure he's glad for your help, but he'll never be romantically inclined toward you."

"We'll see." Millie's menacing gaze reminded Marla of a lioness protecting her cubs.

Marla pointed to a set of tools on the countertop. "You had this same rod and striker blade at the baking demo and showed me how to use them to generate a spark. I didn't realize the rod part could also contain magnesium until I looked it up online." That's what she'd researched on the way there with Dalton. It had clinched the deal for her in terms of Millie's guilt. "In addition to the accelerant used in the restaurant fire, magnesium residue was found on site."

"So what? I was having dinner with my boyfriend when the fire started. We weren't anywhere near the place."

"The owners meant to let you go, didn't they? Was this your way of getting revenge? Or maybe you'd hoped to cause enough damage that people would think you were out of a job due to needed repairs."

"They'd already fired me, you imbecile. They told me I'd have to vacate the premises by the next day."

Marla gaped at her. "You had already been dismissed?"

"That's right. Those cads didn't appreciate anything I'd done for them. They said attendance was down and my cooking was at fault."

"Was it you who hinted to the cops that the owners may have set the fire themselves for the insurance?"

Millie gave a harsh laugh. "Their revenue had dropped. Wasn't it a reasonable assumption? At first, the cops were looking for faulty wiring or a gas leak as a possible cause."

"Yes, until the investigator found evidence that the fire had been deliberately set," Marla continued, hoping to goad her into a confession.

Tendrils of hair had loosened from Millie's bun and framed her sun-worn face. She tucked them behind her ears with a frown of annoyance. "The detectives couldn't pin a thing on me."

"Because of your alibi? Your ex-boyfriend spoke to my husband's associate. He admitted you had left the table briefly for a restroom visit. And wasn't your former establishment across the street? You had plenty of time to run over there, start a fire, and depart the scene before things erupted."

Millie shrugged. "The cops never found anything to connect me to the crime. Those rats got what they deserved."

"What was the evidence that Phil uncovered? That's why you killed him, wasn't it?"

A snarl contorted Millie's face, and she took a step toward Marla. "Phil had been snooping inside here with the same idea I'd had about the missing Confederate gold being hidden among these old buttons. He found my notes on how to start a fire, along with my ferro rod. After he was in here, I destroyed the documents, but it was too late. He'd taken photos with his phone."

"How did you start the fire? You spread paint thinner around and then lit a spark with your tools? Nobody would think of flint as an ignition source."

"Exactly." Millie's chest expanded with pride. "I still had a key to the restaurant. I zipped in there during my restroom break and did the deed. Then I told my boyfriend I didn't feel well. We hoofed it out of the neighborhood before the fire spread." Millie snatched a pair of scissors from the counter.

Marla's pulse accelerated. "How did Phil mean to use this information against you?" she asked, needing to keep Millie talking to avoid an attack. Her ears had picked up a faint rattling sound. Dalton must be trying to unlock the door. Would he be able to get inside?

"With the statute of limitations not yet expired on the arson case, I couldn't risk exposure. Like everyone else on whom Phil had some dirt—which included most of us who work here—he asked for favors in return for his silence. That's how he got away with paying a low salary and embezzling funds from the fairground. But when he found my notes, he wanted money. I said I had something better. I'd found the gold coins."

"For real? Or were you just trying to delay him?" *Like I'm doing with you,* she thought, wondering at the sudden silence outside. Had Dalton left to get help?

Millie pointed to a row of vintage jars on the top shelf. "Would you believe the coins are hidden among those buttons? Lizzy's ancestor was a genius. Nobody had ever thought to look inside these old jars. Not even Lizzy figured it out. I don't know how to fence the coins, so I've left them here for now."

"Did Phil demand you hand over his share right away?" Marla asked, fascinated despite her precarious situation.

"Yes, but I said he should wait until I'd recovered all of it and then we'd figure out a fair amount. The evidence about the arson wasn't the only reason he had to go, however. His discovery only added fuel to the fire, so to speak." Millie cackled.

The hairs on Marla's nape lifted. The woman was becoming unhinged. Marla glanced around for anything to grab as a weapon. She could always smash a jar and use the cut edge.

"What changed to make you kill him during the reenactment?" she asked.

"Phil reneged on his offer to let me run the kitchen at his proposed café. The louse said my cooking stank and he'd find another chef, and that I should stick to my other duties."

"I can understand you feeling betrayed by him," Marla said, her voice oozing sympathy. "It was clever of you to steal Billy's tomahawk. You must have figured the shaman would take the blame."

"It was easy to sneak into the Seminole camp after hours. I'd given an archery class the evening before the battle scene and stayed late. After my students left, I hurried over to the campsite, grabbed the weapon, and went by the pond to stash it in one of those wide buckets."

"How did you get Phil to meet you there?" Marla remembered Violet's claim that Phil had summoned her to the site.

"I sent him a message and said I'd offer him a sample of the gold coins as a sign of good will. But in return, I expected him to eradicate the evidence he had against me."

"I suppose you figured the battle would distract everyone while you met with him. Then what? You stuck the axe in his head while he stood there?"

"I said I'd stashed the coins in the bucket. But what I drew out wasn't any treasure. It was the tomahawk. You should have seen the look of surprise on his face when I swung it at his head."

Marla's stomach heaved but she had to ask the next question. "How did the pearl button end up under his body? The last I'd heard, Gilda had it."

"Henry had given the button to Uriah, who gave it to Violet as a token of his affection. Gilda borrowed it, ostensibly to search among the vintage button jars for similar ones. I'd wondered if she meant to search for the gold there. I stole the button and left it with Phil's body."

"You were hoping this would implicate Uriah or Violet if Billy didn't take the heat with the tomahawk?" Marla asked, trying to reason things out in her mind.

"To be sure, I texted Violet from Phil's phone and said I knew something about Uriah that she had to hear. She thought I was Phil and agreed to come alone."

That's why Violet was at the scene of the crime. She'd been lured there, same as Phil.

"How did you get away from the scene without anyone spotting you?"

Millie chuckled. "First, I had to get rid of my apron. It had blood on it. Luckily, I'd thought of this ahead of time. I tied it, along with the gloves I'd worn, into a ball and weighted it down with rocks. It barely made a splash when I heaved it into the pond. I put on a cloak with a hood that I had brought there earlier and left through the woods."

Marla had been edging around the room. Just a little farther, and she could reach the door. Millie raised the scissors. It wouldn't be long now.

"What made Gilda catch onto you?" Marla said in a last desperate effort to avoid a physical confrontation. Her gaze flitted across the goods strewn on the counter for any sort of defensive weapon.

"After Phil died, Gilda accessed his office," Millie said in a bitter tone. "She had a key as a fairground director. She must have searched through his files and found the printouts he had on me. When she asked for an explanation, I said the fire starter kit was for my position here. As a pioneer woman, I had to know how to start a campfire. Gilda didn't buy it, not with Phil's newspaper clippings about the restaurant fire."

"Did she try to extort money from you?"

"She ordered me to support the developer's deal. I figured she'd get a nice kickback from the sale, but then we'd all be out of jobs."

"You made her poisoned cookies, didn't you? Where did you get the nicotine?" Marla grinned at Millie's obvious surprise. "My husband's lab determined the cause of death."

"Nicotine is readily available. Gilda was oblivious when I gave her the cookies as a peace offering. I pretended to go along with her demands."

Her gaze darkened, and she advanced on Marla. "It's time to end your interference. I tried to warn you off by shooting arrows at you. When you failed to stop asking questions, I sent you tainted chocolates. Guess I'll have to take care of Susan, too, once I'm finished with you."

Marla's fists curled at the threat to her friend. "The game is over, Millie. My husband is outside, and he's heard everything. He's been recording our conversation on his cell phone."

Heavy pounding shook the door.

"Try the window," she yelled just before Millie attacked.

A flash of steel made Marla thrust her arm upward to parry a blow. Skin connected with skin. Before Millie could strike again, Marla ducked, swung around, and grabbed the knitting needle she'd seen on the counter.

As she rose from her crouch, Millie thrust the shears at Marla again. But her swing was too high, and the needle in Marla's hand impacted Millie's belly as she came around.

With a gasp, Millie dropped the tool and sank to her knees.

Marla barged past her as the sound of splintering glass rent the air. Inside the front room, Dalton was attempting to fit his head and shoulders through the cracked window.

"I'll open the door," she told him. "You could get cut that way."

Once he was inside, he rushed over to Marla and grasped her shoulders. "Are you okay?"

Marla's knees buckled, and he caught her in his arms. "I'm fine, but Millie might need medical assistance."

His hard gaze scrutinized her. "Can you walk? If so, wait outside. I'll handle it from here."

For once, Marla was glad to obey her husband.

Chapter Twenty-Five

After Millie had been taken away in handcuffs and the case concluded, Marla got busy sending invites to Dalton's retirement party. It was time to focus on family and the more precious things in life. Thankfully, no other homicides occurred during her husband's remaining workdays.

Two months later, she gathered with friends and family at Antoine's, a fancy French restaurant in east Fort Lauderdale. With a glass of ginger ale in hand, she circulated among the guests during cocktail hour in the upstairs section she'd reserved for Dalton's event. Waiters offered appetizers on trays while a bar supplied drinks.

She caught a glimpse of her reflection in the mirrored wall. She'd worn a simple but slinky black dress with sparkly jewelry. The fit was a bit tight, but she hadn't paid much attention to her diet during the murder case.

"It's too bad Brianna couldn't be here," Dalton's mother, Kate, said as she sidled up to Marla. She looked great with her auburn hair in an upsweep and wearing a forest green sequined top with satiny black pants. Jade earrings dangled from her ears.

"I know," Marla said, feeling a surge of affection for her in-laws. She was lucky they lived nearby in Delray Beach. They'd been supportive of her from the start. "Brie offered to fly down, but school had just started, and I didn't think it would be a good idea. We'll send her photos." Marla's friend Arnie had offered to take pictures that evening.

"You got a nice crowd." Kate indicated the people standing

in clusters around the room. "I can't tell you how thrilled I am that Dalton is leaving the police force. I'll rest easier without him confronting murderers on a daily basis."

"His colleagues were sad to see him go." They'd thrown a surprise party for him at work. He'd been pleased but no less determined to enter the private sector.

Kate gave her an appraising glance. "I hope you'll take this opportunity to leave the sleuthing to others as well."

Marla chuckled. "Don't worry, I am done. Life is precious, and I want to enjoy my..." She caught what she'd been about to say. "We'll have enough to do between Ryder and our other activities. Did Dalton tell you he got accepted for the teaching position at the police academy?"

"Yes. He'll be a wonderful instructor," Kate said with a proud grin.

"They'll provide the syllabus, but he has a lot to do in preparation. And he has hobbies he wants to pursue, like John with his stained-glass art. Any shows coming up?" Marla asked to deflect the conversation away from their personal plans.

"Fall is a busy season for art festivals, so we'll be traveling. I don't mind as long as John tells me in advance so I can plan our schedule accordingly. My bridge group has enough women who can fill in when I'm out of town."

"I'm sure they miss you when you're not there." Marla touched her arm. "Would you please excuse me? Nicole and Kevin have just arrived."

Marla bustled over to the beaming couple who already knew most of Marla and Dalton's relatives from previous events. She'd only invited Nicole and Robyn from the salon. Their other friends plus relatives made up the rest of the guest list.

"How are you guys?" she said, after exchanging air-kisses. "I swear, Nicole, you're busting at the seams. You look as though you're ready anytime now."

Nicole patted her belly. "One more month. We're trying to enjoy ourselves and go out to dinner while we still can.

Tomorrow we're going to the baby store to buy supplies. We've been putting it off, but we'd better get prepared just in case."

"Why don't you wait until after your baby shower?" Marla had one planned at work in a couple of weeks.

Kevin looked handsome in his dress clothes. "We're too nervous. Nicole's hospital bag is already packed. We still have so much to buy since this is our first child."

Marla laughed. "You may think you're prepared, but it'll still be overwhelming." She spied a familiar figure entering the room. "Oh look, Robyn is here."

Nicole's gaze brightened. "I can't wait to hear how you and Dalton solved the case. Robyn wouldn't tell me much."

Marla signaled for Robyn to join them. The salon receptionist bumped fists with them all.

"A yellow streak in your hair this time? I thought you wanted to stick with one tint," Marla told her.

Robyn smoothed down her chocolate-colored jacket dress. "I thought Billy might appreciate the symbolic meaning. The Seminole Nation flag has red, yellow, black and white bands. These represent life in terms of a compass. Yellow is for east, red for north, black for west, and white for south."

"My, you are learning your tribal lore, aren't you?" Marla said with a grin. After the case wrapped, Robyn had started dating Billy, the village shaman.

"The center of their flag has a circle with a chickee hut and a campfire. This represents the tribal council."

"A campfire, huh? I know how to start one now."

Robyn lowered her voice. "I want to hear all about it. You only told me Millie had been arrested but not how you figured out it was her. I'll bet I'm not the only one who wants the details."

"You're right," Nicole said. She'd hooked her arm into Kevin's as they stood by.

Robyn pointed to the doorway. "Whoa, look who's turned up. Isn't that your cousin who works at the village?"

Marla whirled around and stared. Corbin stood in the

doorway, looking awkward in a dress shirt and belted pants. He'd smoothed his hair back and was clean-shaven. She'd never seen him look more civilized.

"Excuse me. I'd better go and greet him," she told the gang before rushing off. "Corbin, I can't believe you came," she said, stopping in front of him. "I'm so glad you made it."

His face flushed. "Thanks. Is Cynthia here?" He craned his neck to peer around the crowded room like a lost waif seeking his family.

"She and Bruce are over there, talking to Julia and her husband." Her cousins were in a huddle together. Marla had greeted them earlier. "I hope this means you'll be coming to Rosh Hashanah dinner at Julia's house a week from Sunday."

"We'll see." He gazed at a spot on the wall before meeting her eyes. "I wanted to tell you that we're grateful at the village for you and Dalton solving the crime. It was scary not knowing who to trust. And Simon finally let me in on his secret. He took me over to meet the neighbor and see his tea plantation. Simon has been helping to cultivate the plants and test new varietals." Corbin sounded proud of his mentor.

"I hope Greg produces teas the average consumer can afford," Marla said. "Artisan tea growers are still a rarity in this country."

Corbin stuck his hands in his pockets. "We're wondering what will happen to the village. Will the developer take over? Will we be shut down? If that happens, I'll be out of a job."

Marla looked beyond him, thinking about his volunteer work. "You didn't bring your girlfriend, did you? She'd probably be happy to have your help full-time."

His face reddened. "Maybe. I'm not ready for her to meet the family."

Marla understood. It must have been hard enough for him to come today on his own. "Dalton has some news to share regarding the village. He'll tell us at dinner. Why don't you go say hello to Cynthia? Your sister will be happy to see you."

After Corbin wandered off, Marla put her empty glass on a tray and joined Dalton who was talking to Arnie. The deli owner had just snapped her husband's photo in front of the gift table. Dalton was prattling on about their son to the father of two.

"Hey, hon, it's almost time to go into dinner," Marla said. It amused her how Dalton's favorite topic had changed from murder cases to child-rearing issues.

He put an arm around her shoulders. "It's a great party, sweetcakes. You know how much I love you, don't you?"

Marla eased from his grip, embarrassed by his endearment in front of others. How many glasses of wine had he imbibed already? As the sober drinker, she'd be the one driving home.

"Arnie, I hope you're giving him good advice now that he'll be a stay-at-home dad."

Arnie grinned beneath his moustache. "He's going to be busier than he was before his retirement. You wait and see. If you'll excuse me, I'd better go retrieve my wife." He headed off toward the corner where Jill was chatting with Tally. Marla had spoken to them both earlier.

She went to round up Anita and Reed. Her mother and stepfather were clustered with Marla's brother, Michael, and his wife, Charlene.

"You can take your places at the table," she told the group, tapping her wristwatch to show it was time.

"All right, *bubeleh*," Anita said with a bob of her tinted blond hair. She'd made the change from natural white after marrying Reed. "We'll go over there in a minute. Charlene is regaling us with some funny tales about her job as a school principal."

"Oh, yeah? You can fill me in later." Marla moved off, secretly glad that Anita and Reed had decided to celebrate their first anniversary privately since it came right before Rosh Hashanah. Marla would give them gifts at the holiday dinner. It was already a busy month with Dalton's last day at work, this party, and then the Jewish holidays.

She alerted Susan and her husband to be seated. Marla had

already told Susan what had gone down the day Millie was arrested, but she'd left out the latest news that Dalton would impart tonight.

Once everyone was seated around the large table in their private dining room, Marla lifted her champagne glass for a toast.

"To Dalton, the best husband and father. May your retirement be filled with joyous events and new memories. I love you and look forward to our next chapter together."

Cheers erupted around the table. Dalton's smile couldn't get any broader as he accepted everyone's congratulations. Marla took a sip of the bubbly drink before placing her glass on the table and signaling the waiters to serve the first course.

Once they were eating their chateaubriand served with sautéed mushrooms, green beans almandine, and pommes de Terre duchess, Cynthia punctured their amiable conversation.

"Tell us how you solved the murder case, Dalton. You know we like to hear the juicy details," said Marla's cousin.

"It was more a process of elimination," he responded, lifting an eyebrow at Marla.

"We can't reveal everything," Marla said, casting a glance at Corbin so he'd realize she meant the tea plantation. "At first, we suspected Simon, the farmer, because of his reluctance to show us his herb garden. We thought he might be growing something unsavory there."

"That's right," Dalton agreed. "Uriah the shopkeeper uses herbs for his medicinal tonics and so does Billy, the Native American shaman. Even Millie and River could use herbs for their cooking. We thought they might all be involved in a conspiracy, but we were wrong."

Dalton gave a rundown on the main suspects, explaining each person's role in the living history village. "We eliminated Simon as a suspect once we saw his herb garden and discovered his activities next door. He was helping the neighboring farmer, Greg Harris, who turned out to be Lizzy's brother. She's the lady who gives tours at Baffle House."

"Billy, the tribal shaman, was also on our list," Marla explained. "Phil's proposal would have eliminated the Seminole camp, and he was murdered with Billy's tomahawk. But Billy had an alibi provided by Henry, the preacher."

Susan's face was lit with excitement. Her staid husband sat beside her with a disapproving expression. "Henry was in our sights, too, at one time," she said. "He'd been earning money acting as a middleman in obtaining costumes for the players. Phil's proposal would have negatively impacted his finances."

"Who did that leave?" Cynthia asked. She nudged her husband Bruce, alerting him to pay attention. Having finished his meal, he'd been fiddling with his cell phone.

"We never really suspected Uriah, the shopkeeper," Marla said, mulling over the prospects. "He'd supported Phil's plan, although it disturbed him that Phil might have hit upon Violet, the schoolteacher. She was a stronger suspect, being the person who found the body."

Susan bounced in her seat. "Someone shot at us with a bow and arrow as we left the village one day. There were three people at the village who gave archery lessons—Angus, Millie, and Lizzy. Angus, the blacksmith, suspected Phil of cooking the books and shortchanging the village of needed funds for repairs. But he had no proof. He competed in axe-throwing contests and knew how to shoot arrows, however."

"But you didn't think Angus did it?" Anita asked. Marla's mother wore a puzzled frown as she took a sip of her cabernet.

"He didn't have a strong enough motive," Dalton replied. He forked a last bite into his mouth, chewed and swallowed. A waiter circulated, refilling their water glasses while soft French music played in the background. "That boiled things down to Millie, who did the baking demos and ran the sewing circle, and Lizzy, the guide at Baffle House."

"Wasn't there a second murder?" Anita asked, pushing her empty plate away.

"That would be Gilda," Marla replied.

"Who was she?" Cousin Julia asked in her characteristic snotty tone. She dotted her mouth with a napkin, while Marla noticed that her roots badly needed a touchup.

Tally broke into the conversation. "Gilda was the fairground's spy who did various odd jobs around the village." Marla's best friend looked great in a maxi-dress, but then again, she looked good in anything with her model-thin figure. Marla had hoped Tally would bring a plus one, but she'd insisted on coming alone. She'd left her son Luke home with a babysitter.

"Gilda was the last person to possess the pearl button that ended up under Phil's body," Marla explained. "Millie confessed that she'd stolen it from Gilda and placed it with Phil to implicate others in the crime. She'd fooled all of us with her heartwarming pioneer act. Millie was even clever enough to search inside the vintage button jars for the missing Confederate gold. When she discovered the stash, she left it there until she found a way to fence the coins."

"How did you figure out it was her?" Tally asked with a crease of her brow.

"Marla is the one who put the clues together." Dalton gave her a proud pat on the shoulder.

All right, the pressure's on me. Marla straightened in her chair. "When Millie gave the baking demo the first day we were there, she showed me not only how to make an outdoor oven to bake biscuits, but also how to start a campfire using flint and steel tools."

Cynthia chuckled. "I remember how you learned to make a smoker to ward off bees on your case at Tremayne Manor. You do pick up the oddest things when you're investigating."

"Right. Anyway, Millie had been dismissed from her job as a restaurant chef prior to her employment at the village. That night, the place erupted in flames. Evidence of arson was found at the site. The accelerant was a chemical commonly found in paint thinner, but the means of ignition remained a puzzle. Traces of magnesium were detected, and they led me to Millie."

"How so?" asked Arnie, holding his wife Jill's hand on the table.

"I looked up fire starter kits on the Internet. You can buy them for your emergency supplies. They come with a metal striker blade and a ferrocerium rod. Some of these include a magnesium component. Magnesium is flammable," she explained. "You scrape the metal blade along the magnesium part to slough off some shavings into a pile of kindling. Then you strike the blade against the ferro rod until a spark ignites."

"Apparently, Millie printed out these instructions," Dalton continued when Marla paused to take a breath. "Phil had the same notion as Millie to search for the missing gold coins among the button jars. Instead, he found her papers and tool kit. He took photos, intending to blackmail her into silence. She decided to kill him to end the threat."

Marla told them how Millie had lured Phil to the fishing shack and then how she'd used Phil's phone to summon Violet to the scene.

"His cell phone records verified that the last call he received was from Millie," Dalton said, his face somber.

They'd never recovered Phil's phone. Millie had said she'd tossed it in the pond.

"What about Gilda?" Cynthia asked, waving her fork. "How did she end up dead?"

Marla explained the best she could. "Gilda accessed Phil's office and discovered his copies of Millie's notes. She meant to coerce Millie into supporting the developer's bid to buy the village. Millie poisoned a batch of chocolate chip cookies and gave them to her as a peace offering. She wasn't taking any chances of the evidence pointing her way in the arson case."

Robyn half-rose from her seat. "She almost did the same thing to you with those chocolates. To think that I might have sampled one of them at the salon!"

"What will happen to the village now?" Anita asked.

Dalton banged on his water glass with a spoon. "Here's the

thing. I've saved the best news for last. It appears Lizzy and Greg still own the village tract along with the farm next door. The attorney who handled the sale must have forged Ian's signature after his unexpected death. He convinced the witnesses that Ian had signed on his deathbed."

Susan skewed him a glance. "No way! Lizzy and Greg own the village? The fairground's directors must be pissed. Can they sue?"

"They could go after the attorney's office for fraud, but Lizzy and Greg aren't liable. They believed all along that the fairground owned the place."

"Lizzy was thrilled to hear this news," Marla said. "She'll sell the gold and use the proceeds to refurbish the village and hire additional staff. She wants to put the property into an historic trust with herself and Greg as co-trustees. But that's enough on the murder case. If everyone is finished eating, Dalton can open his gifts now. They'll serve the cake afterward."

He gave her shoulder a squeeze and looked deeply into her eyes. "Don't you have some other news to share first?"

"Oh, yes." Marla stood, her skin heating. She drew a breath to fortify herself. "It's early yet, but we may be expecting another addition to the family."

Her thoughts slid back to that time they'd been rushed after putting Ryder to bed. Afraid the baby would wake up and interrupt their passion, they'd forgotten about protection. However, considering her age, Marla considered the event a blessing as long as the child was healthy.

Exclamations of joy and congratulations sounded from around the table.

Dalton covered her hand with his and gave her an adoring smile. "We're thrilled. Keep in mind that we're only in the first trimester, though."

"It's the start of a new life for us," Marla told him. "I'm done with sleuthing. Now that you're retired from that job, so am I. Our children need our full attention, as do all of you." She cast her gaze around the gathering. "There's nothing more important than family."

She glowed with an inner warmth, realizing her loved ones brought the only fulfillment she'd ever need.

"Cheers," she said, raising her water glass. "Here's to happy times ahead."

THE END

Recipes

Fourth of July Menu
Baked Brie and Crackers
Blue Corn Chips
Creole Franks with White Rice
Vegetable of Choice
Fruit Platter with Blueberries, Strawberries, & Mini
Marshmallows
Red Velvet Cake

BAKED BRIE

You can use any jam or preserves on hand for this quick yet delicious appetizer. Nuts are optional, and again you can substitute whatever chopped or sliced nuts you have in stock. Try brown sugar mixed with Kahlua for a different topping if you wish. In other words, you can get creative or just serve the melted cheese and jam alone.

Ingredients
8 oz. Brie round
Strawberry jam
Chopped walnuts
Crackers

Directions
Preheat oven to 300 degrees. Place brie in oven-proof dish. Spread jam on top. Sprinkle with nuts. Bake for 15 minutes or until cheese is soft. Serve warm with crackers.

CREOLE FRANKS

This makes a colorful entrée and can be served with rolls and a salad to make a more complete meal. I use Hebrew National Beef Franks. Each 10.3 oz. package contains six hot dogs.

Ingredients

3 Tbsp. olive oil
8 oz. container mixed chopped celery, onion, green pepper (trinity mix)
¼ cup chopped fresh parsley
1 tsp. chopped garlic
(2) 10.3 oz. packages reduced fat beef franks
2 bay leaves
6 oz. can tomato paste
¼ cup water
2 cups cooked white rice

Directions

Slice frankfurters into bite-size pieces and put aside. In a large pot, sauté chopped vegetables, parsley and garlic in oil until tender. Add franks and stir to blend. Add bay leaves, tomato paste and water. Simmer for several minutes until heated through. Discard bay leaves and serve over rice. Serves 4 to 6.

Next Day Brunch Menu
Salmon Mini Quiches
Egg Veggie Bake
Cheesy Hash Brown Potatoes
Bagels and Cream Cheese
Root Beer Cake

SALMON MINI QUICHES

These display well on a platter and provide an elegant touch to your brunch buffet. Quiches that are left over may be reheated in the microwave or oven.

Ingredients
   6 oz. can pink salmon, drained
   1 clove garlic, minced
   ½ tsp. dried dill
   1 shallot, finely chopped
   ½ cup heavy cream
   4 eggs
   ¼ cup shredded Swiss cheese
   Few drops of lemon juice

Directions
Preheat oven to 350 degrees. In a bowl, mix all ingredients and spoon into a greased 24 mini muffin pan. Bake for 20 to 25 minutes until puffed, set, and lightly browned around the edges. Remove to a plate and serve.

EGG VEGGIE BAKE
This is an easy brunch dish that pairs well with other items for an appealing presentation. It saves time if you buy a container of chopped onions. Then you can just toss all the ingredients together after you chop the fresh basil. Feel free to add any other vegetables you have in stock.

Ingredients
   8 eggs
   2 Tbsp. fresh basil, chopped
   4 oz. chopped onions
   12 oz. package cook-in-bag broccoli & cauliflower
   8 oz. package frozen asparagus spears
   15.25 oz. can whole kernel corn, drained
   6 oz. shredded Mozzarella cheese

Directions
Preheat oven to 350 degrees. Combine first six ingredients. Mix in 3 oz. cheese. Pour mixture into greased 9x13x2 baking pan. Sprinkle the remainder of cheese on top. Bake for 30 minutes or until dish is set. Slice when warm. Serves 8-10.

CHEESY HASH BROWN POTATOES

This side dish pairs well with any egg entrée. It's substantial enough to feed a hearty appetite and is suitable for a crowd.

Ingredients
15 oz. can cream of celery soup
1 cup reduced fat sour cream
1 Tbsp. flour
½ tsp. garlic powder
20 to 30 oz. package frozen shredded hash brown potatoes
2 cups reduced fat shredded Cheddar cheese
⅓ cup grated Parmesan cheese
Paprika to taste

Directions
Preheat oven to 350 degrees. In a bowl, combine soup, sour cream, flour, and garlic powder. Stir in potatoes and cheddar cheese. Pour into a greased 9x13x2 inch baking dish. Sprinkle Parmesan cheese and paprika on top. Bake uncovered for 50 to 60 minutes or until browned and bubbly. Serves 6 to 8.

ROOT BEER CAKE

This cake isn't fancy looking but it tastes yummy and will satisfy any chocolate lover.

Ingredients
Cake
15.25 oz. box German chocolate cake mix
1¼ cups root beer
2 large eggs
¼ cup vegetable oil
Frosting
½ cup unsalted butter
7 Tbsp. root beer
3 Tbsp. unsweetened cocoa
16 oz. package powdered sugar
1 tsp. vanilla

Directions

Preheat oven to 350 degrees. In a large bowl, combine the German chocolate cake mix, 1¼ cups root beer, 2 large eggs, and ¼ cup vegetable oil. Beat with mixer until blended. Pour mixture into a greased and floured 9x13x2 inch baking pan. Bake for 30 minutes. Cool on rack.

Meanwhile, melt ½ cup butter in saucepan over medium high heat. Add 7 Tbsp. root beer and 3 Tbsp. unsweetened cocoa. Blend and remove from heat. Add 16 oz. package powdered sugar and 1 tsp. vanilla. Mix to blend. Spread frosting over cake. Serves 12.

****

For more recipes, check out A Bad Hair Day Cookbook (NancyJCohen.com/a-bad-hair-day-cookbook/) available at most online bookstores. With 160+ recipes, plus anecdotes and cooking tips offered by savvy sleuth Marla Vail, this award-winning title will appeal to home cooks as well as mystery fans.

Nancy J. Cohen

Author's Note

Thank you for taking the time to read *Star Tangled Murder*. The inspiration for this story came from Yesteryear Village (https://www.southfloridafair.com/p/yesteryearvillage) in West Palm Beach. I loved the Florida living history village with its costumed tour guides. As for battle reenactments, I've never had the chance to attend one but watched videos online that made me feel like I was there. I was interested to learn button lore and was impressed by the tea production process. Learning something new for a story is what makes each book special to me. I hope you liked reading about these esoteric topics.

Regarding Lizzy's Doll Emporium, I'd read about Judy's Dolls (https://judysdolls.com/) in Longwood. It's housed in a Victorian house and has a unique doll nursery with adoptable dolls, a selection of teddy bears, and other cute items. I visited the shop and loosely modeled Lizzy's store on my experience there.

Regarding the hat lady at the July Fourth festival, I've seen similar displays at local events and their colorful creations inspired this scene in my story.

As for Marla and Dalton, they are starting a new chapter in their lives. Dalton is retiring and Marla is expecting another child. Brianna is away at college. These characters have come a long way since the first title, *Permed to Death*. Hopefully you've enjoyed following their journey as much as I have. If you wish to go back and start with book one, go here for more details: https://nancyjcohen.com/permed-to-death/

If you enjoyed this book, please write a review at your favorite online bookstore. Reader recommendations are critically important in helping new readers find my work.

For updates on my new releases, giveaways, special offers and events, join my reader list at https://nancyjcohen.com/ newsletter. Free Book Sampler for new subscribers.

Acknowledgments

I want to thank the following without whom this book would not have been possible:

My critique partners, Ann Meier and Janice Hardy. Your support and encouragement give me the incentive to keep writing, and your comments always help to improve my work.

My editor, Denise Dietz, with whom I'd worked at Five Star and who still manages to find my flaws and suggest corrections that are right on the mark.

My production team consisting of Judi Fennell from formatting4u.com, cover designer Kim Killion from TheKillion GroupInc.com and Kat Sheridan from BlurbWriter.com. You give my books a professional presentation, which is critical to a book's success.

My friends at Bookloversbench.com—Terry Ambrose, Debra H. Goldstein, Cheryl Hollon, Diane A.S. Stuckart, Maggie Toussaint, and Lois Winston—for answering my questions, discussing the business of writing, and providing reassurance and advice.

My beta readers Taryn Lee, Jan Irwin Klein, and Sally Schmidt. It's so important to get a reader's viewpoint on my story, and your comments are highly insightful. I appreciate you taking the time from your busy schedules to read my work. You catch errors that all the rest of us miss.

Nancy J. Cohen

Truly, it takes a village to publish a book, whether you are traditionally or independently published. A team is necessary not only for the vital work of critiquing, editing, polishing and producing a book, but also for being there as cheerleaders and friends. I thank my industry colleagues and especially my readers for giving me the inspiration to write more books.

About the Author

Nancy J. Cohen writes the Bad Hair Day Mysteries featuring South Florida hairstylist Marla Vail. Titles in this series have been named Best Cozy Mystery by *Suspense Magazine*, won the Readers' Favorite Book Awards and the RONE Award, placed first in the Chanticleer International Book Awards and third in the Arizona Literary Awards.

Her nonfiction titles, *Writing the Cozy Mystery* and *A Bad Hair Day Cookbook*, have earned gold medals in the FAPA President's Book Awards and the Royal Palm Literary Awards, First Place in the IAN Book of the Year Awards and the *Topshelf Magazine* Book Awards. *Writing the Cozy Mystery* was also an Agatha Award Finalist.

Nancy's imaginative romances have proven popular with fans as well. These books have won the HOLT Medallion and Best Book in Romantic SciFi/Fantasy at *The Romance Reviews*.

A featured speaker at libraries, conferences, and community events, Nancy is listed in *Contemporary Authors, Poets & Writers*, and *Who's Who in U.S. Writers, Editors, & Poets*. She is a past president of Florida Romance Writers and the Florida Chapter of Mystery Writers of America. When not busy writing, Nancy enjoys reading, fine dining, cruising, and visiting Disney World.

Follow Nancy Online

Website – https://nancyjcohen.com
Blog – https://nancyjcohen.com/blog
Twitter – https://www.twitter.com/nancyjcohen
Facebook – https://www.facebook.com/NancyJCohenAuthor
LinkedIn – https://www.linkedin.com/in/nancyjcohen
Goodreads – https://www.goodreads.com/nancyjcohen
Pinterest – https://pinterest.com/njcohen/
Instagram – https://instagram.com/nancyjcohen
BookBub – https://www.bookbub.com/authors/nancy-j-cohen

Books by Nancy J. Cohen

The Bad Hair Day Mysteries
Permed to Death
Hair Raiser
Murder by Manicure
Body Wave
Highlights to Heaven
Died Blonde
Dead Roots
Perish by Pedicure
Killer Knots
Shear Murder
Hanging by a Hair
Peril by Ponytail
Haunted Hair Nights (Novella)
Facials Can Be Fatal
Hair Brained
Hairball Hijinks (Short Story)
Trimmed to Death
Easter Hair Hunt
Styled for Murder
Star Tangled Murder

Anthology
"Three Men and a Body" in Wicked Women Whodunit

Nancy J. Cohen

The Drift Lords Series
Warrior Prince
Warrior Rogue
Warrior Lord

Science Fiction Romances
Keeper of the Rings
Silver Serenade

The Light-Years Series
Circle of Light
Moonlight Rhapsody
Starlight Child

Nonfiction
Writing the Cozy Mystery
A Bad Hair Day Cookbook (Companion to The Bad Hair Day series)

Order Now at NancyJCohen.com/Books